JENN LANE

Realmbound

Worlds Echo

To every person whose imagination never cared about their age; keep dreaming. You make the world beautiful.

To the readers who stepped into these realms with open hearts; thank you for giving this story a home beyond my own.

To my friends and family who read the rough drafts, believed in me when I faltered, and stood beside me through every challenge. Your love helped me shape worlds, and your faith guided me back to this dream.

Thank you for believing in a dreamer who chose to imagine again.

Contents

Preface

I dusted off a shelved manuscript after fifteen years to give my heroine, and myself, a second beginning.
In returning to this story, I have found pieces of my own that I thought I had lost.
This book is not just a continuation; it's a reclamation.

Acknowledgments

To my daughter, whose name echoes through these pages.
You loved this story long before you understood it. From middle-school wood carvings to the day you urged me to chase this dream again, you've been part of this journey from its first spark. My love for you has always been unwavering, even when our paths seemed to diverge. It fills me with pride to see you blossom into the brilliant woman, and a devoted mother you are.

To my son, who listened to this story at bedtime with the patience of a saint and the imagination of... well, a bull. Your stubborn strength, kindness, and compassion shaped more of this world than you realize. Elok's heart is yours, even if his horns aren't.
This story bows to you.

To my grandchildren, you bring magic into my days, fresh adventures into my heart, and joy beyond realms.

To my mother, whose courage and enduring love and support gave me the strength to create worlds, your presence anchors me, even from beyond.

To my father, whose quiet support has meant more than he knows.

May you always see in yourselves the qualities I see in you. Never be confined by perceived limitations; you have the power to cross realms, stir hearts, and shape destinies, just as you have shaped mine.

With love, J.L.

Realmbound
Worlds Echo
Jenn Lane

1

Prologue

Marie

We think little about magic or myths once we reach a certain age. By the time you lose your last baby tooth, you don't even bother to put it under your pillow anymore.

Why is that?

Why are myths dismissed while science holds strong? Especially when most sciences start as myths.

Believe me, I'm not here to judge. If you had tried to have this conversation with me a while ago, I would have laughed and asked what Santa had gotten you for Christmas this year.

I was not a believer in magic, myths, or legends. That is until I discovered... Myth was a believer in me.

2

THE CHASE

Marie

I can't breathe. I can't–

My scream scrapes my throat as I run, my chest squeezing like it's trying to fold in on itself. I have to go faster. Faster.

Those paws, god, they're so loud. Slamming into the ground behind me, quaking everything. My pulse, beating against the inside of my skull.

I don't even know what's chasing me. A bear? A grizzly? Some giant freaking dog?

Branches claw at my arms and briars slice my face, but I don't stop. My ankles keep twisting on roots and rocks, pain shooting up my legs, but I can't stop.

Move. Just move.

Crack! Thud!

The forest explodes behind me, trees cracking, splintering; something huge is tearing straight through them. Its snarl rips through the air, deep and furious, paws pounding closer.

No god please. Up ahead. A fallen tree. Massive and blocking my whole path like some nightmare barricade, all thorns and twisted limbs. Natures razor wire.

There's no time. No time to think. I throw myself at it, scrambling over the branches, the thorns biting into my hands.

2

I scarcely register the gully below before gravity yanks me down. My feet slam into the shifting stones of the creek bank, pain shooting up through my ankles.

WHOOSH!

The air blasts out of my lungs as a massive paw slams into my back, driving me into the soggy earth. Sand and grit grind against my cheeks. My ears ring, and blackness swarms into my vision. I can't breathe. I'm gaping like a fish, my mouth opening and closing, trying to drag the air back into my chest.

Not dead. Not yet.

The beast's muzzle curls back, exposing rows of yellowed, dripping fangs. Saliva strings down and pools at the edges, a grotesque prelude to my final moments.

No, not like this.

Something shifts deep within me, small, desperate, and defiant, burning through the fear that has frozen the blood in my veins. It's just enough fire to thaw and to fight back.

I have no idea how; but I move. My fingers clawing at the creek bank, scrambling, reaching for anything, anything at all that could help me fight.

A sudden rush of oxygen floods my lungs; the monster shifted its weight. I thrust my arm forward, my hand closing around a broken branch. With no hesitation, I swing it at the thing's face.

CRACK!

The branch snaps against its enormous skull, splintering in my hands, but the beast recoils for a split second. I twist my body, struggling to crawl away, but the creature isn't done with me.

With a savage jerk, it yanks me off the ground, enraged. My bookbag rips free of my shoulders as its powerful neck whips me sideways, sending me careening into the creek.

I hit the shallow waters and skitter across the surface, my body like a skipping stone with the power of the thrashing.

Drenched. Stunned. But still alive.

Stars swarm in my vision as my chest spasms, coughing, choking on the creek water. Everything feels distant, warped. The rushing sounds of water over stones becomes a murmur. The torn earth beneath me, unreal. In this moment, my body doesn't even feel like it belongs to me; it's just weight, pain, and static.

Reality snaps back in one terrifying instant.

The beast has my bag, jaws locked tight around it, shaking it like a plaything.

I stagger towards the opposite bank, my foot slipping in the mud, my whole body protesting. Blood smears across my palms as I claw at the earth, pulling myself up, higher, closer to escape. But I know I'm not moving fast enough.

The beast charges; its massive form cutting through the water with terrifying ease. Its snarl vibrating through my bones, rattling something deep inside me. The certainty of death.

Then… another sound.

A bellow.

A man, not the creature. His voice is deep, commanding, and unshakable.

I turn, fingers still gripping the side of the embankment, my breath stalled. A towering figure grapples with the creature; its massive arms locked around its throat.

I whip back toward the bank, scrambling again, focusing on getting higher, my escape the only thought in my mind. My fingers catch a gnarled, twisted root, and I use it to haul myself up–

THUD!

The beast slams into the embankment, hurled like discarded prey. The root snaps in my hand, and I fall, hard, back down to the creek bed. I land next to the beast; a Buick-sized corpse, neck twisted at an unnatural angle. My stomach flips. I scramble backwards, away from the still twitching creature, my heart hammering.

Then I look at the thing that saved me, and I stopped breathing.

Not a man. Not a beast. Something worse.

His silhouette looms in the dying light. Horned and imposing; twin crescents curl above his skull, casting jagged shadows across his harsh features. His eyes burn into me, dark and unyielding.

The dog-thing had been terrifying.

But this? This is *intelligence*, staring back at me. Judging me. Calculating.

His gaze drops. He bends at the knee, plucking a coin from the ground. The coin I had in my pocket. The coin that the man in the hood dropped.

His fingers flick the golden disk into the air, catching it with ease.

"Thought you could steal from the Queen, did you? Wretched skinling worm." His voice is deep and gruff and dripping with disgust as he peers at me. "Where's the rest of it?"

I could barely speak. My lips tremble. "P-please –"

"Silence your sniveling, human. Queen Vaira's justice does not bend to the cries of thieves." The Minotaur stalks toward me, and I scream.

3

KINGDOM OF FRIENDS

Marie

I suppose you're wondering how the heck I got into that mess. Well, that makes two of us… Let's backtrack, shall we?

* * *

With the first week of school behind us, Logan was now our ride. His sky-blue Chevy Blazer rattled over a pothole, its suspension groaning in protest as Logan tapped the steering wheel in rhythm with the bass from the radio. The cracked vinyl seats stuck slightly to my thighs, and the faint scent of old pine hung in the air, courtesy of an air freshener in the shape of a pine tree that I'm sure was in here when he bought the truck.

"This thing's gonna shake itself apart," Rene muttered.

Logan snorted. "Nah. She's got good bones. I rebuilt her to survive worse than these crappy Pennsylvania roads."

Rene plucked a random screw that was rattling around at the bottom of the cup holder. "what's this to then?"

Logan didn't even glance her way. "Blazer's evolving." He shrugged. "She's shedding parts she no longer needs."

I watched them over the rim of my coffee thermos. It made me smile, how they spoke to each other like this. Siblings who'd weathered a thousand storms and come out on the other side with wisecracks instead of bitterness.

I'd spent enough time in Logan's garage last summer to know the hours he put into the truck weren't just about getting it to run. It was about proving something; that he could build something steady from something worn out.

The truck creaked as we hit the ridge, causing Rene to side-eye her brother.

Logan and Mr. Darius, their stepfather, rebuilt it over the summer. Rene had called them 'wrench warriors,' half-mocking but half proud.

Logan and Rene had it rough growing up. Their bio-dad was a drunk, the kind whose anger left holes in walls and bruises beneath clothes. However, it was never brought up, and frankly, I can see why. Which is also why I only know pieces of their story; several hospital visits, caused by that asshole, and a final fight that led to handcuffs for a man who should've been locked away years prior.

Riding with Logan now, watching the quiet control in the way he drives, I don't see a boy shaped by violence. I see someone who decided somewhere deep down that he wouldn't be the echo of someone else's damage.

Rene leaned back, humming to the song on the radio as I sipped my coffee and let myself admire them both; not just for surviving, but for surviving gracefully.

Maybe that's what I was learning from them, without even asking to be taught.

Senior year had made Logan king of our small-town high school, laid-back charm, lopsided grin, and all. His confidence was enough to make any girl swoon, including me, though I'd never admit it out loud. I'd made it my personal mission to keep his ego in check. Even if that meant hiding the butterflies in my stomach whenever he flashed that lopsided grin my way.

"So, Marie;" Logan glanced back at me in his rearview mirror while he drove. I sensed his unspoken question when I entered the vehicle. "How are things going with you and Charlie?"

Charlie Moore was my boyfriend. We've been dating since school ended last year, and throughout summer break; but why would he ask about him?

Logan thought Charlie was an ass. He loved sending us sideways, teasing jabs throughout the summer. I scooted over to get a better read of Logan's face. He didn't look like he was trying to be a smartass; he was smiling, but sarcasm and teasing were like a second language.

"Fine, I guess. He's been pretty busy with tryouts and all. Why?"

I was telling a half-truth. Charlie had been avoiding me the entire week, and told me he was busy with tryouts, but too busy to call? Too busy to meet me between classes like we had last year? Too busy to send a text after school? I'd been wondering if I was being dramatic.

"Just wondering." He shrugged.

I was still trying to decode Logan's shrug when Rene spun around like a top.

"Hey! Did you hear about Taz?!" she asked abruptly.

She turned in her seat and clapped her hands together in excitement. Rene, Logan's little sister, had been my closest friend for as long as I can remember. Her bubbly, glass-half-full personality, regardless of her past, always seemed to brighten my day.

I giggled at her excitement. "No, what happened?" She seemed on the verge of exploding.

"He has a girlfriend!" She blurted out, bouncing in her seat.

"Oh my god! Who? How do you know?"

Taz is such a lovable, silly, and entirely oblivious person when someone tries to flirt with him.

Logan shook his head at the two of us, half amused, half exasperated. "Guess the rumor mill is officially open for business today."

"Maggie Nelson!" she exclaimed, ignoring her brother. "He called her last night and asked her out!"

"Mags!?" I squealed. "She's perfect for him! How come he didn't put it in the group text?" I pouted. We were all very close; an update was practically law.

* * *

We pulled into the student parking lot and scanned the courtyard as we walked toward the school.

Southeastern Eagles is small for a high school; but what it lacked in grandeur it made up for in beauty. The student parking was just beyond a large island of tall oak and maple trees. A sidewalk made of laid brick cut through the island's center, leading to the courtyard by the student entrance of the school. The walkway, lined with blue and black light posts, the school colors, had tiny eagles perched upon each one, clutching lanterns in their beaks to light the way.

The courtyard itself displayed a large, majestic stone eagle, our mascot, beak open, wings spread wide and ready for flight. On its base, the school motto inscribed read, *"Wings of Wisdom, Soar to Excellence."*

Several students sat along the base, under the shade of its massive wingspan. A long, low brick wall enclosed it, along with many benches.

My group hung out on a brick partition wall that separated the courtyard itself from the grass, which I supposed could be called the school's lawn? We sat at the far end of that wall, where it was the highest and most open. Most of us seemed to have unspoken assigned seats along the top of it.

Logan had taken his seat at the peak, as I said, the king. Rene and I sat a little farther down; we were only juniors, so we were lucky to have a seat on the wall at all, as seniors mostly occupied it. The rest of our friends hung out on the benches that ran parallel along the wall, talking, finishing last-second assignments, or playing on their phones.

As we settled in, I surveyed my surroundings. I couldn't help but feel a sense of belonging. That was our spot, like being the lords and ladies of a royal court; that was our little corner of a high school kingdom.

My eyes scanned the other students, grouped out in their corresponding cliques.

The nobility lounged near the entrance, polished smiles, practiced laughs, and names everyone knew. Their kingdom came with inherited status and curated playlists.

"What'cha smiling about?" Rene asked as she tried to find my source of amusement.

"Our kingdom of course," I declared extravagantly, gesturing to the students who lingered around us.

"The palace staff," she murmured, nodding at the yearbook kids.

I snorted. "Clergy's over there, preaching calculus."

"Foreign diplomats," she added, gesturing towards the exchange students. We both laughed.

I glanced at the stone eagle, noticing how it seemed to shimmer in the morning light. The sunlight glinting off its granite feathers. For a second, it felt like the eagle's eyes could watch us. I guess in a way it did. It's customary before any big football game that you touched the base for luck. Failing to do so could cause you to lose a game, fail a test, not make a tryout, or whatever else you could hope for that's school related. Superstition, of course, just people wanting to control the uncontrollable.

"The Kingdoms gargoyle?" I asked, nodding at the eagle.

"'Tis the kingdom's deity, of course." She quipped, forcing an old English accent. "All who dost lay eyes upon it must render homage with a touch, lest they suffer grievous consequences."

Taz entered the courtyard and drew our attention. He was grinning so wide it looked like his freckles were trying to escape his face. His shaggy red hair swayed with every step as he swaggered into our circle, Maggie at his side.

Maggie suited him, a plump young woman who wore it well, with a round face that always glowed with her smile. Today, though, her cheeks were flushed as Taz introduced her to us as his girlfriend.

By the wall, a few of the usual suspects perked up, Kyle with his nonstop flirting, Jay, the mouth, and Abby, who looked like someone told her smiling was a felony.

"Way to go, man!" Kyle King called, slinging his arm around Taz's shoulder. "Dude, is her sister single?" he added slyly.

Jason Root and Abby Browning weren't far behind, Abby with her gum pop and Jason already winding up with something inappropriate to say.

Abby rolled her eyes. "Congrats, I guess. Don't expect me to plan the wedding."

Jay snorted a laugh. "So, Maggie, you ready for those late-night study dates with Taz?"

"Oh, c'mon, man." Taz begged.

Jay ruffled his shaggy red hair. "You're a lucky leprechaun." Taz pushed him away and tried to fix his hair. "You show her your pot of gold yet, bro?" He wiggled his brows.

"Ok, mouth." I warned from my perch on the wall. "Don't be disgusting."

Maggie was a good sport, though; she smiled and rolled her eyes. "Jay, don't you worry about our *'study dates.'* I'm sure Terry could provide some notes if you're lacking."

"Ha!" Logan laughed from the wall.

The banter buzzed around the couple; harmless jokes tossed like friendship confetti. Watching the two together, though, I couldn't help thinking how natural it looked. Mags had always seemed like the missing piece, and now the picture was finally complete.

Abby strolled up to where Renee and I sat, leaning against the wall between us. "So, Terry finally asked her out," she stated indifferently, popping her gum. "That's cool."

I wasn't surprised by her flat tone. Abby always seemed to suffer from emotional constipation. If deadpan were a personality, Abby had it.

I'd seen her light up once last fall, only for a moment, when she thought no one was watching. She just had trouble with feelings, especially the loud ones.

Rene huffed at Abby's lack of enthusiasm and jumped down off the wall.

"That's awesome." Rene corrected her.

Rene didn't like Abby much; she only tolerated her for my sake. Even I tired of Abby's constant stoic demeanor sometimes. Still, she'd always meant well; she just had trouble showing it. Rene moved to Maggie's side, evening the odds against the boys.

"So... How's Charlie?" Abby asked without a hint of emotion on her face.

"Why the hell is everyone asking me that?" I snapped, jumping off the wall and was about to ask what was going on when I saw Charlie sauntering through the courtyard. "Wait. Don't answer that; I'll find out for myself."

"Goody..." Abby sighed dryly.

I made a beeline for Charlie, but Logan got to him first. They were scowling at one another. Neither had noticed me, so I froze and ducked behind a group of chatting students.

Logan had caught Charlie by the arm, his voice low and sharp. They were talking in an aggressive, yet secretive manner. I couldn't hear what was being said, but they seemed irritated as they spoke; Charlie's scowl deepened, and for a moment they looked like two bulls about to lock horns.

What the heck is going on? I fumed, ready to march over, but the loud clang of the bell cut me off before I could start my aggressive questioning. Logan dropped Charlie's arm, and the two men split fast: Charlie bolting through the doors without even glancing at me and Logan turning straight into my path.

"Oof!" I gasped as I slammed into the wall of his chest. His hands closed around my upper arms, steadying me before I could stumble backwards.

Logan towered over me, at least a foot taller, and his touch sent a prickling current racing up and down my neck all the way to my fingertips. He exhaled hard, looking down at me.

"Geez, Marie!" he chuckled. "Sorry, I didn't see you there."

I blinked at him like an idiot, uselessly nodding, still rattled.

"You'd better get to class, shorty. You're all the way over in the math wing first period, right? Mr. Molson's a douche when you're late." He released me, and jogged unabashed to the wall where he left his books. "Trust me, he's a douche," he added over his shoulder as he passed me again and headed for the doors.

I looked around, bewildered. This wasn't the first time Logan had fried my nerves. Damnit. Now I had to wait until lunch to corner Logan, and Charlie had been so elusive lately, I wasn't sure I'd catch him at all.

The first bell shrieked, and it startled me. "Damnit!" I blurted. "I'm going to be late." Running to the wall, I grabbed my bookbag and darted into school.

I ran to my class.

Logan was right, Mr. Molson was a douche.

4

THE NOBLE ASSHOLE

Marie

After class, I grabbed two lessons' worth of books from my locker, hoping that'd give me more time to catch Charlie before his next one. I hurried over to the stairs, the fastest way from Charlie's tech class to his government.

Peering over the railing, I watched students funnel in below. From the top floor, I should be able to see him headed up.

Finally, I spotted him. He was halfway to the stairs when he looked up and met my eyes. I smiled and casually waved my fingers at him. He glanced away and spun, changing course and bumping into people. I frowned and dropped my hand, embarrassment and uncertainty hitting me like a punch in the gut. I glanced around, hoping no one had witnessed the unspoken rejection, then headed for class.

What had I done? I couldn't remember fighting about anything. Why was he being so evasive? My mind flashed to Logan and the way he gripped Charlie's arm that morning, and the way their expressions changed. Whatever he said to Charlie, had him acting weird as hell, and I'm not about it.

"Logan." I hissed. "I am going to kill him." I growled as I stomped off to class.

* * *

Rene was in my history class. It's almost impossible to stay mad with her around. She must've seen my face the second I walked in, because she mirrored my pout, lip out, eyebrows furrowed.

"What's wrong?" She asked as I slid into my seat beside her.

I shook my head. "It's just Charlie… and your stupid brother."

Rene's gasp was full of drama. "What'd he do? You want me to sabotage his dinner tonight?"

She tried to look menacing, but she just looked cute, like an angry kitten.

"Tempting," I muttered. "But no. I'm not positive, but I think Logan said something to Charlie. Now he's acting weird."

I avoided looking at her face; she was trying way too hard to make me laugh, and I wasn't ready to let go of my righteous fury just yet.

"Charlie? Logan doesn't even talk to him. What do you think he said?"

"No idea… but I'm gonna find out."

I slapped my palm on the desk and regretted it, wincing and rubbing the sting. Rene tried not to laugh, which didn't help. I cracked a smile.

Mr. Case, our squat, aging history teacher, stood at the front of the room. His glasses magnified his eyes so dramatically that it was like being taught by a disgruntled owl. He read from the projector slide while another student clicked through the PowerPoint.

"In Greek mythology," he intoned, "centaurs were creatures with the upper body of a man and the lower body of a horse. Their wild and unruly nature was known for excessive drinking and lustful behavior.

One boy in the class grabbed the sides of his desk and started making humping motions, accompanied by a concert of whinnying. Some boys thought this hilarious and began to chuckle and bray along. Steve, one of them, turned towards us and winked at Rene, clutching his wrist and displaying his clenched fist, as if it's his unit.

"Ew," she muttered, recoiling. She leaned on her desk and whispered, "Did you see that? He winked at me."

I nodded and shrugged. At least he's not shy, I mouthed back. Then looked again. "Kind of cute though." I teased. "Court jesters?"

She rolled her eyes like I'd just told her the cafeteria was serving wet cardboard again.

"Mr. Parker!" Mr. Case didn't sound amused. "Would you like to add something to the lesson?" he snapped. "Or you would care to tell the office what you find so hilarious?" he asked, eyeing the boy over his spectacles.

The boy blinked innocently and shrugged as if to say. *Who, me?*

Mr. Case adjusted his glasses with a grunt. "In contrast to their baser cousins…" he said, glaring, "…was the centaur Chiron, renowned for his wisdom and gentler nature. He was even said to have trained heroes like Achilles."

Why are we still doing this? I thought. Who even cares about ancient creatures that never existed?

Rene and I passed notes and whispered through most of it. She doodled a unicorn with Mr. Case's glasses, which scored a snort of approval from me.

* * *

Charlie's cold shoulder stung less after class, a temporary return to normalcy before lunch.

Our group sat at the usual table, across from Logan's, but he wasn't there.

Everyone else chatted, Terry and Maggie, about upcoming clubs and new teachers. I tried to keep up, nodding in the right places. I was happy for Terry… but I couldn't focus. Staring down at my slice of pizza, chewing absently, I replayed the courtyard scene in my mind for the hundredth time.

What had Logan said? Why was Charlie avoiding me?

Why didn't he just tell me if he wanted to end things? I'm not clueless. I'm aware I'm not his usual type.

Logan walked into the cafeteria, looking ticked off. But when his eyes met mine, his expression softened.

I should've let it go. I should've finished my pizza and pretended it didn't matter.

But it did.

I dropped my pizza onto the tray and pushed back from the table, almost knocking over the chair in my rush. Conversation stalled as heads turned. I heard someone whisper, "Oooo… she's pissed…" followed by a chorus of muttered reactions behind me as I strode toward him.

My eyes did the talking. I didn't ask for answers; I demanded them.

Logan caught my wrist and led me through the cafeteria doors, into the courtyard where fewer people lingered.

When I felt we'd gone far enough, I planted my feet, yanking my hand from his grip. I will not be dragged around like some damn puppy.

"What is going on?" I demanded, my breath coming faster than I'd like. "What did you say to Charlie this morning?"

Logan exhales, eyes narrowing. "Charlie's no good for you, Marie."

There it is. So damn matter of fact. So confident, like he gets to decide. The audacity of this man!

"Oh, really?" I threw my arms up. "And what makes you think it's your decision to make? Don't you think that should be up to me and Charlie?" I paced once and then spun back around before Logan could interrupt. "He looked right at me, from the bottom of the stairs, and then bolted! Was that because of you?"

His jaw tensed. "Maybe. Or maybe he's just too chickenshit to deal with it."

"Deal with what, Logan?" My hands planted on my hips now.

"I… He's…" He hesitated, then dragged a hand through his hair, frustration settling on his face like he was the one being wronged. "I don't want to see you get hurt, okay? That's it. So I had some words with him."

I crossed my arms, glare sharpening. His ridiculous protectiveness. His concern.

"Some words?" I repeated. "What are you talking about?"

He paused, running his tongue along his teeth like he's deciding whether to argue or let me win. Finally, he exhales. "Fine. You're right. It's your decision."

I sighed too hard, like it could push the whole tangled mess back down where it belonged. I didn't want his control or his judgment. I didn't want his… his stupid concern; a concern that didn't feel so stupid when I looked at it.

Because the truth was… I knew him.

He wasn't arrogant. He was loyal. He wasn't just bold. He was protective. Thoughtful. And unfortunately, infuriatingly attractive… which made everything so much worse!

He didn't even notice, which might've been the most maddening part of all.

An audible growl of frustration slipped from me as a loose lock of raven-colored hair had fallen into his face, just enough to make him look annoyingly perfect. He brushed it away, and those damn stormy eyes, sharp and clear like glass, locked onto mine.

I realized their power in seventh grade, and they hadn't let up since. If anything, they'd gotten worse. Logan had aged like fine wine, and I was tempted to take a drink.

"I don't think you see how much better you are than him," Logan insisted, shaking his head. "He doesn't deserve you."

"Oh, pfff." I scoffed, rolling my eyes so hard I half expected them to roll out of my sockets and onto the ground.

He smirked slightly.

"Marie," he warned. "He's an asshole."

"So are you!"

He laughed once, dry and short. "Wow. Okay."

I shrugged. "Well, you are. The noble, pain-in-the-ass best friend kind… but still an asshole."

"Fantastic. I'm a noble asshole. Do I at least get a badge with my title?"

"I'll make you one. Out of paper clips," I replied, grinning before I could stop myself.

Something shifted in his expression; his voice dropped low. "He's going to talk to you after school," he muttered.

I paused. "Talk? About what?"

Logan didn't answer, just eyed me, and in that instant. I knew.

No, no, this isn't. He wouldn't. Would he? Charlie was gonna break up with me.

The thought slammed against my chest so hard that I forgot how to breathe. I swallowed the sting rising in my throat.

Of course he was; it made sense. Every avoidance would've stemmed from that. Somehow, Logan noticed it and said something, and now Charlie's done with the forgettable girl next door who never saw it coming. *AKA me.*

Logan shifted his weight beside me, his posture suddenly too careful. He read me like a book.

"I can't say exactly." he said.

I bit my lip hard, forcing myself to hold it together, but my body betrayed me. He noticed before I could hide it, and before I could tell him not to, he wrapped me in his arms.

"It's alright," he murmured.

His voice was steady, and his warmth folded around me like a shield. "Whatever happens, just remember, he's a smooth-brained bastard." He pulled back just enough to catch my gaze. "But if you're into that, who am I to judge?"

The breath I'd been holding came out in a cracked laugh. "You're impossible."

"You're welcome."

Pine and something warm filled my lungs, and I despised that I leaned into it. He felt like calm. Like safety. Like everything I shouldn't have wanted in this moment.

He held me for a second longer, then eased back, his eyes scanning mine. "If you want me to go with you, I will."

"No." I shook my head, slower this time, trying to pull myself back into shape. "I'll handle it. I just need to… get a grip."

His head tilted as his jaw flexed, words bottled behind clenched teeth. When he spoke again, his voice dropped an octave and carried something sharp beneath its softness. "He's asking for trouble, if he doesn't talk to you, and I'll be happy to deliver."

"Brute."

"Well which is it? Noble asshole or brute?" brushing me off with a smirk.

"I'm not sure I can keep up with all these titles."

"Logan..."

"Hmm?"

"Shut up." I teased.

He smiled. "Just saying, I've got your back if you need it. I'm not leaving. Not now. Not ever."

I nodded, the corner of my mouth twitching. "I'll be fine. It just... sucks."

"In that case, I'll wait for you by the student lot?"

"No, it's alright. I'll take the bus."

He sighed through his nose, then softened when he saw me swipe at a stray tear. "If you change your mind," he replied gently, "or if you need me... or Rene, just text. We'll come get you."

That smile, lopsided and lazy, hooked the corner of his mouth, and there I was, watching his lips. Again.

Curiosity flickered, sharp and dangerous.

What would they feel like... against mine?

I shook the thought away and pressed my lips into a firm, embarrassed line. Get a grip, Marie.

"You good?" he asked, brow raised like he already knew the answer.

Heat flared in my cheeks. "Yeah."

He slung an arm around my shoulder without fanfare, as if it's no big deal. "C'mon, I'm starving."

We started back toward the lunchroom. I snuck a glance up at him from beneath his arm, and his eyes found mine just long enough to make me wish they hadn't.

"It's gonna be okay," he reassured, grin widening. "I've got your back."

Then came the wink.

A stupid, gut-punching, heart-melting wink.

"Noble asshole..."

5

RIFT IN THE WOODS

Marie

Bus number 700 sat in the lineup beside my school, and I hiked the backpack strap higher over my shoulder as I made my way to it.

I peered between the two buses as I walked, toward the student parking lot across the way, last chance to change course and ride home with Logan and Rene.

No, I needed to know what was going on, or it'd eat me alive; not that it hasn't already been feasting on my nerves all day.

I climbed the stairs to my bus and turned to examine the familiar faces already seated, one of whom looked up and met my eyes. His brows rose, and then he looked down at his phone and started texting fervently.

I made my way down the aisle, turning my hips to avoid the band girl with the enormous tuba she had in the seat with her.

My seat was on the left, third from the back; its brown vinyl cracked at one seam. I flopped into it, pulling my backpack onto my lap and pressed my forehead to the smudged glass. Outside, students swarm the sidewalk, laughing, shouting, and shoving past each other. I scanned the crowd while I waited, hoping, stupidly, that he'd show up and everything would feel normal again.

But then I saw him.

He strolled toward the bus with a girl clinging to his arm. She was tall,

20

blonde, and glossy in that magazine-cover way. Her laugh carried over the noise, high and sharp, and then, because the universe has a sick sense of humor, he kissed her.

Forget a quick peck or a casual farewell; I'm talking about the kiss that used to quicken my pulse, the kind he'd given me just last week.

For a beat, my brain refused to process what I was seeing, maybe trying to spare me, but the image stuck. My stomach dropped, and I went still.

"Asshole," I muttered as I shook my head, trying to shake the image loose like an old Etch-a-Sketch. "Cheating asshole."

The self-doubt monsters crawled out from the corners of my mind, knives in hand, already carving into whatever confidence I have left. I felt so stupid…

Someone behind me gasped, Evelyn, I think.

"Oh my god, is that Ava?"

"Totally. She told me they hooked up at the party last weekend."

"Wait, aren't he and Marie still together?"

A face briefly appeared above the tall seat, scoffing. "Guess not anymore."

I shrunk down in my seat, my heart racing. The bus felt smaller, louder, and my face burned with embarrassment. I stared out the window, hoping the crack in the vinyl seat would open up and swallow me whole.

Charlie climbed aboard, still grinning. Ava on the sidewalk, waving like she'd won something. He walked to me, paused just long enough to sigh, then dropped into the seat beside mine like we're still fine. Like he hadn't just detonated my entire afternoon.

Across the aisle, a kid snorted. "Awkward."

Logan knew. He must've seen them. That had to be what lit the fuse this morning. And our talk at lunch, it all made sense now.

How long had he known though? He'd asked me about Charlie this morning during the drive. But he hadn't told me. He'd let me stumble into this mess alone.

I kept my eyes on the glass, watching the building pass as the bus pulled away from school and started its long route.

Charlie shifted beside me, like he was about to speak. I felt him glance at me, felt the weight of his silence pressing against my ribs.

We rode like that for miles. With the trees blurring outside, shadows dancing across the window as the bus crested the hill, groaning down the slope, and turned onto the long, wooded stretch toward my house.

Right on cue, Charlie exhaled like this was hard for him, like he's the one blindsided and humiliated in front of the whole bus.

"It's not you. It's me," he said, like he'd practiced it in the mirror. Like he thought I hadn't heard that line in a hundred movies and a thousand memes.

I didn't react to him, just stared out the window as the bus rattled over a pothole, which sent a collective jolt through the seats.

"I've got tryouts," he went on. "I'm under a lot of stress, you know?"

I imagined how awesome it'd be if the bus had ejection seats. Although I couldn't decide which of us I wanted launched first, maybe both of us, only his would malfunction and send him flying off to the side, slamming into a passing tree. The image played out in my head like a cartoon: limbs flailing, that smug expression wiped clean. It made me crack a smile.

"My parents expect a lot from me. My grades. Work…" He pushed his tongue into his cheek, like my silence was the real offense here. "Someone like you wouldn't understand. It's just a lot of pressure."

Behind us, someone snorted.

"Dude, she's not havin it."

"Bet she's gonna slap him when we stop," someone else whispered.

A phone camera clicked.

I didn't turn around.

The bus groaned around another bend, tires crunching gravel. A freshman up front was trying to rap along to his music, off-beat and too loud. Someone near the back is laughing at a TikTok. The world kept spinning, like my heart hadn't just been stomped on in public.

I kept my eyes on the glass, not because I'm calm, but because if I looked at him, I might cry, or scream, or both.

* * *

When we reached my stop, I stood and stepped off without looking back. My skateboard was still in Logan's truck, figures. I sighed, adjusted my backpack, and veered into the woods beside the road. There's a trail that cut through the trees, tracing the edge of my property to the driveway, so I followed it.

Tears fell as the forest shadows engulfed me, and the sunlight faded. Silent at first, then sharp, violent. I sobbed as if I'd held it in for days.

I clenched my jaw as my grief shifts, curdling into rage.

"Stupid prick." I kicked a rock off the path. "Self-centered, egotistical, cheating prick!"

The insults didn't help the situation, but they sure helped keep me from falling apart. Better angry than sobbing.

The trail bent, and I spotted the clearing ahead to my driveway. Two cars; Dylan's white pickup and Willy's Jeep, were parked out front.

"Oh, great..."

My older brother and his best friend, the human embodiments of loud reactions and dramatic overkill. If they found out what happened, Dylan would go full big brother berserker mode, and I'd never live it down.

I paused at the edge of the driveway, looking at the red Jeep and the silhouettes that moved behind the screen door.

"Nope. I'm not walking into that today."

I spun on my heel, wiped my cheeks with my sleeve, then took the narrow trail that led toward Rene's instead.

I was not trying to vanish; I just figured if I didn't stand out, I wouldn't fall apart.

Our property stretched across four acres, with forests enclosing us on three sides. The trails curved, splitting in different directions, giving me plenty of space to wander without straying too far.

Just as I settled into my steps, an awful realization hit me.

"Oh, crap." I spun around to look back towards my house.

I was supposed to go into town after school and fill out an application at the market. With a groan, I rubbed my temples.

I was 16, quickly approaching 17, and Mom and Dad didn't have the extra cash for a car, so I was getting one myself. No complaints; I never expected them to buy me one, but now that school was back in session, my babysitting and dog-sitting gigs had slowed down. I was hoping Mr. Mike might have needed a part-time helper on weekends.

But did I go after school?

No.

Because I was too busy being emotionally obliterated by my cheating, spineless ex.

I blew my hair out of my face with an irritated huff. "Stupid boys."

Returning home wasn't an option. Dylan and Willy would have way too much fun at my expense. My tear-streaked face and general air of devastation would make their day.

I sighed, tugged my phone out of my bag only to find a black screen.

"Dang it." I whispered. I'd forgotten to plug it in last night.

Dead.

Frustrated, I shoved it back into my bag and looked up at the trail winding deeper into the woods. I could cut through to Rene's house. Just like old times.

Most of my childhood played out beneath this canopy, climbing trees, building forts, ducking behind brambles to escape my brother's ambushes. I've walked this trail so many times with Rene and Logan that I could navigate it in my sleep. There's no reason I shouldn't remember the way.

I exhaled hard through my nose, swiped at my face with my sleeve, and nodded as if sealing the plan with myself. Rene would get me out of that mess. She always had. And it was Friday evening, which meant her mom; predictably soft when it came to two teenage girls pleading for a sleepover; wouldn't say no. That'd have given me the entire weekend to recover, dodge my mom's worried questions, and reset. By the time I crawled home on Sunday, my tears would've dried, my temper would've cooled, and I'd have figured out how to pretend I was fine.

Mostly, anyway.

Logan would be there too. I'd thank him right after I let him have it for keeping Charlie's bull crap a secret. I know he meant well, but he doesn't get a pass. Not this time.

Rene and Logan had always been my constants, anchors in this nowhere town where nothing ever happened and everyone knew too much about everything. Lifelong friendships were sort of inevitable in a place like this, but I'd never take them for granted. I'm lucky to have them.

Although the idea of Logan felt different.

I didn't want it to; he's almost family. The boy who hauled me out of a ditch when my bike ate a tree root in second grade. He's supposed to be my big brother, not… whatever this fluttery mess in my chest was becoming.

"It is what it is," I grumbled, giving a half-hearted shrug as I pushed deeper into the woods. The trail curved toward Rene and Logan's place, worn smooth by years of shortcuts and shared secrets.

I'd tell her everything. She'd listen. She'd say all the right things; call Charlie a flaming hemorrhoid; remind me I'm too good for him; throw on our power chick playlist and stuff our faces with junk food until the sting dulls into something almost laughable.

That's the plan. And it's a good one.

It didn't involve my family, which was ideal because they just didn't get it. My mom always tried to give advice, but what does she know? She's been with one guy since high school; my dad. They're sweet, sure, but comparing their fairytale to modern dating? It's like handing a sword to someone in a gunfight. Ghosting, DMs, social media traps; it's a jungle out here.

I walked a little faster.

The woods seemed darker than they should've been at that hour. The canopy pressed low, a tangled ceiling of shadow and leaves, the light above fractured and thin. It felt… off. Just enough to make my arm hairs prickle.

I slowed, scanning the trees, expecting to see the clearing, the one where we built our crooked tree fort, the one that often became muddy after a hard rain, where we'd pretend to be Atreyu attempting to save his horse from the muck. The imaginary kingdom where we ruled with flower crowns and stick lances.

It wasn't there.

Instead, I was knee-deep in ferns. Thick ones. And not the flattened, well-trodden kind that usually hugged this trail. These look untouched and pristine, like no one has been through here in ages.

But the ones beneath my feet were crushed.

I froze.

Had I really come through there? How did I get that far without breaking through the rest?

A chill tiptoed up my spine.

I turned slowly, expecting to see the trail behind me, but it had vanished beneath a carpet of wild, undisturbed ferns. The path I thought I'd been following wasn't there. Only the signs of my passage, bent stems and broken leaves.

I swallowed hard.

Took a wrong turn, I told myself. Lost the trail for a second. It happens.

"Okay…" I muttered.

I pivoted and retraced my steps, eyes scanning the underbrush as ferns bowed under my boots. A few strides in, I told myself I'd find the trail just behind the next cluster of trees.

Nothing.

I stopped and looked again.

The trees looked bigger, older, somehow. The air felt thicker, heavier, the scent of damp earth, richer, stronger. There's no 'No Hunting' signs anywhere, or familiar trees or branches with carved initials on them. No tree forts or discarded toys. No trail. A well-worn path, after years of use by kids and bikes, vanished.

I stood listening for a second. With my head cocked to one side, breathing lightly, so I could hear better. I had passed a small group of kids playing in the creek a little while ago. I should still have been able to hear them playing somewhere in the distance; after all, I'd passed them just five minutes earlier.

Nothing.

Cupping my hands to my ears, I swiveled back and forth like a rabbit or a satellite.

Nothing.

Baffled by the strange silence, I cupped my hands to my mouth.

"Hello…?" I yelled. I stood there listening for the little boys again, but still heard nothing. Befuddled, I dropped my hands and continued to walk.

Maybe I walked farther than I thought. I started weaving my way through the ferns and underbrush, looking for the trail or anything that would get me back on track.

Wonderful Marie, I joked to myself. You're the only local in town who gets lost on the trail behind your own house. I had always wanted to have the spotlight, at least once, to be known for something a little less ordinary, but this was not what I had in mind.

"Breaking news! Local girl gets lost in her own backyard! Witnesses say she's an idiot! More news at eleven." I announced to no one in particular, giving my best newscaster voice.

The longer I looked, the more I felt panic closing in on me. Overhead, the sky had shifted into a bruised blend of pink and purple, stained with dusk; I didn't know how much time had passed since I veered from the path. I started walking faster through the ferns, scanning the ground for the trail that should've been there, had always been there, but no matter where I looked, the familiar markers were gone.

"This is so stupid." I laughed at myself, but it's too flat to convince myself that this might be laughable. The sound evaporated into the trees, as useless as the comfort it offered.

Before I could take another step, a sudden explosion of wings erupted from the canopy; dozens of birds had burst upward from the branches, their cries slicing through the silence in chaotic rhythm. I froze, heart jumping, breath caught in my throat as I stared at the spot where they vanished.

For half a second, I thought the forest had stilled again. Something was moving.

Not just wind or wildlife, but something else, or someone, faster, carving a path through the underbrush with a purpose I didn't understand.

"Hello?" My voice came out thin, strained, stretched tight like a thread that might snap if anything answered.

From a thicket of brush, a man with ash-brown hair burst through the undergrowth. He wore a strange, hooded cloak, his eyes wild and wide with surprise, as he barreled into me, consequently dropping a cloth bag and its contents as we made contact. He spun on his feet and caught himself; I did the same.

"What the hell? What's wrong with you?" I asked, irritated and stunned.

He crouched, snatching up a jumble of small, glinting objects and shoved them back into the bag. His eyes darted behind me, above us, as if the forest might spit out something worse.

"What is that?" I asked. "And seriously… what the hell are you wearing?"

He hesitated, met my gaze. His amber eyes flicked across my jeans, my hoodie, my shoes, then snapped back up to my face with a deepening crease between his brows, like I was the strange one here.

"What in the black depths are you supposed to be?" he muttered, exasperated, not slowing his frantic movements. He bent and scooped up a silver goblet and another handful of odd, glinting coins, shoving them into his bag.

"Excuse me?" I asked, frowning.

"You…" he gestured vaguely at my shirt, jeans, shoes, as if searching for words; his brows were drawn tight in frustration. "You look like you're dressed for some fool's festival!"

I gaped at him, my hands on my hips as I shot back. "Yeah okay, Red Riding Hood."

"If I were riding something, I wouldn't have crashed into you, would I?" His tone wasn't cruel; its bewildered, maybe even a little unnerved. "There's no time to linger." He moved again, stuffing the last of his loot into the sack before peering over his shoulder, as if expecting someone, or something, to come crashing through the brush after him. "I should've been gone three breaths ago. As should you."

The young man teetered around me, giving me a small salute gesture as he once again bolted into the forest.

I stood rooted for a moment, stunned, watching his dark figure slip out of sight, swallowed by the thick underbrush as if the forest itself planned to keep him hidden.

Something glinted in the greenery near my feet, a flicker of gold catching the last light. I looked down and spotted a coin half buried in the ferns.

"Hey, guy! You dropped one!" I called after him, raising my voice as I stepped forward, but the forest offered no reply; he was already gone.

I crouched and scooped it up; larger than any coin I'd ever seen, its weight surprisingly heavy. A stylized bull's head stamped on the surface, its eyes in an expression somewhere between wildness and regality. I turned it over, studying the backside where odd, curling symbols snaked along the rim in a foreign language.

Without thinking, I slid it into my pocket and straightened, glancing back in the direction he had vanished, then scanning the trees around me as a knot formed in my stomach.

"Where the hell am I?" I whispered, though no one was there to answer.

The brush rustled behind me, not the wind this time either, not the soft sway of leaves.

"Hello?" I called, more hesitant now. "Weird guy?"

Silence stretched for a beat, then broke beneath a low, deliberate growl.

The ferns at the margin of the clearing shuddered, parting as something emerged. I couldn't budge, couldn't speak, couldn't do anything but stare as a creature stepped forward, slow and measured.

My breath caught somewhere between lungs and throat, locking in place as a chill spilled down my spine, thick and immediate, rooting me in place with a weight that felt like drowning.

The enormous, hulking beast was unlike anything I had ever encountered. Its nightmarish, lupine body was gigantic and grotesque, easily the size of a grizzly bear. The monster's coat was as black as coal, matted into large, ugly knots of fur. It stood on all fours, its massive head held low to the ground, its muzzle pulled back to reveal a menacing row of sharp teeth.

A long, low, malevolent growl rumbled from its throat. The dog-like fiend skulked toward me slowly, its evil smile oozing a long, glistening glob of drool.

Frozen with fear, I stood immobilized, but also spring-tense.

It watched me, and I watched it, and in that split second, we both knew I was the prey.

My mind screamed, pleading for my petrified bones to soften, and with a sudden surge of warmth, whether from panic or divine intervention, I thawed, turned on my heels, and fled.

Running as fast as my feet could carry me, darting through the trees, I heard a menacing snarl rip from the creature's throat behind me.

Terrified, I pushed myself forward, into the thick underbrush of the forest, hoping to evade the thing that hunted me. The brush relentlessly pulled at my hair and clothes as I ran. I tripped over a branch and stumbled to keep from falling. Each step was a battle; the forest itself was trying to consume me, trying to swallow me whole!

Run!

* * *

Now that we're all caught up.

6

THE MIDNIGHT QUEEN

Marie

As a kid, I used to dream about adventures, real ones. Knights, magic, ballrooms, monsters I could actually beat. I'd picture myself as someone special, someone pretty, someone people wanted around. I'd save kingdoms. I'd marry a prince. All that stupid fairytale stuff.

This nightmare, however, was not one of them.

In my dreams, I was always free. I never imagined a daydream where my hands were bound, I was blind and stumbling in the dark, with bruised cheeks and ribs that ached with every breath.

It's not real. Not real. Not real.

I whisper it in my head, over and over, clinging to it like it might hold me together.

But the dark doesn't answer. And my body doesn't believe me.

My teeth bit down into the cloth gag that tugged at the corners of my mouth, and I moaned my new mantra through it. "Ishh nohh rehhl, ishhh nohh rehhhl." The sound came out muffled and washed in fear and agony.

No, this wasn't in any of those childhood fantasies. They aren't real, and neither was any of this. I'm asleep. Having a horrible nightmare.

But the pain said otherwise.

Terrified. My insides were a quivering, knotted mess as my captor guided me to God knows where, by the arm. I darted my face this way and that.

31

Trying to see anything I could through the hood that he had thrown over my head.

I tried to ease the tremors of my nerves, and I practiced my breathing, in through my nose, out through my mouth, long focused breathing–Oh shit! My mind jolted with panic as I felt my balance falter, and with no way to stop my fall, hands bound and blind, I was sent to the ground as I tripped on an unseen obstacle. My body twisted, my hip crashed onto the floor with a crack.

I screamed in pain through the gag, and he hauled me back to my feet with a snort.

"Keep your feet, rat." He blew the words from his snout.

As we wandered through what I imagined was a building, from the smell of fire, and echoes of people talking within the confines of walls and roof, doors opening or closing, and the sound of my captors boots on a stone floor rather than dirt or tundra.

"Are you ready to meet your Queen, skinling?"

I shook my head and hissed through my gag. Unable to protest further. I'd much rather wake up from this madness.

"Be wise to leave the sharp tongue human. Queen Varia don't take kindly to wildling human filth." He growled as he prods me forward.

* * *

The trek from start to finish felt endless. For most of it, I was slung over his shoulder, kicking and screaming. That is, until he set me down so roughly that my legs protested and I was slammed into the forest floor, followed by a punch to the face.

I'd blacked out then.

I awoke to darkness. Fabric clung to my face, covering my eyes and nose, damp with my hot, stale breath. As my consciousness stirred my awareness into focus, I'd found myself hooded, gagged, and my hands tightly bound. I was draped over his shoulder, the blood rushing to my head, which was pounding thanks to the blow I took to the face.

There were voices, male. "No, I had to kill the beast." The one carrying me said.

"Shame. The queen likes her pets." A second male voice.

"Leave that part out, I'd say." A third voice.

"It was bent on killing this one," he said as he adjusted his grasp of me. "With the rest of the gold missing I think this skinling might be worth more alive."

"For now at least." The second voice said, with amusement in his tone.

"Awake are you?" He must've felt me stir.

A low laugh signaled from the other two as he set me on my feet.

He yanked the hood up and locked eyes with me. His face just inches from my own. "Walk. I am not a horse."

The sight of his bull-shaped head atop a human body ripped the breath from my lungs. Terror had seized me so hard that I lost control, urine soaking my legs. He rolled his black eyes, jerked the hood back down over my face, and barked his command again. "Move human."

I did so, barely.

* * *

Nearing our destination, my mind was wrecked. None of this made sense. My head pounded, my face was swollen from the punch, and exhaustion was dragging my every step.

The queen awaited.

"Kneel, skinling." He commanded as he shoved me onto my knees, which barked in pain as they slammed onto the stone floor. "Her stench mingles with that of another, Majesty, the true thief who carries the bulk of the tributum. This one may yet serve as a guide to their wretched camp, where I believe the rest of your offering lies. The filth was found with this."

A bored sigh sounded ahead of me, lighter than the grumbling of the Minotaur beside me, and more feminine.

My face turned beneath the hood, casting around for the source of the sound.

Sudden light, blinding and stark as the hood was pulled from my head, along with a few of my hairs. I yelped in disagreeing pain. I blinked against the sudden brightness; the world stabbing into my vision.

For a brief, desperate second, I thought, I hoped, this was still some terrible dream. But the sharp sting of the bruises flowering across my body and the cold, unyielding stone beneath my knees told me the truth: This was happening.

When my eyes focused, I peered up to behold a Minotaur woman wearing finery. Jewels. A crown. Gold bands that cuffed her black horns.

The Minotaur at my side stepped forward, placing my school bookbag into the hands of a slim, younger female Minotaur beside her. She inspects it, pulling my books and papers from inside; a pen tinked to the ground.

The two regal looking females looked over my belongings with mild interest.

"What is this?" The queen asks, holding my textbook upside down and squinting at the text.

I shook my head, unable to answer her through the gag.

She sighed, unamused. "It's of no matter."

She opened her palm, and the guard placed the coin into it, the coin I had found on the forest floor.

"So this is the skinling thief,"

The Queen's voice was smooth as silk, but there's an edge, like a blade hidden beneath. She turned the coin between her fingers, admiring it as if it's far more valuable than the broken creature kneeling before her.

"All limb and tremble. I imagined something less… soggy."

She didn't look at me like a person. I am something beneath her, something she was deciding whether to crush beneath her heels.

I shook my head, blinking, my voice straining behind the gag, muffled and raw with fear.

"Where are the others?" She asked almost conversationally. "The rest of your grubby herd."

She clicks her tongue as she flicks her fingers at me indifferently; the gag is yanked from my mouth. The rough fabric scrapes my lips, and I gasp.

"Herd... I don't know... I."

She lifts the coin, inspecting it like one might consider a fly stuck in a web.

"I collect secrets," she murmured. "You carry none." With a flick, she pocketed the coin. "Then you may offer blood."

She paused, considering.

"Whispers reach my ears from the outer provinces," she said, voice curling like smoke. "They speak of unrest. Skinling filth rising from the mud, imagining crowns atop their dirt-smeared heads."

She was beautiful; her human body was as black as night and shone with a golden hue. She wore a long, sleek gown of smooth black fabric, its curves accented with golden trim. Her cow-shaped head was the same deep black. Her eyes were like wells of midnight. My captor averts his gaze as she speaks. Even he dares not meet those eyes of pitch.

"Tell me where they are, human, and I will set you free..."

"But I don't know where they are!" My words slipped out in a panic, too fast, too desperate. "I didn't steal anything! I found it!"

"You found it?"

"It's the truth." I cried.

"You found a sacred coin in the dirt? How very poetic." The queen made a sound, a soft tutting of disapproval.

And then, impact.

A violent crack against my skull. White-hot pain burst through my head, sending me sprawling forward, onto my hands and knees.

I gasped, but there was no air, only the swirling nausea of being struck.

"And the strange writings? You found these too I suppose?"

I croaked out a cry, unsure how to answer her.

"If you will not aid me with answers," she was practically singing, unbothered by my suffering, "you will serve me, human." Her voice was calm and filled with amusement. The corners of her bovine lips tilted upwards in what I could only imagine was a coy grin. "Your garb is foreign. And your tongue... not bred from these lands."

I stared at her, my breath uneven, sharp and jagged, like broken glass in my lungs. I knew I'd be hit no matter what I said; I was too afraid to speak.

"There are whispers," she continued, "of skinling societies to the west. Primitive. Hidden. Crumbling. Are you one of them?"

I blinked at her, my lips trembling.

"Out with-it girl. Your queen asked you a question." The beast beside me growled, prodding my shoulder.

"I don't know what to say; I'm not from here." I stammered.

The Queen curls her ringed hand into a fist, as if ending the conversation with her grip. "I despise riddles," she said. "And rats. To the mines with her. Until I decide what she's good for."

The words settled in my stomach like a stone. Mines. My body trembled at the thought, underground, prisoner, no escape, no freedom.

She waved her hand to dismiss us, then paused. "And captain…" she added, her voice light as silk. "Don't ever bring me another skinling before first dipping them. Filthy vermin reek of piss and muck."

He bowed his head. "Yes, majesty."

She watched me for a moment longer. Sneering.

As if weighing whether I was worth the breath it would take to kill me.

With a flick of her wrist, a dismissive gesture. My fate was decided as easily as one might throw away scraps.

Grabbing me by the arm, he hauled me out, yanking me back out of the throne room before I could gather my thoughts. A forceful grip pulled my hood down.

Darkness returned. But it's not just the darkness of the hood. It's the darkness of hopelessness, of knowing I might never wake up from this nightmare.

7

THE MINES OF MAW

Marie

I was thrown into the cart with such force that I landed painfully, colliding with other prisoners, who groaned in response. Prisoners crowded me on all sides. I couldn't see them, but I felt their body heat and the stench of sweat and fear.

The hood clung to my face, suffocating me, and the gag chafed the corners of my mouth. The ropes used to bind me bit into my wrists, making my hands tingle and go numb. Before I could gather myself, the cart lurched forward again.

The cart's wheels groaned over the cobblestones. The sounds outside my hood were a cacophony, voices shouting, merchants calling, kids laughing like this was normal, as if our forced procession were some kind of spectacle. The crowd's roar intensified, their jeers and curses pelting us like stones. I couldn't see their faces, but I felt them. I felt their eyes crawling over me, and I wanted to disappear; I wanted to wake up in my bed; I wanted this to not be real.

Someone whistled and clucked, driving horses forward as the groaning of enormous gates opened, the iron shrieking. Once outside the city walls, the voices faded; the cart rattled on into emptiness. This road was rough and vacant for what felt like a long time, with only the crunch of wheels and whimpers of prisoners.

Eventually, through the hood, the world assaults me with fresh sounds and smells. Distinct cries pierced the air, mingling with the sharp cracks of whips, the grinding of more wagon wheels, and the relentless clinking of pickaxes, hammers, and chisels. The acrid scent of smoke clawed at my nostrils, mingling with the damp, earthy stench of decay.

Someone beside me whimpered while another muttered words I couldn't understand. Too fast, too broken, and sobbing. One captive rambled, his words a garbled stream of panic, too low and thickly accented to decipher.

The wagon crept to a halt as the guttural bellow of a Minotaur guard cut through the din. Commanding the cart to halt.

The muttering man's voice rose, frantic and strained, his words spilling out in a feverish torrent. "The chosen one will come! You'll all bleed for this! She will come; the gods demand it!"

"Drag him out!" barked a guard, his voice dripping with cruel authority.

Keys jingled as a lock clicked, and the creaking door to the cart swung open. The man's protest turned to screams as he was dragged from the cart, his voice cracking with desperation.

"Out! Move, filth!" commanded another.

"No, no, please! No! I'm a half-blood! I'm part Faye! You can't do this to me! I don't belong here! This is a mistake!"

"A mistake, you say?" The guard's voice was mocking, almost amused. "Eh now, half-blood, maybe you shouldn't be here after all."

A sickening whisper sliced through the air, followed by a wet, gurgling sound. Warm droplets sprayed against my hooded face and arm, the tangy scent of iron flooding my senses.

"Now you're free; and so is half ye blood." The guard sneered, his laughter echoing as his comrades joined in.

Strong hands yanked me from the cart, my feet stumbling over the lifeless body of the man who had just been silenced.

The scent of blood flooded my senses. My stomach lurched, and bile rose in my throat. I clench my jaw, swallowing hard, forcing the nausea down. If I vomit now, I don't know if they'll let me live long enough to remove the hood or wipe my mouth.

I was shaking. I didn't realize it until my knees buckled. I couldn't stop.

I'm shoved into a line, colliding with the person in front of me, as another stumbles into my back. The whip cracked so close to my ear that the sound reverberated through my skull. A scream from the person behind me followed, a raw, agonized cry as the whip tore through her flesh. We shuffled forward, unable to see, away from the sound of the whip.

The hood clung to my face, damp with breath and sweat, sour with blood and whatever filth had soaked into it before. I couldn't see, but I heard the slosh of water on the ground, the scrape of boots, the bark of orders that snapped through the air. Hands seized my arms, rough and unkind, dragging me forward until my sneakers struck stone. My sneakers. The converse I had put on that morning. Converse. I didn't belong there.

Rough hands grabbed at my hoodie, yanking it upward in one violent motion. I tried to hold on to it with my bound hands, but another hand clamped around my wrist and cut the ropes and the hoodie free. Fabric tore. My t-shirt went next, pulled over my head and tangled in the hood. I reached for the hood on my face to see, but my hands were grasped hard and twisted.

I cried out in pain.

I gasped, blind and breathless as they stripped away my shoes, my jeans, my socks.

The laces caught on my ankle, and someone cursed and kicked my shin until I stumbled.

They left me in nothing but my bra and underwear, cotton, pale blue, printed with tiny stars.

There was a low snort behind me.

Then laughter, deep and grating, cruel. "What in the pits is this?" one of the minotaur growled, voice thick with disgust and amusement. "She wrapped herself in whores cloth."

They laughed harder. One flicked the waistband of my underwear with the tip of his finger. I flinched again, cheeks burning, stomach twisting.

"Strip her proper," he said. "I'd not had a tramp with such soft skin before."

But another voice cut in, sharper, colder. "Leave her. She's marked for the mines, not your lust."

Laughter erupted from them as the one guard withdrew his finger from the band of my underwear.

"Heh, she looked to be a filthy tramp anyways." He grunted. "Time for a bath whore."

Then the water came.

It hit like a wall, ice-cold and soapy sour. I gasped, but the sound was swallowed by the hood. My skin seized, breath vanished, and I doubled over, choking on the shock.

Around me, others scream or sob, or go silent. My body convulsed as another wave of water hit me; my teeth were chattering. Someone beside me sobbed. Someone else retched. The water was hurled from all sides of us. Buckets of ice-cold, soapy sludge slammed into my skin, soaking through my undergarments, stinging every cut and bruise I was unaware of.

A voice bellowed through our cries and the sounds of water, calling us "clean," though it sounded like a cruel joke.

The hoods came off at last. Torchlight stabbed at my eyes, and I squinted against the sudden brightness. It flickered and smoked, too intense after the darkness for me to focus.

A rough bundle of fabric was shoved into my un-bound hands. I blinked, my vision swimming, and saw the others. Dozens of us, men and women, soaked and shivering, clutching robes that felt like sandpaper against raw skin.

They herded us down a corridor slick with runoff, the walls sweating, the air thick with rot. A man ahead of me broke rank, bolted toward a side passage, barefoot and fast.

He didn't make it five steps before a guard's spear punched through his back. He dropped, gurgling, clutching at the spearhead protruding from his chest.

No one moved.

A scream rang out as a woman rushed to him. She was intercepted. A large, armored hand fisted her hair and yanked her backward, sending her flying into me, sending us both to the ground, her atop me.

Face to face. A whip cracked, and she screamed, eyes wide and pained, before she was yanked off of me.

The same gauntleted hand grabbed my arm hard enough that I was sure it would snap and pulled me to my feet.

"Keep moving, filth." His voice was a deep bark of warning.

Another prisoner stumbled.

Another whip cracked.

He didn't cry out, just folded in on himself, blood blooming through the robe where the lash had landed.

The cell they shoved us into reeked of sweat, sewage, and lantern smoke. Straw littered the floor in clumps, shaped into nests by too tired hands.

In the corner, someone coughed. Someone else muttered to themselves, rocking. Others watched us as if we're fresh meat.

I curled into myself, knees drawn tight, arms wrapped around my middle. The robe isn't helping; I'm still cold. Still shaking. Still stripped bare, not just of clothes, but of everything.

* * *

I awoke sometime later to the sound of a guard pushing a cart whose wheels screeched and squealed. Food lay in wide-mouthed, shallow pans stacked high, accompanied by porridge and bread spilling from metal buckets.

One cell at a time, he pushed a pan and a bucket of bread through an opening in the bars near the floor, locking it shut afterwards.

Once he'd moved to the next cell, the prisoners got up and dug their bread and a spoon from the bucket, and then sat to eat from the pan. The pan was communal. Just wide enough for a few people to sit around it and eat together.

I got up, curious, and another prisoner rushed me.

"Not your turn, new one!" She was wide-eyed and thin; dirt clung to her face, and her hair was in knots. She might have been in her twenties, if I had to guess.

I backed up slowly, not interested in the food, or any sort of dispute.

41

One of the eating prisoners started coughing over the food, which drew her attention.

She cursed at the man as another corrected him.

"Cover your mouth, stupid!" the man across from the coughing one yelled, holding his hands protectively over the pan. "I don't want whatever's got you!"

I sank back down against the wall, my mind in a horrible fog.

I lost track of time underground, with no windows to mark the passing hours. Unfortunately, my surroundings remained the same.

Dim torchlight, walls of chiseled stone and iron bars surrounded me. People still huddled together on gathered piles of straw, or curled into themselves, waiting their turn to eat from the pan, though a few prisoners paced the cell floor.

I rested my head against my knees again, as a gentle, lilting voice whispered, "There now, isn't it just the prettiest clover ye ever did see?"

I lifted my eyes to see a slender hand holding a dried bit of clover pinched between a pair of dirty fingers. "I find treasures all the time, though you best not be tellin' them cud-chewers." She jutted her chin toward the door down the hall outside our cell, then continued. "I tuck them away, nice and safe."

She pulled a stone loose from the wall behind her, revealing a hollowed-out patch in the crumbling stone, and nestled the clover inside. A wide grin spread across her face as her eyes met mine, darting back to the little trove with a twinkle.

"Here now, this one's for you. A gift. For my friend." She darted, grabbing my hand before I even recoiled. A small, shining stone, quartz maybe, rested in my palm. "See how it gleams? It's pretty, yeah?" she waited a moment, then added, "Hold it when things get heavy. It won't light the way, but it'll remind you the way exists."

I nodded, unable to speak, not from injury or ailment, but from shock. My head still swam; the nightmare pressed against my mind, thick and suffocating.

The woman turned and ruffled her straw pile, separating it into two small nests. She's thin, too thin; her face is sunken, pale circles shadowed her weary eyes. Her hair is long, wiry, blonde, knotted locs that fall from within her hood as she moved.

"Now you won't be needin' to lie in the filth." Her smile met her eyes despite the gloom, as she offered me my nest of straw. "I'm Tessa. What are you called?"

A tear slid down my cheek as the pebble in my hand tinked onto the stone floor. I let my head fall back to my knees, curled inward again.

"That's alright, friend, I'll keep it safe for ye. For when you're ready." Her slender fingers scoop up the pebble, and I hear the stone slide back into place, sealing the tiny treasure trove once more. "Safe and sound."

I closed my eyes, only to be jolted from my curled position by a loud, hissing, snarling scuffle beside me.

I scrambled away from the sound, eyes wide, and heart hammering.

A man had a handful of straw clenched in his fist that he had pulled from the nest she's made me. Tessa's hands hold tight to his wrist as he attempted to twist from her grip. "She doesn't want it, and you gave it! I will take it!" he snarled.

A long guttural hiss coiled in Tessa's throat, sharp as a blade. "You will drop it, or you will pull back a bloodied stump for a hand!" she spat, flashing a pair of elongated teeth. The man recoiled, releasing the stolen straw as if burned.

Tessa lurched forward like a cat, her movements fluid and wild, hissing again. Her hood fell back as she moved, revealing a set of pointed ears.

Pointed ears. Not human.

The man cursed under his breath about her being more animal than human. Tessa only rolled her eyes before mockingly preening, dragging her tongue across the back of her hand and smoothing it over her wiry hair, a blatant, taunting display.

She turned back to face me. "Don't listen to him; he's just prejudiced against mixers."

"Mixers?" the word croaked out of me as if it's been buried in centuries' worth of dust, and I coughed.

Tessa raised a brow. "Mixers? What, were you raised in a hole with the rats?"

I hesitated, my throat tightening, and she lets out a muted sigh, amused but not unkind.

"Half-bloods, wild-born, those with natural Mythborn and human tangled in their veins. The pure don't like what doesn't fit into their neat little boxes. Pure Human," Tessa shot a pointed glance at the man, "or pure Mythborn boxes. But I fancy myself well enough."

"It's not that way everywhere." A young boy's voice whispered from the cell beside us. His head leaned against the bars, so small he could almost fit through them. "In the great city, all sorts live together in peace."

An older man beside him cut the boy off. "Dreams like those will get you killed, boy. Better to keep 'em to yourself."

"Dreams are the only things them bulls canna take away from the lad." Tessa countered. "But the old bugger is right; best to keep a tight lip on the matter."

The boy huffed through the bars at them, then returned his gaze to me. "It's not just a dream. It's true. My papa told me." Then he stuck his tongue out at Tessa and the old man.

"Brat." The man chuffed.

"My name is Rat, not brat." he retorted as his drifted to a small bit of knotted cloth and straw that vaguely resembled some four-legged animal, a horse, or a dog, perhaps.

Tessa moved with uncanny grace, shifting between feet, hands, and knees. She almost floated across the cell floor to fetch the ladle from a wooden bucket of water. Not a single drop spilled.

She shifted the ladle into my hands, tilting her chin toward it. "Go on now, drink. No sense lettin' yer tongue go dry when there's talk to be had."

Cautiously, I sipped the water. The liquid, though unclean, soaked my dry throat and tasted fine, so I finished it.

I moved onto the nest of hay after returning the ladle. Tessa watched me, her catlike eyes flicking between my face and the trembling fingers clutching the robe around my shoulders. She didn't pry; instead; she shifted closer, settling against the stone wall beside me with a quiet sigh.

"Marie…" I said at last, "my name is Marie."

"Marie. That's a fine name. It sounds like joy in a breath." She noted.

"How long have you been here?" My voice faltered, unsure if I wanted the answer.

Tessa tilted her head, considering. Her eyes searched mine for something. "Been long enough to see friendship turn to grief too many times. For a time I kept to myself, so grief wouldn't find me. But now? I reckon the time's worth it. So if ye gotta mind for it, we'll call each other friends."

Shifting, I curled my fingers against the rough fabric of my robe. "Could I hold the pebble again?" My voice murmured, raw and uncertain, caressing the question.

Tessa tilted her head, her eyes flickering with something unreadable before a smile tugged at the corner of her lips. Without hesitation, she reached beneath the loose stone, retrieving the tiny quartz and pressing it into my palm.

"There ye go, friend," she murmured. "Safe and sound."

I closed my fingers around it, feeling its cool weight against my skin. It was small, insignificant really, but for the first time since my arrival in that place, that world, I possessed something solid, something tangible.

I exhaled.

My body ached, and my mind reeled. I was exhausted, in more ways than I had ever known possible, but I forced myself to ask, "What happens now?"

Tessa huffed a soft laugh, though there was no joy in it. "Now?" She glanced around at the others, the hollow-eyed prisoners watching from their own nests of straw. "Now we survive."

8

THE DISAPPEARANCE

Logan

Marie went missing on Friday after school. By nine that night, the Blooms were calling around, first to friends, then neighbors, then anyone who might've seen her. Mrs. June's voice cracked through the phone when she called me and Rene for the fourth time, asking if Marie had come by, or heard anything.

We hadn't.

When that turned up nothing, they called the police.

Dylan's been sending out mass texts to keep people updated, but none of it feels like enough. I have this pressure in my chest, like I'm missing something.

At about one in the morning, I couldn't sleep and gave up trying. I resorted to pacing the kitchen, restless, and munching on a box of dry cereal.

I kept staring out the window, watching the woods between our houses, now a dark expanse only lit by our porch lights and whatever light trickles from the moon behind broken clouds. That trail we used to walk all the time, it's been tugging at me, but I don't know why. It's a small, yet well-traveled path that cuts into the wood line from the backyard. On any other day, when my eyes landed on its opening, they landed softly and unbothered. Tonight, however… it looks more like a black mouth trying to consume what little light dared to stretch in its direction.

My skin prickles, and I pace again.

Then… I see movement. Just a flicker on the treeline; a figure slipping into the woods.

My heart kicks inside my chest, and I move, not thinking.

Shoes, no socks, and no flashlight. I fly halfway down the porch steps before I realize how dark it is, how quiet, but I don't want to lose sight of whoever's wandering around out here.

I step into the forest, and the silence swallows me whole. There's no wind to rustle the leaves, or insects singing, just the crunch of my shoes against the dry forest floor.

Up ahead, two figures stand in the shadows, backs turned, hunched over strange devices that tick and pulse with soft light. They don't appear to be hikers or hunters, and neither group should be here this late. The canopy swallows the moonlight, leaving their faces hidden, only the glow of their instruments hint at their features. I glance at their belts, scanning for weapons; thin, dressy belts, they aren't dressed for an outdoor adventure. Their posture is tense, though focused, like they're measuring something. The devices look like Geiger counters, but sleeker and more angular.

One of them speaks low.

"Is it unstable?"

"…levels spiking the further we go. Could be a tear."

I take another step. "Hey, what are you doing out here?"

They freeze. Their shoulders stiffened as their heads tilt toward each other like they're deciding something. "Shit…"

One shifts, his hand moving toward his belt. "I'll deal with it."

I wished I had woken Darious before running out the door, completely unarmed, like a goddamned idiot.

That's when everything goes sideways.

A third figure grabs me from behind, arms like steel cables. I thrash, yell, and try to twist free, but it's useless. Whoever has a hold of me has a grip of a vice.

The man with the device steps forward. "Never seen levels that high in one person before." He waves the device over me, the pulse quickening.

"He a breach?" the man holding me asked.

The other snaps, "Would you shut him up already?" Something sharp pierces my neck. The cold in my veins spreads fast. My limbs go heavy, and the forest tilts.

I wake up in my bed.

* * *

Early morning light bleeds through the blinds. With my head still on the pillow, my eyes adjust as I blink around at my room.

I jolt upright. I'm in my room?

My shoes are by the door. My phone is charging on my nightstand. I swing my feet out of my covers and stand, looking down at myself.

I'm in sweats... I don't remember putting on sweats.

Standing here for a moment, barefoot, shirtless, assessing. My heart hammering as I try to retrace my memory, or try to make sense of my complete lack of it.

It had to be a dream. Right?

But it didn't feel like one... was I just fucking abducted? Wouldn't that be the most stereotypical bullshit? 'Trailer house kid claims abduction in small town,' would be the headline right next to one about some guy seeing a Sasquatch.

I move, stumbling to the mirror in alarm, tilting my head, checking my neck. There's no mark, bruise, or sign proving injection or getting my ass handed to me. I scan my room again; no proof of anyone being in here. But... something's off.

I dart out of my room and crack my sister's bedroom door. She's asleep, our cat curled beside her head on the pillow. Down the hall, I can hear my mom and stepdad talking over the soft sound of the coffeepot brewing.

Everyone's fine... all good... just a weird ass dream?

* * *

It's Saturday morning. Less than 24 hours since Marie disappeared.

The cops started questioning people early, anyone who saw her last, anyone close. Rene and I were on that list. We're her best friends, and we live the closest. Walking distance through the woods that separate our houses.

The properties butt against each other, but there's a lot of space between them. It's a rural area, rolling hills, farms, and thick forest. If you don't count the town itself, which is Main Street, lined with small businesses.

Dylan's been doing his best to keep everyone updated. According to him, they were up all night searching. Marie's mom stayed home in case she came back, calling everyone she could think of. Her dad and Dylan, her brother, were out driving around until dawn.

The phone buzzes across the table, snapping me out of my daze. I am still shook from the dream last night. My stomach churns as I reach for it. What if those dudes in the forest abduct her? What if my not saying something about last night hurts our chances of figuring out where Marie disappeared to?

It's Dylan with another mass text.

My heart plummets.

Marie was spotted in the woods, the same woods I walked last night, in the same woods where I saw them… did I see them?

If it's a dream, why do I remember the cold in my veins? Why do I remember the strength of that steely grip? That guy's arms were like… I used to wrestle. That hold was not normal. I know how to spin out of someone's grip. But if it were a dream, it might have mirrored those kinda dreams where one runs underwater, sluggish and frail. I look back out the window at the trail that led to Marie's house.

My brows furrow.

I've had an overwhelming feeling that I needed to walk our old trail for days now, prior to all this. A weird, restless feeling, like a whisper in the back of my mind, warning me, urging me, but I ignored it. Told myself it's nothing; I have a truck, so why the hell am I gonna walk the woods?

I feel… guilty.

I should have guessed that Marie might walk here after the whole Charlie thing. I was even surprised when Rene and I hadn't heard from her yesterday, and then when Marie's mom called looking for her last night. I should have known something was wrong. It wasn't like her to just take off without telling anyone.

I shook my head.

No, it's not my fault, and even if I told someone, then what? It wouldn't change anything. What was I gonna say? Hey umm, yea so, I think I had a premonition that some fuckery went down in the woods, and then last night I think I was abducted by the men in black that flashed my memory clean. That's crazy as hell. I'd probably end up a suspect, for Christ's sake. Given my background, they would try to pin this shit on me. I grew up with a drunk, abusive father, until I finally got him caught…

I ran my hands through my hair and looked down at the table.

"It's just a coincidence." I murmured to myself.

It had to be; the gut feeling and the dream, it's all just a stupid coincidence.

Rene and I both tried calling her cell last night, but it went straight to voicemail, which at the time meant one of two things. Either she was upset and didn't want to talk to anyone, or the phone was dead again. Marie was known for forgetting to plug it in. My sister left a message asking her to call us back and told her that her mom was looking for her, but she never got back to us.

I look over at Rene, who was just receiving a text; it's most likely the same one I had just received. I cringe. For her, this text would mean one thing and one thing only, trouble.

Rene knew as well as I did that if Marie was last seen in the woods, she was headed here, and if she were coming here, she wouldn't have gotten lost. There's a better chance of getting hit by lightning on a sunny day than Marie getting lost in those woods.

Rene reads the text and cup her hand over her mouth; she's shaking her head slowly. I push my chair out from the table and heave myself to my feet. I can't stand seeing girls cry, especially when it's my little sister.

I walk to where she's sitting on the sofa and plop down next to her; she drops her phone and leans her forehead into my arm.

She points blindly at her phone, which lies face up on the floor.

"Did you get that text?" Her voice trembling. "They're doing a search party."

"Yea, but that doesn't have to be a bad thing." I tried to sound reassuring. Her face peeks up at mine. "Maybe she camped out at our old tree fort?" I explain.

Rene nods and sniffles. "You think she would do that? Stay all night in the woods by herself?"

I could tell she wasn't buying it.

I shrug. "You never know."

"Marie would have come over by now, though. She would have gone home, or into town. She would have called someone!"

My sister is having a meltdown; her voice cracking as she sobs. I pull her in for a hug. She's right; Marie would have done all those things.

A familiar, unspoken intuition stirs within me as I thought of the woods.

My arms tightened around her awkwardly as I wished I could take away her worry. But words felt useless, and I hated how powerless I was to fix this.

She stops crying and gets up after a bit.

"I'm gonna go call some girls." She sniffs. "Maybe they'll want to help with the search."

"You, ok?" I ask.

She forces a smile and nods . I'm not convinced, but I let her go.

"The guys were asking what they could do to help. I'll call them too." I add as I cross the room to grab my phone from the kitchen table.

I call Kyle first, my best friend. "Hey, man? It's me. You get the message? You down with helping?"

"Yeah. I'm down."

"Good. You good to grab Jay tomorrow on your way?"

"Yeah, will do. Dude… you believe this shit? Marie's just gone. It's crazy. My mom's freaking out too."

"Yea, crazy." I rub my temples, staring out at the woods. "We'll meet at her place, alright?"

"Yeah. See ya there."

"See ya."

I hang up and scroll through my contacts, tapping Taz's name next. The phone picks up immediately.

"Can you believe this shit?" Taz blurted before I say anything.

"No man, its nuts. You good for tomorrow?"

"Yeah. Maggie's already set to meet me at my place, we'll catch a ride with you if that's cool? This whole thing is so messed up."

"Tell me about it. Rene's calling the girls so we'll have them covered."

Taz exhales hard. "Alright. Maybe I'll bring some gear? Flashlights, bats… you know, just in case. I'm not showing up empty handed."

"I don't know. Dylan never mentioned needing anything, but it gets dark out there. Bring whatever you've got. Couldn't hurt."

"Alright, bro… We'll find her."

His voice carries more conviction than mine, but I let it stand.

* * *

The following day, Rene and I pull into Terry's drive. He and Maggie wait on the front stoop of his parents' long rancher. He holds a huge megaphone in his hand.

He smiles and blasts the siren. "Taz-tastrophe incoming!" The megaphone screeches.

"Oh shit. Where on earth did you get that?" I ask him as they climb into the back seat of my truck.

"My dad, he used to use it when he coached," he said, smiling, his fingers hovering over the controls. "Prepare yourselves. This beauty comes with sirens, echoes, and wait for it, a button labeled 'DISTRESS.' I haven't figured out what it does yet, but I intend to!"

"NO!" we all yell together.

There's no such buttons on the thing, but regardless, sounding that thing off in my truck would blast our eardrums.

Maggie snatches the thing from his hands. "Let me see it."

"Whoa, whoa! That's highly classified technology! The dramatic speech mode hasn't even been beta-tested yet!" he said sarcastically.

Mags rolls her eyes and hands him back his megaphone. "Just don't make us deaf before we find Marie."

"I make no promises. But I appreciate your trust," he mused as he kisses her cheek.

Maggie is a good sport; she's kind and patient. Two things you need if you are going to be spending a lot of time with the chaos of Terry.

He smiles and nods his head; keyed up about his new toy. "This thing has everything! Also, if anyone needs a glow in the dark compass, or a whistle that supposedly summons ducks," he pulls a duck call from his pocket and hands it abruptly to Rene, who eyes it with sudden joy as she blows into it. "I've got you covered."

Rene giggled at his *supplies*. "Can I see the compass?"

He hands it up to her and watches her inspect the glowing for herself, holding it in the darkness of her cupped hands.

He's like a walking toolkit. No matter what the situation, he somehow always has the perfect, unexpected tool for the job. I am glad Taz is here. He's an easy friend, and we all love his antics.

* * *

When we pull up at Abby's house, Rene goes to knock on her door. Abby answers, says something to Rene, then spins around, her dark, macabre goth skirt twirling as she darts back inside the double-wide.

When Rene turns to face me, I mouth the words, 'What's she doing?' to her. She shrugs and peeks back inside the door.

Finally, Abby comes out of the house carrying a big plastic grocery bag. She has it doubled up and filled with something heavy. She and Rene jog down the sidewalk and hop into the truck.

"What's in the bag?" I ask.

Abby's nose is buried in the bag as she rummages one fingerless-gloved hand through it. "Ah, there it is." She pulls a small black flashlight out of the bag. "Flashlights. Bright, huh?" She deadpans, flicking the light on and off directly in my eyes.

I squint and push her hand away. "Yea thanks, Abb." I quipped.

"Obviously, I'm taking the black one. Black. Like my soul."

"There's a big surprise." Terry jeers.

She reaches into the bag and pulls out a middle finger for Taz, a dry smirk on her face. Then turns to Rene, skipping him altogether. "What color do you want, Rene?"

"What colors have you got?" she asked.

"Umm, blue, gray, yellow… red."

"Blues fine." Rene half smiled as she takes the light and turns it on to check its strength. "Think we'll find her?"

"Not like she got swallowed by the void." Abby shrugs, then appears to contemplate a void, "probably." and smirks. "So, what color mad Mags?" She asks, holding out a few to her and Taz.

Maggie smiles. "Whichever."

"Just take one; don't make me regret sharing."

"You think we'll even need these?" Maggie asked as she took one and tried to find the on switch. "I mean, it doesn't get dark till seven or something, right?"

Abby shrugs, "Depends on whether Marie feels like being found."

Rene's smile vanishes; she hadn't thought about it taking a long time to find Marie. Her face pales, concerned about Marie being lost and alone in the woods again tonight.

Abby catches the air of dread in Renne's expression. "You're panicking. I don't do panicking. Try blinking… or something."

"Well, it'll get a lot darker a lot faster in the woods." I interject. "We'll most likely need the lights when we start. Chances are, with all the help, plus the megaphone and all these flashlights, we'll find her before dinner." I hope that keeping a positive mindset will help settle some of Rene's anxiety.

Abby seemed to understand what I was doing and played along for the rest of the drive, which was out of character for her, but I was grateful.

9

THE SEARCH

Logan

Marie's house nestles back in the woods down a long driveway, which brims with cars. As I pull in, Kyle and Jay stand near Kyle's battered Harley-Davidson, their heads bent over it like they are debating whether it will survive another ride. The thing is stubborn, runs when it feels like it, but Kyle refuses to give up on it. "A work in progress," he always insists, though between the bike and himself, I am not sure which is the bigger project.

I park the truck and step out, eyeing the bike. "Got that thing running again, huh?"

Kyle ran a hand over the seat, nodding like it had just passed some endurance test. "Yeah, well. She needed some motivation, but she came through." He mutters something under his breath to the bike, like it had earned his blessing.

I turn to Jay, raising a brow. "Didn't think you'd be caught dead riding pillion. Guess that makes you Kyle's official backpack now?"

Jay snorts. "Backpack? Please. I'm lucky I'm not an obituary. This asshole corners like he's trying to ditch the cops."

Kyle grins. "Don't lie, you liked holding onto me. I felt the cling, bro. Real tender."

Jay rolls his eyes. "Yeah, tender like a guy clinging to the only parachute

55

in a crashing plane. Take a corner like a normal person and I'd not have to hang on."

"Can't help it. She's got torque." Kyle beamed at the bike. "You held on. That's love."

Jay flips him off. "That's survival, jackass."

I clasp Kyle's hand, then Jay's. "Thanks for coming out guys, in more ways than one apparently." I chuckle.

Kyle grinned. "Logan calls, we answer. Simple as that. Besides, its Marie, like we'd be anywhere else?"

Jay sighs, rubbing his neck. "So, what's the plan? We pretending this is no big deal, or do we admit we're actually scared shitless?"

Abby rounds the truck, handing out flashlights. Kyle and Jay took theirs with a nod of thanks, and I exhale, glancing towards the house.

"Guess we'll figure it out when we get over there."

* * *

There's a bunch of people gathering in Marie's backyard. Among them stands a middle-aged gentleman in dress slacks, polished shoes, and a crisp button-up shirt. His brittle blond hair, buzzed short, and his pallid face, as pale as ash, catch my eye. Smoke meanders from his cigar as his eyes sweep the mob with detached calm.

He looks out of place among people ready to tear through the forest.

At first, I think maybe he is family, someone in from out of state, but he doesn't look worried. In fact, he doesn't look phased in the slightest.

A badge glints at his belt when he shifts, catching the light. I squint, but the emblem is unfamiliar and too far away to get a good look. It doesn't look like the local police, or any badge I recognize. Maybe a private detective?

I start towards him, thinking I'll ask, maybe offer some help, but before I can reach him, Marie's parents intercept me, arms wrapping tight, voices thick with gratitude.

By the time I pull free, the man has drifted deeper into the crowd, his cigar smoke trailing behind him.

I push through the crowd, smiling and nodding at familiar faces as I move, craning my neck looking for the detective.

Freaking Houdini, this guy.

A whistle sounds from my right. Dylan stands with a large group of college-age kids; his friend Willy is at his side.

Familiar faces, Adam, Billy, faces I grew up with. Adam has two fingers in his mouth, ready to whistle again, until our eyes meet. He waves me over to the group.

Adam and Billy are first-year students at the community college. They were all seniors last year; we used to play backyard ball together as kids. The only person I don't recognize is a slim, beautiful, dark-eyed woman with high cheekbones and long dark hair, who looks to be native.

She has her arm weaved through Willy's, looking around as if she is lost.

"That's Willy's new girlfriend," Rene's voice appears on my left.

"Geeze Rene…" I said, slightly startled. Then, glance past her into the crowd the detective had slipped into.

"What's wrong with you?"

"It's nothin.'"

"Uh huh…" she had one unconvinced brow raised. "May." She said, as she points her chin toward the woman at Willy's side. "She's new in town, moved here from Alaska." she remarks, pursing her lips. "Pretty, huh?"

I nod. "Yea. How did you know who she was?" I ask.

She shrugs and holds up her phone. "I asked, of course." She taunts as her phone dings, announcing a new text.

I look up and realize that Willy has his phone out and is texting my sister.

I roll my eyes. "You know you could've walked over there and introduced yourself."

Rene snorts. "Why?" She looks up from her phone, baffled by my suggestion. "I know her now… see." She waves at May, who smiles and waves back. "You're so weird sometimes."

"Just because you can text doesn't mean you should." One brow raised at my sister.

"Orrr… I can text. Efficiency, duh," She shakes her head at me. "So very analog of you to think otherwise."

Jay walks up, slinging his arm over Rene's shoulder. "I'm with her, bruh. You're weird. And I don't even know what we're talking about."

The two of them chuckle.

The sheriff calls everyone to the deck; his voice strains to get everyone's attention. As the crowd huddles together around the deck, Sheriff Drum begins his instructions. He yells over the enormous crowd of volunteers when Taz bounds up to him and hands him his megaphone. He beams as usual, happy that the sheriff takes it without hesitation.

While the sheriff went over the plan of action, I scan the crowd of people. There's a hundred people here, maybe more, including my own parents. Not to include my asshole father, who even after his release from jail, has been estranged for years. My stepfather is here, though, with my mom at his side. The two of them are shaking and slapping a large flashlight with a bad battery connection, passing it back and forth.

That's when I notice May; she's staring at me with this creepy look on her face, like she's waiting for something to happen, or like she suspects me, like I had something to do with Marie being missing. I glance the other way and notice the detective beyond a large group of people.

He too is staring at me; surprised, I look down at my feet; I don't know why, but their stares make me feel uneasy, guilty even. Which is ridiculous, I remind myself.

When I look back up at May, her expression had changed. She's smiling; she raises her fingers and wiggles them at me in a kind, girlish gesture. I smile back and nod before turning to glance at the detective; he is no longer where my eyes had left him, having disappeared again.

Weird... I thought to myself.

* * *

We spread out into a single line, flashlights slicing through the shadows. Marie's name echoes through the woods, overlapping with the sharp crackle of leaves and snapping twigs beneath our feet.

There's no way she wouldn't hear us if she were here, especially with Terry blaring her name through a megaphone like he's calling for lost cattle.

I keep walking, but something gnaws at me. A pressure deep in my chest, like I'm standing on the edge of something I can't see. The woods feel off; the air here is too still, as though it's suspended. No wind. No rustling branches. Even the usual buzz of insects seems absent.

Close. I'm close. To what exactly, I have no clue. But the feeling is suffocating, thick as a storm rolling in, the hairs on my neck rising.

Then, all at once, it hits me. A jolt of urgency tears through my body like a live wire; my heart kicking against my ribs.

Move. I don't know why, but I need to move.

My steps turn erratic, weaving through the thick ferns, following something unseen. I am chasing it, no, following it. I feel like a fish following a lure.

Rene rushes towards me, her voice breaking through the static in my head. "Logan, what's the matter? What are you doing?"

I shook my head, scanning the ground. "I don't know. I just have a feeling... have you ever felt like you knew something would happen?"

She pauses, watching me with cautious eyes. "You mean like déjà vu?"

"Yeah. Kinda like that." The words feel too small for the weight pressing into my skull. I swallow, forcing myself to focus. "There's something here, Rene. I know it."

Another wave of something unexplainable rolls over me, sharp and tingling. The sensation make the hair on my arms stand up.

Marie was here.

My flashlight sweeps across the ground. A glint, just for a second. I hesitate.

No.

It couldn't be.

I angle the beam back. A small rectangular shape, half buried in the ferns. My pulse slams against my ribs. I stoop, brushing aside the leaves with shaky fingers.

Marie's phone.

Dead.

I stare at it; the dead screen reflecting nothing but my own uneasy face. She had been here; there's no mistaking that. But she never made it to where she was going.

Something happened to her.

Rene's breath hitches beside me. "That's, that's–"

"Marie's phone." I cut in; the dread in my voice is more audible than I intended.

She cups a hand over her mouth, eyes wide with disbelief. I exhale, shaking my head.

"She could still be close." Her voice wavers as she turns in circles, scanning the woods like she expected Marie to suddenly materialize. "She could be hurt! Maybe she can't yell for help! We've got to help her; we have to find her!"

Her panic climbs fast, turning into something sharp and desperate. She knew now. We all did. Marie wasn't camping out somewhere. She wasn't visiting a friend. She was gone, and nobody knows why.

But I know one thing. Whatever happened. Somehow, deep in my gut, I was sure of it; she's *supposed* to be gone.

The thought chills me.

I grab Rene, pulling her into a firm embrace as she sobs into my shirt. "Rene, we'll find her, I promise. Even if we don't find her today. We will find her."

She lifts her head, her confusion spilling into her eyes. "How can you be so sure?"

I swallow hard. "I don't know. Just a gut feeling." I exhale. "We'll find her, I promise."

I turn, calling for the sheriff. The woods erupt with movement as everyone rushes over, flashlights bouncing in the dark. The moment they see what I am holding, everything changes.

Marie *had* been here. That was no longer a question.

Her disappearance wasn't a mistake. It's something else.

When I spoke to the sheriff, my gaze flickers towards May. Her expression

struck me like a brick to the chest.
    She's smiling.
    Not in shock, or in relief, but calm. Knowingly.
    Like she's been waiting for this.

10

NOT BROKEN BUT OPENING

"She won't be what they expect, lad. She doesn't come glowing. Not shining, not grand. She'll come wrong-stumbling, soft, and split at the seams. But the Realms'll feel her all the same. Like a whisper that lingers too long. She won't raise a sword. She'll carry a change no one sees coming."
~ Papa.

Marie

Working the mine stretched time until it frayed, until the edges curled and split and lost meaning. I didn't know how long I'd been there, weeks, a month, maybe more, but the days bled together, marked only by the ache in my body and the weight of the pickaxe that seemed to grow heavier each time I lifted it.

My arms trembled before the shift even began. My palms were blistered and split, calloused in patches, raw in others, and the robe they'd given me rubbed against my wounds like it was trying to finish what the whip had started.

The lashes still burned. Not fresh anymore, but deep, cross-hatched scars that throbbed when I moved too quickly or breathed too sharply. I'd learned to keep my head down, to move just enough to avoid attention, but not so fast that I stood out. The guards didn't need a reason. They only needed a mood.

Somewhere in the dark, a whip cracked. The sound sliced through the air like a blade, followed by a scream that echoed once and then vanished.

No one looked up.

No one flinched.

We had all learned that reacting was dangerous. So was sympathy. Even curiosity posed a risk.

This was the rhythm of the mines.

Swing. Crack. Bleed. Obey.

The tunnels were narrow and slick, carved through stone that sweated and groaned, and sometimes shifted beneath our feet or over our heads. The air was thick with dust, smoke, blood, and piss. Death too… they let the bodies rot in the shafts sometimes. A reminder of their cruelty, and of our worth.

We worked by torchlight; shadows danced across the walls, making monsters out of the people beside me.

Rumors, not loud. Never loud. Just threads of sound passed between mouths too tired to speak and hands too practiced to fumble. I saw things exchanged, scraps of paper or folded cloth, slipped from palm to palm and tucked into sleeves before anyone saw. I didn't ask what they were. I didn't want to know. I was almost certain that knowing was just another way to end up on the floor, bleeding, or worse, rotting.

The guards watched everything, or they pretended to. Sometimes I thought they missed things on purpose, just to see what happened.

I hadn't spoken in days, and my voice felt like it belonged to someone else. Someone softer. Someone who wore jeans and sneakers and believed in things like fairness and safety and home. That girl was gone.

I swung the pickax again. The stone cracked. My hands bled… and the mines kept stealing my hope.

Rat, the boy, slept in the cell beside mine, though "sleep" might have been generous. He was rarely still.

At night, he slipped between cracks in the stone, his small frame vanishing into spaces the guards didn't check.

At first, I thought he was hiding, just another kid trying to stay invisible long enough to survive. But that wasn't it. Not anymore; he's not a coward, not a shadow, not a boy in survival mode, but a thread of promise in the walls of rock. A whisper of hope.

Once near the oubliette — they don't call it that, not out loud, but I've heard the word whispered by mixers with haunted eyes.

The pit.

The place they throw the dying, the defiant, the ones who screamed too loud or fought too hard. If the guards don't kill you outright, they'd drag you there, broken, bleeding, and still breathing; they'd drop you into the dark. No food. No water. Just time. Time to finish what their fists and whips had begun.

I paused near the edge, careful not to draw attention. The grate was rusted, slick with something I don't want to say. I glanced down, expecting nothing but shadows.

And then I saw him.

Rat.

Half in darkness, arms stretched through a fracture in the wall I hadn't noticed before. A scar in the stone, narrow and jagged, just wide enough for him to slip through. He wasn't stuck. He was climbing, leaning, and reaching.

He handed something to the man below; a bundle wrapped in cloth. The man took it with trembling fingers, his eyes slitted, his lips cracked and bleeding. He didn't speak. He only held the bundle like it was the last thing that tethered him to life.

Rat didn't linger. He vanished back into the wall, swallowed by the stone.

I said nothing; I didn't move. I just stood there, watching the grate until the shadows settled again.

The guards didn't feed the pit. They didn't check it. They just waited. They let the oubliette do the work. But Rat... Rat fed them. The dying and broken prisoners left for dead; he was trying to help them.

I've learned a few things since I arrived. The Queen of these Bull bastards hates humans. That part is obvious. Accused of some random crimes and sent into the mines to work and die. No one is ever alive to see their sentence fulfilled. The beatings, the whippings, the way they spit when they say "human." This isn't a prison; it's this realm's version of Auschwitz.

Humans aren't native to this realm, or so I've heard. How we got here I've no idea, maybe the same way I got here. Just walked in clueless and unaware. Regardless, the queen sees us as an invasive species, as some sort of blight on her kingdom.

There're creatures here I've never seen before. Not just humans or Bulls, but Faye beings, hundreds of them, maybe more. Some with wings. Some with scales. Some with eyes that glow in the dark, and almost all of them have human blood in their veins. Mixers, half-breeds, or hybrids.

All being killed off by Queen Vaira, a secretive genocide.

It's hard to tell the race of beings down here; the signs aren't always obvious, and most of us keep our heads down.

Tessa, for example, she looks human at first glance, with light skin and blonde, dreaded hair. But her ears taper to points, and when she talks, you catch a glint of longer than usual canines. If you piss her off, you'll see her claws, and not metaphorical ones either, real ones.

They're curved and fast, sharp enough to draw blood before you even realize she's moved. Her movements are strange too, almost feline; she doesn't walk so much as stalk. Even when she's just crossing the cell to sit down.

I've seen her crouch with a small stone, tilt her head, and make a sound so soft and pleased it could only be called a purr.

She told me once that her father was a pooka, a shapeshifter who could take the form of any animal he pleased. Her mother was human, and that makes Tessa something in between. She can't shift fully, not like her father, but she can change in pieces. Summon claws, teeth, or eyes that flash gold when the torchlight hits them just right. And she's not the only one.

Others were hybrids of humans and nymphs, sprites, or even a dragon.

I've no idea how that's possible, and frankly, I'd rather not know. But I had seen one of them once; dragon mixer.

The bulls had been dragging prisoners down the corridor as usual. I hadn't even been looking at her at first, just another figure in rags, head down, moving like the rest.

But then the torchlight had hit her skin.

Scales shimmered across her arms and throat, shifting like oil on water, colors sliding over each other. She was beautiful. Her breath had steamed in the cold air, and when her eyes had lifted, they had been slitted and bright.

The bull holding her chain had yanked too hard, and she'd turned; the sound the chain made when it snapped had been like a sharp beat of freedom.

Everyone had stopped, and I swore the wave of hope that had swelled in our work line had been a tangible spark.

When she roared, a wave of warmth hit my face; the surrounding air warped from the heat of it.

The bull had staggered back, bellowing from the steam.

She moved so fast and fluid, nothing but a streak of heat and scales, tearing down the corridor. The torch flames had guttered as she had passed; she had been so fast.

Then she vanished into the dark, slipping between shadows like a snake into a hole.

I hadn't breathed for a full minute, and neither had anyone else.

Rat said she was caught; they had thrown her in a cage. How he'd known so much about this prison mine was intriguing.

The guards hadn't seemed to notice him, or maybe they had pretended not to?

He'd slipped between cracks, vanished into walls, and reappeared in places no one should have been able to reach.

Sometimes I wondered where he goes. How he gets there. Why he doesn't run.

If he can move without being caught, why stay?

But then I remember the man in the oubliette. The way Rat leaned through the stone with that bundle of food, and the outstretched fingers that took it…

My pickax struck the stone, again and again as my mind wandered, and I didn't remember when I started swinging, just that my hands hurt.

Tessa's voice pulled me from thought.

"Yer workin' like a ghost, Marie. What's got your mind in a twist?"

I blinked, the pickax still swinging in my hands, only making a thud now with my tired strikes. I don't know how to answer her.

"Just thinking."

Tessa snorts, shifting her grip on her shovel.

"Thinking doesn't get you far down here. We break rock. That's what we do." She glances back at the guard as he casually patrols. "Until we don't."

Rat slipped past, just a shadow between the rubble. He's barely visible and easily unnoticed. I watched the way he moves. Quick and careful.

Tessa watched him, too. "He's a rat, alright."

I frown.

"Rats survive." She said, casting her eyes away from the tiny boy as he disappeared into another shadow.

He was always near when the cracks formed, exploring the edges of collapse, chasing shadows where they deepened. Similar to last week's Minotaur disappearance, the walls' collapse felt suspiciously convenient.

The whispers of gossip had curled between bars, straw nests, and work lines. Attempted escape, an explosion in a lower shaft, walls that cracked too cleanly to be natural. They were called knockers; I didn't understand the term.

Now, they had us clearing the debris.

Boots scraped behind me, picks rang against fractured stone, but Rat stopped moving.

I hardly noticed at first, just a stillness behind me. Stillness usually meant the crack of a whip would follow, so I glanced back to see if the coast was clear. When I turned, Rat was crouched, hand to the wall like it might rise under his palm like a breath. He moved his ear close to the rock. Eyes narrowed, head tilted, as if listening.

I dropped my voice. "What is it? We need to keep moving before they see." I warned, pointing to the Minotaur guards with my chin.

He didn't blink. "The stone's wrong here," he murmured. "The wall's not solid."

I stared at him, waiting, watching, hoping the guard wouldn't notice us.

He ran his fingers across a vein in the rock. Like he's reading the mine with his fingertips, trailing them over the rocky surface like braille.

"Felt the air tug. Mama says we can go this way."

My grip shifted on the pickax; it felt heavier now. "What way? Your mom? Rat, what are you talking about — a passage?"

"Mhm, not one on the maps," he explained, tapping his temple with a dust-smudged finger, implying he had mental maps, then added, with a flicker of a smirk on his lips, "But the dust moves through the air that way. It's breathing."

As if that clarified everything.

He stood, brushing dust from his knees. His pants hung loose, cinched with a rope belt. He didn't wait for permission, or backup, or a second glance. He just vanished into the splintered supports ahead with a confidence I hadn't seen in anyone down here.

I followed him, my steps clumsy in comparison.

Then, just once, he looked back, his eyes catching mine.

There's no warning in them. No fear. Just… Joy.

The kind that swells beneath the surface and never makes it to a smile. The kind you don't share unless you're sure it won't be ruined.

It hit me then; for a boy born underground, new tunnels were his sky.

I watched him as he slipped through the rubble with ease. This slope, a little harder for me to traverse, had me positioned in an uncomfortable sideways crawl. While his compact frame fit through the smallest of places. The way he moved through the vein was so fluid and graceful, unlike myself, knocking a bit of stone loose as I moved. He seemed to read the mine, like the whole place was stitched beneath his skin.

He stilled again, fingertips brushing the fractured wall, brow furrowed in concentration. It wasn't just instinct; he was listening.

"There's space behind it, sure of it. Something waiting."

"Waiting? Rat… wait. Is it safe? This whole place is barely holding."

As if summoned by the warning I'd just hissed, the ground betrayed me.

Stone cracked wide, my breath caught short, and then I was falling.

I clawed at the air. Rat's hand clutched mine, holding before the force pulled him with me. We dropped together; limbs tangled in a blur of dust and stone.

I hit hard. Everything throbbed. Rat groaned somewhere nearby, scrambling upright. My torch lay a few feet off, still sputtering light.

He snatched it up, tied a dirty scrap of shirt over his mouth, then waved his hand, slicing dust from the air in trembling arcs. He coughed, the sound rough and thin, then held the flame high.

I rolled onto one elbow, spitting the grit from my mouth. "Yeah. Definitely broken," I rasped, dragging breath through my teeth. "So much for 'barely holding.'"

Rat didn't answer at first. He stepped forward, eyes locked on something beyond me.

The dust thinned.

And there, rising from the far stone wall, was a mural.

A gate crowned in jagged peaks. Beasts and humans trading goods and stories. The colors were faded, pigment cracked, but it still told its story.

Rat stared.

"Not broken, Marie," he said, voice soft and awed. "Opening. Like you."

I didn't answer; I just stood there, lungs raw from the dust I'd breathed in, shoulder aching from the fall.

Rat held the torch, the flame wavering just above his head.

I trailed beside him, my boots crunching across the fallen stones. The chamber stretched around us, pillars sagging inward, ancient shapes carved into them. Paint still clung in places, bruised by time but untouched by the collapse.

I reached out and took the torch from Rat's hand.

He didn't resist. He kept staring, letting me raise the light higher.

"Ayrah Gates…" Rat spoke as if remembering a dream. "My papa told me them stories." His brows furrowed. "Says they was open long before the realms belonged to themselves."

I stepped closer, torch raised, eyes scanning the small painted shapes, the humans, the beasts, the Fae, the quiet trade of knowledge and goods, and the gates open wide.

"Realms?" I murmured.

Rat nodded. "Your papa didn't tell you much, huh?"

I couldn't take my eyes off the painting. If there're gates… then there's a way home too.

"No," I mumbled. "I guess not."

I moved my torch to the next panel; chaos unfolded in its depiction. Tribes clashing in bloodied reds, creatures crowned in bone, swords held high and twisted faces. War. A stark contrast from the previous harmony and trade of the first panel.

Then Rat stepped forward.

He slipped a tiny satchel from beneath his shirt, the size of a baby's fist. From it, he drew a sliver of pale white light. It shimmered in his palm like captured starlight.

"Holy crap, Rat? What even is that?" I gasped at the strange, secret light he produced from the satchel.

He grinned, "Lumo, was my mama's. Half-broke, but it still works fine." He raised one small eyebrow at me, like he was waiting for me to catch up. "How do you think I see in the dark?"

Before I could ask what a Lumo was, the light caught another painting.

A single figure, standing alone, drawn not with grandeur, but with intention. Centered in the panel. He held no crown, only a blade pressed into the ground. Others gathered around him.

"Kabane" Rat stated, touching his two knuckles to his forehead in reverence. "He saved the realm."

A deep tremor shivered through the ceiling. Dust rained in a soft hush. Above us, the work drums began their slow, steady beat.

Rat snatched my hand. "We need to go. If they notice you're gone…"

I turned to follow, but something caught the corner of my eye, a crack in the far wall, wide enough to be more than just a seam. A doorway? Old and intentional.

"Did you see that?" I whispered, my torchlight flickering against the hidden arch. "That passage… a door."

Rat didn't look back. "Not now," he insisted, voice taut. He was already scanning the fractured stone behind us, eyes searching for footholds among the broken architecture.

He moved fast, hands finding the crevice we'd fallen through. The collapse hadn't sealed. Rubble had choked the gap but not buried it. Its jagged edges jutted like ribs.

"This way," he guided, weaving his fingers into a cradle.

I stepped in, my barefoot sliding. Grit bit into my palms as I reached up. The tunnel wasn't high, but the climb was steep. My legs shook with every upward push, muscles jolting from the previous fall.

Rat braced beneath me, solid despite his size. As I hauled myself over the rim, the air shifted, colder, louder. Climbing up, I noted a stone jutting upward at a tilt, different from its surroundings. This would be my marker; I will return to this place.

The echo of the work drums filtered louder, now back into range, steady and unforgiving.

I turned, breath ragged.

Rat scaled the structure, fingers nimble, weaving through the fractured supports as if it were routine. When he reached me, neither of us spoke. We'd seen something in the mines, and now we had to decide what to do with it.

Together, we retraced our steps in silence, Rat ahead, flickering in and out of the light from the torch I had left behind, still burning. It wouldn't burn much longer.

The tunnel felt smaller now. Tighter. Like it might close us in if we took too long.

The glow of torchlight from the work corridor returned as we neared the opening, voices shouting, pickaxes clanking, carts being pushed. Then the sharp crack of a whip and a cry that turned my stomach. They'd noticed someone slacking.

Rat pressed a finger to his lips and eased forward, crouched low behind a fallen beam. I followed him. Ducking beneath a cluster of collapsed timbers. The shadows here were shallow, exposed.

"Wait," he murmured.

We watched the guards pace, circling the prisoners like wolves. One of them barked something, kicking a boy barely older than Rat in the ribs before moving on.

My breathing was too loud, but my thoughts grew louder.

The painted chamber. The Ayrah Gates. That doorway.

I wasn't done there. Not even close.

Rat touched my arm. "Now."

We moved.

I slid into the work line mid-motion, bending to lift a chunk of stone with hands that disobeyed. Rat had already melted back into the cracks, gone like a shadow.

My fingers shook; the stones slick against my skin. Not from fear, though I knew fear intimately; this place had been my teacher. This tremor was different. It was the mural, the Ayrah Gates. That painted doorway, a gateway to a familiar world, burned in my mind, brighter than any flame. The shaking came because something inside me had changed, a pulse of hope, a glimmer of possibility. A way back.

If those gates were real, and that chamber meant what I thought it did, then maybe this place wasn't my prison. Maybe it was a map, and all I had to do was figure it out.

"Where did you go?" Tessa asked, ceasing her efforts to push the cart filled with dirt and rubble.

I hoisted a stone onto the cart, gasping for breath. "I followed him, Rat."

Tessa narrowed her eyes. "Oh aye? Have a death wish, do ya?" She wiped the sweat from her brow.

I huffed, "Don't start with me, Tessa. Don't you get tired of this..." I gestured to the stone, the chains, the endless dark, the very situation. "This?"

She gave a humorless chuckle, then pushed the cart forward with a grunt. "Course I do. We all do. But I'd rather keep my friend this time, is all."

I sighed and mouthed back, "I'll be careful, I promise."

Later that night, I waited for Rat to return to his nest, my thoughts consumed by the desire to examine the murals that adorned the walls below. However, he never returned to his cell.

* * *

Rat

I remember a lot, but not my real name. Mama whispered it once, but Papa told me never to say it out loud. Said some names ain't safe in places like this. So, I guess forgetting's not so bad. If I don't remember it, I can't tell it, now can I?

My friends call me Rat. That name's easier. When they say it, it means something good. It means I can move through cracks they can't. It means I see things others don't. It means I'm hard to catch. The Bulls call us all rats, but not for good reasons. They say it like they're spitting out rot.

Yesterday, a man died in the mines. Just collapsed mid-swing. The Bulls never even looked. I waited for the cart to pass, then dragged his body to the crevice behind the red pillar. Gave him a burial. No black fire here to make the soul clean, like Mama had told me they do. But Papa said you don't need flames if you have faith. I whispered the words of the dead, just like they told me, then covered him with dirt and stone like blankets. Now he can rest good.

The Bulls count heads, not faces. That's how I move folks in and out. Sometimes they leave the dead where they fall, don't even bother tossing 'em into the pit. Let the bodies rot in the open. Papa told me that the dead scare prisoners better than the whip. I see that too. Some folks work faster just so they don't end up lying next to the bones.

Now that Ren's here, he needs help. I call him Ren; he said I could. But he's called Lyren. He and six men stand just beyond the treeline above ground. I have a secret door, but I don't like it above, too open.

They're too many. I buried one body, messed up the bulls' count just enough. If they're quiet, I can slip a couple past the guards. But not all.

"Too many," I say, shaking my head.

Ren leans in, keeping his voice low. "Rat, I'll need my men to clear debris in the shaft."

"No," I said. "Too many. Too big." I look at the group. Some wear armor that squeaks. One drags a hammer behind him like it's a showpiece.

That's when I heard *him*.

One man breathes through his nose like it's trying to blow down trees. Big and round, with hairy nostrils that whistle every time he exhales. I can see his breath making noise through his nose hairs. I grimace without meaning to.

"Too loud," I say, nodding right at him.

He scoffs and steps forward. "We aren't taking orders from a mole," he said, puffing out his chest like it makes him smarter. "We can take the right side. Shadows look thicker there. We'll slip in unnoticed."

"Not even your breath is slippery," I say. "It whistles through your nose hair."

His face twitches. I know he wants to yell, but Ren cuts him off before he can open his big, snorting mouth.

"Who can I take, Rat?" Ren asked, calm but sharp.

I point past Big Nose, to two with quiet boots. "Them. And you."

Ren nods. Big Nose keeps grumbling behind his breath, whistling like a teapot, but doesn't say another word.

* * *

Marie

Another week slips past, each day bleeding into the next, marked only by the rhythm of the mines and the absence of Rat. I scan the cracks between shifts, listen for his soft-footed scurry, watch the walls like they might show where he's gone. But nothing. No shadow. No hum. Just the ache in my worry, and the absence in the mines where Rat used to linger.

Today, the absence feels different, though, more like a dare.

I spend the shift gathering courage in fragments, between swings of the pickax, between the whip cracks and the screams that follow, between the moments I catch my breath and remember I still have lungs. The fissure waits. I've watched it for days, a jagged seam in the wall, narrow enough to vanish into, deep enough to swallow old secrets and pictures of gates. We slipped through it once, and I swore I'd go back.

When the shift horn blows and the guards bark their orders, I see my opening. I set my pickax beside a half-loaded cart, careful not to let it clatter, and reach into the rubble pile where I buried the torch yesterday. My fingers close around the handle. It's still there. Still dry. Still mine.

I move with the line, shoulders hunched, eyes low, mimicking the shuffle of the others. The torch feels too bright in my hand, even unlit, like it's shouting my intent to every Bull in the corridor. I tuck it close, make it look like part of the gear, something I was told to carry. No one stops me.

Then I make a break for it.

I weave between two fallen, charred beams, their wood splintered. I huddle in the shadows they cast. Up ahead, a narrow, jagged fissure gapes open; I push through it. The air is noticeably colder and more humid here.

Boots echo past.

I freeze.

The Minotaur's shape looms on the cave wall before me, huge and warped by the dancing torchlight. Its horns create matching shadows that curve like talons. It pauses. Directly in front of me.

I hold my breath.

From the shadows of the crevice, I watched. His snout glistened, wet and twitching in the light. His tongue darted out, dragging across a nostril as he sniffed the air, searching for something. He took a step, and then another, finally nudging my discarded pickax. The clang against the stone echoed, a sound that made my stomach lurch.

Shit.

I didn't hide my trail. His eyes tracked the footprints, mine, pressed into the dust, leading directly to the shadows where I was concealed. I flattened myself against the wall, my heart pounding, lungs frozen. And then Tessa showed up. She jogged past as though late for an appointment, then stumbled purposefully, I realized, right into him. She sprawled across the dirt floor, her body covering the tracks he'd been examining. Her robe billowed, her hair tangled in the dust, and for a second, it looked like she'd simply tripped.

But Tessa wasn't falling. She was saving my ass.

The Minotaur's enraged bellow echoed, a guttural roar against the stone walls. His massive boot rose, looming, promising oblivion. But she was gone, a flash of movement, twisting with a grace that only belonged to Tessa. In a heartbeat, she was on her feet, darting into the mass of prisoners, swallowed by the chaos. The bulls stormed after her, roaring, torchlight swinging wildly across the crowd.

I stay frozen for another breath. Maybe two. My hand presses to the wall, steadying the quake in my chest. She risked her life for me. Again.

The moment the guards turn the corner, drawn by the commotion, I slide deeper into the fissure. The stone closes around me, cool and tight. I hug the chasm wall as I move; the torch clutched to my chest, my heart pounding against my ribs like it's trying to get out ahead of me.

The deeper I go, the less I feel the mine's heat. A chill crawls over my skin, the air getting thinner, touched by something foreign. The smell changes too, not to decay or dampness, but to something buried and ancient.

The shaft is quieter now, away from the work lines and foot traffic, but still dangerous. No torch: I can't risk being seen from above. I move by touch, my hand tracing the veined, cracked stone.

I'd memorized the path. The ridge where Rat had almost knocked loose that chunk of stone, the slope that forced a sideways crawl. I counted my steps, knuckles brushing every edge until I found the marker, the wedge of stone tilted just so, the one we'd shifted during the fall.

I crouched, fingertips combing the rubble. There, the gap. Narrow, uneven. Rat had slipped through it like water last time. I was slower.

Twisting sideways, I pressed into the crevice feet first, limbs awkward. The walls closed in. "Dammit," I muttered. The stone scraping my back as dust coated the inside of my mouth.

Imagined hands tugged at my ankles in the dark, whispering nonsense my brain insisted on conjuring. I exhaled through clenched teeth.

"Deep breaths. No one's down here but me. No one but me." I repeated.

I wriggled free from the last choke point and dropped into open space, almost toppling over on the uneven ground of debris. The crevice had pinched closed since I was last here.

I lit the torch, and it flared against the dark, smoke curling up into the ceiling. And there it was, the chamber. I turned and peered up at my entry point; a large stone had rolled and wedged itself in the opening. That explained why it was so tight now.

As for the rest of the chamber… untouched. Unchanged.

Yet not the same.

It felt denser now. Not just a secret, but a promise. The kind you don't speak out loud unless you're prepared to follow it all the way through, and I wasn't planning on going back.

I raised the torch, my jaw tight.

The murals waited in shadow.

"Let's do this," I whispered.

I stepped further inside, and the torchlight caught on the mural of the gates again. I stared at it, trying to burn it into my memory. The gates are on top of mountains in this mural. I'll need to get out of this mine and find mountains that look similar to this mountain range. I wish I had something to write on, to trace the horizon, to draw the surroundings. I stood there, trailing the torch over the image, photographing every detail into my mind's eye.

I paused only a moment this time, glancing at the other images, not wanting them to wash clean the image I'd just tried to score into my memory. My eyes already drifted past them to the crack in the far wall. The one I hadn't had time to explore.

I crept toward it, torch raised.

The fissure widened into a narrow passage. Rubble cluttered the mouth, but it had once been a hallway, arched and beautiful.

The carvings changed here. Older and deeper, beautiful craftsmanship. They lined the base of the wall like a border, each one etched with such care and precision. Some of them were crumbling; others were scorched. My torch caught the carvings there, low to the ground, not art, but writing.

Then I saw the bones.

Sprawled just beyond the first arch, half-crushed beneath a fallen stone the size of a basketball. Ribs twisted. One arm outstretched toward a rusted blade, fingers still curled like they'd been reaching.

My throat tightened.

Whatever this place had been, it hadn't just been hidden. It had been sealed. Some sort of disaster, maybe?

I treaded through the corridor, the dust thick as snow. A set of footprints was set before my own. Rat must've been here; that's why he hadn't been in his cell. No... multiple sets. Boots?

Rat's prints were easy to identify, small, light, narrow, close to the wall like he was sneaking. But the others...

Larger and heavier.

They couldn't have been the guards; they wouldn't have fit through the choke points. But someone had followed him.

I scanned the shadows again, torch lifting.

"Rat, where are you?" I breathed.

My throat tightened, but I moved forward. I had to. I need to find a way out, and I need to find the gates, but I also need to find him. What if he's in trouble?

The passage gave way to a sloping staircase, half collapsed, leading down into the hushed heart of a ruined city.

The city opened all at once. Vast.

The flame in my hand shrank against the dark. It skimmed the nearest column, let alone the far walls, that curved away like ribs from a hollow chest. My light felt swallowed, its flicker dancing along nearby stone, clinging to it as if it too might be afraid of the dark.

Shadows hung high overhead, beyond the torch's reach. Shapes hinted at balconies and bridges, crooked rooftops and broken archways.

This wasn't just a cave. It's a city. One that must've been grand.

I made my way along the broken staircase onto the descending boulevard, now choked by time. Stone buildings lined either side; arched rooftops sunk at odd angles, doorways half buried. The city's hush was so deep that my footfalls echoed off of broken walls, regardless of being barefooted.

Carvings covered every surface; sharp, angular script unfurling like vines across doors and pillars. The wall carvings curved in spirals, function, and elegance, braided together; it had been beauty blooming underground.

I passed collapsed homes, and still hearths rimmed in soot. Faint outlines of murals still clung to the stone; elves with cloaked shoulders, bowing not in submission but in counsel. Council chambers. Gathering spaces. One wall showed a procession of guards in etched armor; spears raised in vigilance.

A small glimmer from a once grand mosaic tile caught my eye, and I stopped to investigate. I'm sure it had once beamed with color, blues, and coppers, under this crumbling arch. I brushed it; the paint now flaked off under my fingertips.

Beneath the debris, bones of some poor souls lay undisturbed; Elven judging from the murals and the clothes that still draped their now hollow bodies. Their robes were long rotted, but fragments remained: woven black cloth, inlaid with metallic thread and faded symbols, covered in blankets of dust. One hand still grasped a spear shaft; the other held a scroll sealed in wax. Curious, I plucked the scroll from the elf. The paper cracked as I split the wax, which became flakes and powder at my touch, and unfurled the scroll. Swooping letters in a language I didn't know covered the document.

I frowned and tucked it into the large pocket I had sewn into my robe. Maybe Tessa can read it, or Rat.

There're several armed skeletons here, guards. Protecting something.

I moved deeper.

A cracked plaza opened ahead, centered by a broken spire that had once been beautiful. It slumped sideways now, wrapped in stone vines. At its base, the statue had fallen, its face destroyed. But across its shattered plinth: a carving of an eye. One. Singular. Set in a thorn-woven design that seemed to watch from every angle.

My stomach twisted.

Crouching by the broken plinth, I saw it. Nestled there in the rubble, something glinted. A coppery chain holding an amulet, smooth and curved. I handled it with caution. The metal was oddly warm, despite the cooler air, and at its center: a blue stone, round and gleaming, so blue. So vivid and deep. Set in the shape of a watching eye.

"Beautiful…" I whispered as I appreciated the stone's depth and the sweeping detail of the metal.

My heart pounded then.

I gripped the amulet tighter.

The torch hissed, and the world tilted.

For a second, images not my own, swarm in my vision.

A massive stone door slammed shut. Elves yelled in panic. A tremor. A shadow bleeding into corridors. Creatures attacking. Slaves. A War. The dog-things from the forest. A whisper not spoken but felt:

"Free us. Return the eye."

I gasped. The vision snapped shut, and silence returned.

I stumble back, clutching the amulet. Around me, the murals seemed to breathe. One nearby showed a gathering; dark elves, gathered in a circle, passing something from hand to hand. The eye, this eye; I stare at it a moment, then back at the pictures.

Their faces weren't reverent; they were afraid. They hadn't worshiped the Eye. They'd hidden it, and Solrek — The name came to me as if the blue eye had spoken it out loud; he had buried them here. Buried them and this eye, and now it wants freed.

I straightened; the amulet still warm in my hand. The vision: if that's what it was, still clung to the edges of my mind, like smoke that wouldn't leave your clothing.

"You're not supposed to take things from the dead," advised a voice behind me.

I spun. Startled.

Rat stood at the edge of the doorway; hands tucked into the rope belt that held up his too big trousers. His head was tilted as if he were trying to listen to my thoughts.

"Rat! You're okay?" I said in relief.

He smiled.

"I didn't know you were there," I stammered, heart still racing.

"I was quiet." He stepped into the chamber, glancing once at the fallen statue, then at me. "You saw something."

Hesitating. "It's nothing. Just… weird light."

Rat didn't argue. He just gave a half-nod, like weird light was answer enough. I quickly tucked the eye into my pocket, out of sight.

His bare feet scuffed against the floor as he peered up at one of the cracked murals.

"She doesn't come glowing, you know," he recounted, as if continuing a thought he'd already been having.

"Who?"

"The one from Papa's stories." He scratched his ear. "She's all wrong. All out of place. Like water in your shoes."

I frowned. "Okay…?"

Rat smiled faintly.

I didn't have a reply to that. Not one that would make sense.

He turned to me again, and this time his eyes flicked briefly to my pocket, where the amulet pulsed softly against my robes. I pressed my hand to it as if that would better conceal it.

"You took it," he stated, not judging. Just stating.

"I found it."

He nodded. "Same thing, sometimes."

A silence stretched between us. Dust shifted overhead.

Then he added, "The stone likes questions, I think."

I blinked. "What?"

But Rat was already moving toward an arched tunnel.

I watched him go, more uncertain than ever. Not just about what I'd seen, but about what he knew.

11

THE EMBER PATH

Marie

I followed Rat through the cracked corridors and buildings into different parts of this broken city. The amulet heavy in my pocket.

He didn't speak. Just moved, silent as always, his bare feet soft against the ancient cobblestones and dust. The dark, cavernous city slumbered around us, pillars cracked, painted murals faded and chipped, doorways lay yawning like open mouths.

The little Lumo glowed white in the dark, gleaming in his hand. It sent long shadows crawling up the walls, slithering and streaking across broken arches and behind shattered statues.

The dust hung in the air, catching the flicker of the torch in my hand, making a yellow, hazy orb, loud, beside the pale whisper-white of Rat's light.

I glanced back over my shoulder. The room with the eye is now hidden by shadows. My imagination sends a shiver up my spine, conjuring unseen dangers that lurk wherever shadows pooled.

"Where are we going?"

Rat's answer came after several steps, tossed over his shoulder like a thought mid-formed: "To meet someone."

I frown. "Who?"

I remembered the footprints in the dust within that initial chamber. "Rat, there were footprints in the chamber with the gate." More of a question than a statement. "did you bring someone down here?"

He glanced back at me, expression unreadable. "He doesn't know about you yet."

I halted. "Wait, what?" My pace quickened after a beat. "Who? Rat?"

Rat didn't answer, just threw a crooked smile over his shoulder. His pace shifts, quicker now but not reckless. His bare feet grazing the stone, so sure of himself. He doesn't seem lost or exploring anymore. The little exploratory rituals he used to do are all gone. Instead, he moves with ease, like the tunnels are already memorized.

He hums, a steady and cheerful sound that bounces off the walls. Not the usual breathy sound he makes when he's nervous or squeezing through holes. This one is different. It rolls through the corridor like a heartbeat, slow and certain and damn near happy.

I bite back a smile.

At seven years old, he's practically skipping through ruins like a play-ground. I adore him, I really do, but I could also do without all the cryptic bullshit.

"Are you sure this is the right way?" I asked, stepping over a crumbled threshold.

"Mhm." He doesn't look back.

"And this person we're going to see?"

He shrugged one shoulder. "Not really a person. Not like us."

I groan under my breath. Good Lord, this child… "Rat, wh-what's that supposed to mean?" I stumble over a stone I hadn't seen, catching myself on the wall.

"They'll get you where you need to go." A flash of a grin. "Nyltak's a long way, and the gates don't open for just anyone."

I stop dead. Again. "What did you say?"

He paused and gave a sheepish little smile. Like a secret slipped from his lips, just to keep me guessing. "Nothin.' Keep up, Marie."

And then he was moving again, his bare feet quick against the stone, arms swinging like a pair of metronomes. His little Lumo shard sways in his fist, throwing his shadow high, then low, like he's some pint-sized grand

Marshall, leading a parade of one.

Light flickered, and warmth crept through the ruins, carrying the scent of wood smoke and the distant crackle of a fire. Rat's humming trailed off, his head tilted.

"We're here."

The cobblestone path curved and narrowed, transforming into stairs before widening once more. He waved up, above his head and into the darkness, where I notice shadows stir along a broken walkway overhead. Within the shadows, a metallic glint. Weapons maybe.

"Rat…?"

Firelight flickered ahead, low and steady. Not the erratic sputter of forgotten torches, but tended flames. Shadows shift and stir against its light within the chamber.

I creep closer. The faint mutter of conversation hovering in the air.

The chamber had once been a council hall. Half its ceiling collapsed, but the bones of its structure still stood, arched rafters, broken pews and tables, cracked mosaics lay underfoot. Firelight spills from iron sconces hammered into beams on rusted brackets, and from a small cooking fire in the corner.

A half-dozen figures are gathered in the room, some wearing patchwork hoods, others in armor. No one was in uniform, suggesting they were there for a clandestine meeting of sorts.

A horned woman leaned against a pillar, sharpening a curved blade, her eyes narrowed on us as we entered. Tucked beside a crumbled window, two squat figures hunched beside the fire, grimy-faced and snub-nosed, with eyes that glittered like cave glass. They whispered to each other as they side-eyed us, their knobby fingers twisting bits of wire into traps for vermin.

"Knockers." Rat hinted, following my gaze. "Mine-spirits"

I nod; I'd heard stories from the prisoners to beware of them in the mines. Said they'd thump on stones and cause a cave in when angered.

One of them looked up at me. Grinned. A single tooth gleaming in the firelight.

"Rat's bringin' someone again," the Knocker chirped.

Rat gave a theatrical bow. "Only the important sort."

The group shifts but doesn't move to greet us.

A man steps from a deeper shadow on the left, his hood drawn low. His posture's relaxed, but the sort of relaxed that could snap into something else at any moment.

My stomach drops. That cloak. That hood.

You've got to be kidding me.

The Red Riding Hood guy.

His face looks sharper in the firelight: high cheekbones, stubble dusting a strong jaw, and those same gold-amber eyes that had darted over me before vanishing into the trees. His gaze passed over me now without a flicker of recognition.

"You," I snap.

He pauses.

I step closer, robe tugged tight around my elbows, the city's cold stone biting into my bare feet. "You're the one who barreled into me. You dropped your loot and took off like a lunatic!"

Still nothing.

"I called after you!" My voice echoes harder than I mean. "You left me to be torn apart by a goddamned dog."

That got his attention.

"Wait…" He blinked, squinting. "Fools festival?"

I throw up my hands. "Unbelievable."

His mouth quirks more at himself than at me. "Right. Okay. That… yeah. That may've been me. Sorry about the Cerberus. Genuinely. That wasn't my cleanest exit."

"You think?"

"I didn't recognize you with that…" He gestured vaguely at my robe, then changed tactics. "That face."

"This is a uniform of captivity, genius."

"Mmh. Indeed… glad to see you made it out. And in one piece as well." He mused.

Rat lingers behind me, arms crossed, grin twitching like he's watching the circus. He steps forward. "She found the city," He stated simply.

"I didn't…" I started.

Rat shakes his head. "You did; you found the door. I wouldn't have come back to explore it if not. And none of them would've been here either."

Riding Hood's expression shifted. Not awe, not exactly, but a hint of recognition. "I owe her thanks, then," he said, hesitating.

"Marie." Rat added, then continued. "This is Lyren; he's the First Flame, the founder."

Lyren nods. "Thank you, Rat, and to you, Marie."

That stirred something up because from the edge of the camp, a guttural voice sneers, low and rough: "She and the mole? Praise comes cheap these days."

A dwarven mixer stepped from behind a cracked column; a broad-shouldered figure, yet not short, clad in heavy, layered armor that creaked with each shift of his body. He leaned a battered crossbow against the stone; its iron arms scarred from use; the pouch at his hip clinked, filled with bolts.

His peppered gray-black beard was long and thick, and he stroked his hand over it once as he eyed us both. His bulbous nose cast its own shadow in the firelight. As the flames danced, they illuminated the engravings etched into his pauldrons. I couldn't help staring at that nose; swollen and crooked, like it had been broken more than once.

"Some of us bled building this rebellion before they were born." He growled in distaste, voice like a grinding stone.

Rat narrows his eyes, and I swear I thought I heard him hiss at the man, but another voice answered, purring and sharp. "Then mind yer tone before I bleed ya now."

Tessa stepped into view, graceful and lean, her eyes sharp and narrowed, her teeth bared. The way she'd defended me on my first night here, she held herself like a blade drawn halfway from the sheath.

My breath caught. "Tess!"

The last time I saw her, she was darting into the crowd of prisoners, a bellowing minotaur thundering after her. I thought she might have been captured. I hoped she had vanished. How the hell did she get down here?

But here she was, alive and well.

Relief surged so fast it made my knees weak. I almost laughed and cried at once. My chest cracked open like something frozen had thawed.

"I say this girl stays."

Ren crossed his arms and laughed. "You heard your general! Fools' festival…" He paused to correct himself, "Marie… stays. But not in this chamber, not at this moment."

I almost didn't register his words. My eyes were locked on Tessa, who gave me the smallest, knowing nod.

I glared at Ren as Rat, delighted, grabbed my sleeve and tugged me from their council room. "I'm a messenger," he beamed, declaring his title.

* * *

The space beyond their council area buzzed with muted movement. I didn't expect so many Mythborn packed into one place. Most wore prison robes, seemingly ushered down into the city.

Tents sagged between broken pillars, stitched from cloaks and drapes that looked like they'd survived more lives than I had. Torches and lanterns burned, throwing small, trembling circles of light around each one. Cooking fires crackled in old cauldrons, smoke curling into rafters that struggled to hold. Someone smeared unfamiliar sigils onto walls near doorways with paint.

Every flame becomes a point on a map I can't quite see, scattered lights in the dark, like a trail. An ember path. The thought hits me before I can stop it.

Some of them were clearly warriors, with decent clothes and more muscle, having snuck into the city undetected. I couldn't help but worry about being discovered down here. The others were prisoners: thin, filthy, but purposeful, focused on rebuilding. It was chaotic, no doubt, but there was a flicker of hope, a spark in their eyes.

A duo of knockers skitter passed, pickaxes as long as their arms clattering against the stone floor behind them. They mutter and rhyme as they go:

"Stone's asleep, we'll tickle it."

"Wake the path, then triple it."

One winks at me, teeth like river stones. I clamp my mouth shut before I gape like an idiot.

Further down, I caught sight of a tall figure adjusting scaffolding with three arms. His skin like the bark of a tree, fairy, maybe, or something plant-like? A young human boy trailed behind him, balancing a stack of dented helmets that looked like they'd been hammered from old scrap.

Food was cooking somewhere, vegetables and something meaty. My stomach growled, but I didn't ask.

A medic crouches beside a minotaur, wrapping a bandage around his leg. My chest tightens, and I feel queasy. Why help a bull? Wouldn't he just go charging back to his bitch queen the second he could run? The beast growls through clenched teeth while the Elvin woman flicks her fingers through a jar of ointment, muttering in a sharp yet musical tongue. I stare too long, then hurry past, not wanting the bull's eyes on me.

* * *

After receiving a warm meal of stew and a cup of clean water, still warm from boiling, we headed back to the council chamber. We stood to the side, out of the way, and away from the cranky male with the enormous nose.

The war table, cracked granite and worn smooth, had maps sprawled across its surface, held down with bits of stone and scavenged blade hilts. A Knocker snored on one corner of the large table, using a rusted bracer like a small pillow.

Ren stood at the center, hands braced over the tabletop, gold-amber eyes flicking from curve to cross-mark like he could see ghosts of passages no one else noticed on the paper.

"Our scouts have been pulling some outstanding reconnaissance here. Theres much more to explore and map, but so far…" He tapped a spot labeled Cavern 9B. "Assuming these passages haven't collapsed, they were once trade routes, wide, reinforced enough for carts or wagons. If we can clear them, we open up exits to the upper tiers of the prison mines. Perhaps even the surface."

The surface. He said it like it's possible, like it's right there waiting. My chest tightens at the thought of sunlight, air that doesn't taste like dust. But all I hear is *prison mines*. Right back at the enemy's doorstep, the one place I swore I would never crawl back into. I can feel hope and dread tangle together like a couple of snakes in my mind.

A hawk-eyed mixer grunts from the left.

Broad brown wings were folded hard against his body, lifting and adjusting, trying to keep them from dragging along the ground or banging into things. I couldn't stop staring; wings, real fucking wings, tucked tight up against his back.

"Clear them fast. I want my wings in open air, not stone corridors." His voice clipped, teeth grinding like he's chewing on the fact that he's stuck down here, below ground. "This place feels like a gods-damn tomb."

I nod before I can stop myself, even though I'm not part of this conversation.

Firelight slides over his long, wavy blonde hair as it brushes his shoulders, then catches the short beard that frames his mouth. His armor is neat but worn, silver pauldrons, bracers, and a leather chest piece. A sword rests at his hip; hilt carved with exquisite details.

His wings twitch again, and his eyes flicked to the ceiling, seemingly measuring space that will never be enough. He's underground, and he hates it. God help me, I hate it too.

Ren didn't lift his head. "Knockers know the stone better than any of us. They say they can find the way out."

Tessa stood just behind him, arms folded, her expression unreadable, yet calculating.

"We're feedin' nearly a hundred as it stands," she cautioned. "But if we crack those mines open... we'll be facin' thousands. They'll need food. Water. A place to put their bones that isn't iron or stone. And, gods help us, they'll need arms."

A man shifted closer to the table, broad shoulders hunched, burned scars climbing his arms and throat. His grin is wide and crooked, and made me wonder if he was laughing at something only he could hear.

"The old forges could hold." he rasped, voice rough. "Reactivate them, and we can arm a hundred at a time. Maybe more, if the fire doesn't bite."

Ren's golden eyes flicked towards him, sharp but amused. "Dangerous work. Those forges have slept longer than empires. If we wake them wrong, they'll bite harder than any blade."

The scarred man's grin widened, delighted. "Then let them bite. They've marked me before, and I'm starting to like it. I'll take their teeth again if it means they burn for us."

Ren smirked. "So be it, Khett. The forges are yours, forge master."

So the forges are dangerous, and this Khett guy is going to start them up? *Great...* a half-mad pyromaniac with burn scars to prove it, grinning like fire is his best friend, about to light a potential bomb in a city that's already half collapsed. Perfect, absolutely perfect.

Ren looked up, tapping three points on the edges of the map, fine with all of this, and ready to move onto the next topic.

"Outposts," he explained. "We'll need to send someone through the prison to deliver a message to the Astomi. They can run messages to the Triune faye and to our outposts if necessary. We'll need supplies and hands here."

A grumble sounded across the slab table I recognized now as Borun.

"I'd trust my underarms to send clearer signals than those flutter-things the Astomi call wings," he muttered. "What good are messengers that can't speak and float like lazy feathers?"

I rolled my eyes. Is he always this cranky?

"They don't speak," Tessa retorted coolly, "but they understand. And they've never failed us."

"She's right," Ren agreed, smirking faintly. "I've trusted slower legs to carry worse news."

His eyes flicked to me.

"And besides, we've got a precedent for unlikely assets."

Heads turned toward me, and I raised my chin, hoping my posture would help my mind feel less uncertain.

Ren's gaze locked with mine. "Welcome to the Ember Path," he announced.

"Now figure out how you want to matter." His words hung in the air, heavy with unspoken expectations.

Easy for him to say…

No greeting, yet no one ordered me away. And just like that, I was in. I was part of the Ember Path.

The rigid set of Tessa's shoulders, the proud lift of her chin spoke volumes. The decree was silent, the feeling palpable: *I demanded your presence.* She seemed to say without speaking.

The horned woman stepped forward, her stature lean, long brown hair brushing the scaled plates at her shoulders. The hilt of her blade peeks between her shoulder blades. Her two horns curl forward like a goat's, framing her pointed ears and steady brown eyes.

She hands me a rolled bundle, no wasted effort or flourish with trying to be hospitable. "Boots," she said. Her voice was serene, clipped, but not unfriendly. "Fit you or don't, they're better than bare stone. Name's Caleen. I'm the Tactician."

"Thanks." I said, trying not to stare at her horns, which catch the lamplight, but it was her gaze, sharp and assessing, that pressed against me. I chewed on my lip and then found a place to sit and try on the boots.

The leather was cracked and stiff; one heel patched with hide, but they fit well enough. The insides were lined in a soft fur, warm… my feet were warm. I stood staring at my feet, wiggling my toes, and smiled. One boot squeaked with each step, but I didn't complain; these were perfect. It felt so good to wear shoes again.

No one lingered near me long, and no one asked questions. But I felt the way they watched when they thought I wasn't looking, like they hadn't decided yet what kind of "asset" I might be.

Later, after the council thinned, a wiry girl with almond-shaped eyes, cropped silky black hair pulled back, and fingers black from drawling, nodded in my direction.

"You Marie, yes? Fingers good. Come." Her words were clipped, softened vowels, and sounded a lot like the Asian ladies at my favorite salon. Her familiar yet broken English caught me off guard.

I followed her into a narrow side room she had claimed as her workspace. The air here smells of resin and smoke, the kind of scent that clung to ink jars and old parchment. Dust moats drift in the lamplight, settling over papyrus scrolls pinned beneath stones; parchment sheets rolled tight lie against the wall, as well as wax tablets etched with half-finished corridors. Clay jars of ink stand beside reed pens cut into sharp nibs.

She gestured at a parchment spread across the floor, its surface lined with careful strokes in colored threads marking routes. She handed me a stub of chalky wax and pointed to a corridor marked with spider scratch notes.

"Rat say you saw path near mural. Walls, carvings? Show. Show me, yes?"

I kneeled, adjusting the new boots beneath me, and drew. The arch. The sloped descent. The vault door, etched with flame-marks I hadn't understood but couldn't forget. My lines weren't perfect, but the woman didn't criticize. Instead, she slid a thread across the parchment to mark the slope, pinning it with a Pebble as if anchoring the path itself.

She watched for a moment, then picked up the chalk she'd given me. She set it beside the reed pens, as though any disarray might somehow contaminate her meticulous maps.

Then murmured, "Useful. I am Venn. Cartographer. Much work ahead if city is to live again. You learn trade, yes?"

It's the first thing anyone had said to me all day that didn't feel like either a threat or a warning.

"Absolutely." I said with a nod.

Around us, the camp shifted again. Someone shouted for replacement brackets, a Knocker laughed about "ticklin' stones," a Medic was hauling supplies toward the wounded.

In the middle of it all, I kept sketching, listening, and learning.

Because for the first time in what felt like forever, I had something to offer, something that mattered.

Days passed, and I was getting pretty good at cartography. The work kept my hands busy and my mind just distracted enough to stay ahead of the darker thoughts. My group was small, just me, Venn, and two knockers who never left each other's side. Since they didn't name themselves, I started calling them Peas and Carrots. It wasn't clever, but it fit. They were always together, always moving in tandem, always finishing each other's half-sung verses.

They were thrilled, actually thrilled. Peas clapped so hard I thought that the reverberation might cause a cave in, and Carrots almost dropped his lantern. They spent the rest of the shift introducing themselves to anyone who passed, voices echoing down the stone corridors like they've just been crowned.

After that, it caught on. Other knockers started asking if they could have names too, but I wasn't prepared for it. I'm not imaginative under pressure, so I defaulted to whatever came to mind. One wore green every day, so I called him Green Eggs; his companion, naturally, became Ham. Then came spoon who always carried one, and Blanket, who kept nodding off mid briefing period. I named them like I was handing out nicknames at summer camp, and they took each one like they were a badge of honor.

It didn't change the mission. But it shifted the mood. They started carving their names into their gear, humming new verses with their names stitched into the rhythm. And when we passed other groups, they introduced themselves like they'd always had names, like they've just been waiting for someone to say them out loud.

It's strange how something so small could shift the air down here. The tunnels were still cold and in disarray, but the knockers smiled more, and that felt good because so did I.

As the cartographer's assistant, I wasn't just drawing; I was etching possibilities onto parchment. If I could map enough of this underground city, trace the old veins, mark every collapsed corridor and every overlooked hatch, I might find a route out, and not have to sneak through the prison mines above us, where guards work us until there's nothing left, and a filthy human worm found out of place wouldn't be a breathing worm for long; but I can escape under it, around it, in this secret city that no one remembers.

It's sad when you think about it. Looking at this place, discovering a little more of it every day, I can't help but realize that this place, with all its grandeur, must have been stunning when its people were thriving.

Venn passed behind me with a fresh strip of cloth-map, nodding toward the far tunnel. "Knockers say the stones shallow here. They'll dig while we sketch."

I nodded and followed without complaint. That was the deal now. We sketched; they dig. Venn and I weren't friends, not yet, but we were something better than cellmates or slaves. Acquaintances? Trust comes hard with this bunch, but we're all trying.

The Eye warmed in my pocket.

Not again...

I felt it pulse, faint. Not like a physical movement or a heartbeat, but like a pulse that pulls on my sensory system, like a direct line of electricity, the same as my body uses to signal the brain and vice versa. It's subtle, yet so very clear, as clear as understanding if your fingers are touching something hot.

A memory surges into my mind on that electric current; it bubbles up beneath the ruin that my waking eyes can see, replacing my vision with another. Not my memory. Theirs.

The dog's vision came unasked: the corridor intact, torches lit, armor racks gleaming beneath sigils carved in the old tongue.

This dog was walking side by side with an elf, appraising fine swords. Friends maybe?

I scoffed through the vision; the dog I'd met in the forest wanted to eat me. Not be my friend. I can't imagine these things being friendly to anyone.

This city was once a place that had stood proud before Solrek's fire and magic stripped it to ruin. I've never heard of him until these visions, but I already hate and fear him. The eye has shown me several times the atrocities he's capable of, and all I can do is hope to God that he wasn't immortal or long lived like some creatures of the realm. If he was, I have to hope he was captured or killed by now.

I stumbled, heart kicking once against my ribs as the vision melted into a fog before I could get a hold on it. Slippery things to grasp, these visions.

I marked the point anyway. It's another vault, half buried and untouched. The eye had shown me what it remembered, a moment left behind in calm friendship or trade with those monsters.

Thankfully, no one seems to notice my reactions upon receiving or losing a vision. Venn is talking to a Knocker who keeps wincing at falling dust. I stood alone, still sketching, sighing, hoping to glimpse a little more from the eye.

As if in answer, the Eye pulsed again.

A female running. Elven. She's armed with a sword and moves like a ghost. More than once, she glances back at me… at the dog… before she reaches a dead end. She turns to face me, pleading. Her words are muffled; the sounds in these visions are almost always muffled or distorted. I think she knows this dog, whose eyes I'm seeing from. The dog is whimpering. He's trying to focus on anything but her, but can't. The Elven warrior kneels, laying her sword on the ground. Surrender? The dog howls in anguish; it's nearly deafening… and then… lunges for her.

I dropped the chalk in surprise. It cracked against the stone as the vision snapped closed in my eyes.

Peas scrutinized me, but didn't ask. I retrieved my chalk and continued working.

The Eye didn't hurt me… It just knew things I didn't, and sometimes the things it knows are horrible and shocking. Still, it shares its stories with me, and sometimes it answers me.

I pondered that thought for a moment. "The stone likes questions." Isn't that what Rat had said the day I found the eye?

"But why didn't you stop?" I whispered the question, the words just reaching my lips. "Why attack her?"

I waited a moment.

No answer.

I shook my head, still trying to let go of the chase, of how the elf had refused to fight the dog… the way the beast cried out… not in anger, but in grief, in defiance, maybe both.

If it kept doing this, the eye, showing me things, doorways no one's seen, caches no one's remembered, or memories too brutal to invent, I might get out of these mines, but I might just lose my mind. I don't sleep well as it is.

On a better note, I could at least guide others through this maze of a city, better than blind guesses or luck.

When we had finished, I tucked Venn's maps under my arm, pages firm and rolled tight. Rat spotted me first.

"Marie!" He bounced from behind a barrel, skinny legs kicking up dust. "Are those ones the tunnels?" His grin split his face wide. Pointing at three of the rolled maps tied together.

"Marked and sealed," I said, handing them over.

He looked at them like they might turn into treasure. "I'm gonna run them to Lyren and then maybe steal one of Jorrun's feathers. For... reasons."

He dashed off before I could ask what kind of reasons.

Caleen was perched nearby, elbow propped on her knee as she scraped a dagger with rhythmic flicks. She glanced at me once, then back to the blade.

"You've got a funny way of talking," she said.

I stopped. My mind searching for a rebuttal.

Jorrun swooped down behind us, feathers rustling as he landed. "You're not from anywhere local." His eyes scanned me like he was reading a map Venn hadn't drawn yet.

"No..." I said.

Syl had been listening, quiet as usual, sorting scrolls on a low shelf. "Where were you raised?" she asked, like she was noting it in her ledgers.

I swallowed. They weren't interrogating, just... curious. Still, the truth tangled fast in my throat.

"I'm from a place called Keystone," I said after a beat. "Small village up north."

Jorrun raised an eyebrow. "Keystone," he said, testing the word.

Caleen tapped her blade once against the crate. "Never heard of it."

"It doesn't make the maps," I replied.

Borun trudged by, grumbling something about brass fittings, and Syl laughed under her breath.

The sound of boots on stone turned heads before anyone spoke. Lyren emerged from the far hallway. His cloak was dusted at the hem, as if he's been pacing every dusty corridor in the ruin.

"You've been busy," he said, reaching for the two remaining scrolls under my arm. I handed them over without a word.

He unrolled them halfway, eyes scanning the marks Venn and I had made. After a beat, he nodded. "This'll do. We'll start mapping the northern runs tomorrow. Good work."

Then, a glance at Syl. "That last ledger, does it mention a surplus in rations, or did I dream that?"

Syl blinked and then nodded. "Two crates from Cintara's shipment. Unopened."

"Move one to the second barrack," Lyren said. "Let the crew eat something that isn't dried root, or salted meat for once. Rat would like that… Probably more than feathers." He said, eyeing Rat, whose small hand had been reaching out from behind a wooden barrel to pluck one of Jorrun's feathers.

Jorrun's wings flared as he turned and eyed the boy who darted out of hiding, abandoning his quest for Jorrun feathers, and presented Ren the three, banded scrolls.

"Thank you, Rat." Lyren smiled, then turned back to us. "Get some rest, we'll pick back up here in the morning."

12

SEVENTEEN CANDLES

Logan

I wake up gasping in the darkness of early morning. My heart hammers like I'd just run a marathon. My sheets are twisted around me, damp with sweat. For a second, I imagine the heavy, steady pounding of hooves, then it disappears. Just the occasional hum of cars on the main road and the faint rattle of my ceiling fan.

It isn't the first time.

Lately, my dreams are full of places I've never been, and the sounds and smells of forest and smoke seem to linger in my mind.

I wake up sore and restless. Stress, just stress, fucking with me.

I roll onto my back and stare at the glow-in-the-dark stars Marie stuck on my ceiling when we were kids, swearing she mapped out constellations NASA missed.

I never take them down. I can't.

They glow faintly when it's dark, reminding me she isn't here to sprawl across my bed and argue about whether "The Platypus Princess" is a real constellation. Today, they feel like they are mocking me.

Seventeen candles, and she isn't here to blow out a single one.

My phone is already in my hand, and I type "Happy Birthday" to her number before I am awake enough to think better of it.

The screen stays blank. No reply, just me, gazing at the cut off text thread.

I hear Mom's car crunch down the gravel drive at exactly 7:00 am.

Exhausted and wide awake have become my new norm, and today is no exception. I drag myself to the bathroom. The mirror catches me mid-yawn, hair sticking up, eyes hollow. Marie would tease me, call me "Logan the Lame" for sulking on her day. I lean in, splash water on my face, and freeze.

For a second, the reflection blurs. A flank, the shimmer of something equine flashes behind me. My heart leaps, and I blink, and then it's gone.

Just me, with toothpaste foam clinging to my lips. "You're a horse's ass alright," I murmur, half smiling at my imagination, but my pulse doesn't slow.

Back in my room, I flop backward on my bed, letting my legs dangle off the edge and sigh.

The stars overhead grab my attention again. One peels loose and drops onto my chest. I pick it up, thumb brushing the faded glow. I should have tossed it in the trash. Instead, I stand on my bed and press it back into place.

"Not today," I whisper to the star.

My voice cracks. I run my hands over my face.

"God, I miss that girl," I say into the quiet.

The room stays still. No reply.

I turn toward my headboard. Two plastic Scopes hang on the bedpost, one red, one blue. We get them during a beach trip when the girls are six and I am eight. I reach for the blue one, hers. The frame clicks between my fingers. Inside is a photo I haven't looked at in forever: me lying belly-down in the sand, Marie stretched across my back like I am a lumpy beach blanket, laughing over my shoulder.

Her smile isn't perfect, but it's honest.

I rub my hands over my face, then reach for Lenoir, my guitar. She sits in the corner like she's been waiting. I haven't played "You and Me" in months—not since Marie disappeared. It used to be our song, the one she would hum while doing homework or spinning circles in the driveway.

I take a breath and start slow. The opening chords fill the room, shaky at first, then steadier. My voice cracks on the chorus, like it always does, but I push through.

The door creaks. Rene leans against the frame, arms crossed, flyers clutched in one hand. She says nothing at first. Just listens.

By the second verse, I can't keep my voice steady. The words catch in my throat, so I let the guitar carry them instead. The melody fills the silence between us, heavy and familiar, like muscle memory.

When I finally let the last chord fade, Rene wipes at her eyes. "She loved that one," she whispers.

I nod, throat tight. "Yeah. She used to hum it while she did homework. Drove me nuts."

Rene gave a watery laugh. "You never told her it was about her, did you?"

I shake my head.

For a moment, neither of us speak. Just the hum of the ceiling fan and the faint traffic outside.

Then Rene plops down beside me and nudges my shoulder. "Logan, you can't keep blaming yourself. You're doing everything you can."

I swallow hard, staring at the guitar in my lap. "Doesn't feel like enough."

"It is," she says firmly. "And when we find her, you can tell her how you feel."

She stands again, shifting the flyers against her hip. "Mrs. Blooms' setting up something in town. Cupcakes, photos, a card for people to sign. It's not much, but it's something. You should come."

"Cupcakes?" I asked, trying to keep it light.

"Cupcakes," she says, half smiling.

She gives me one last look, then turns for the stairs. "At least take a shower. You smell like B.O., and Marie wouldn't tolerate it."

I smirk despite myself. "She also wouldn't tolerate me skipping her birthday," I murmur.

When she leaves, I sit there a minute longer, staring at the ceiling stars. Then I set the guitar aside, grab the cleanest dirty jeans I can find, clean boxers and shirt, and head for the shower.

Once ready, I grab my skateboard. If I can't bring her back, I can at least move.

* * *

Out on the street, it feels good, damn good. The moment my wheels hit pavement, I can breathe again.

The board's rhythm against the asphalt and the wind whispering across my skin soothe me.

But I haven't ridden since Marie disappeared. Not once. Her board still sits in my truck, like it's waiting. She left it there the last time I saw her, and I can't bring myself to move it.

Now, rolling through the neighborhood, it feels like she is with me again. The wind in her face. That sharp laugh of hers, always half daring, half delighted.

For a second, it feels like someone's watching me. I turn to check, but notice nothing. Just leaves scattering across cracked concrete.

A car honks its horn and then jerks to a stop, the tires biting pavement harder than necessary. I dodge it as it noses out of a side street.

My palms hit the hood as I veer past. "Asshole!" I snap.

I keep rolling and flip the guy off, but something in the way the driver stares makes me glance back.

The man behind the wheel doesn't baulk. He doesn't reach for the door or lean out to yell. He just watches me through the windshield, locking eyes with me, one hand resting on the wheel, the other out of sight.

I kick harder; the board catches speed, but my chest tightens. The detective? I turn again, watching the car ease into a slow turn, heading in the opposite direction.

I face forward, toward town, and kick harder; the wheels hum beneath me, the wind slices past my ears. I don't look back again, but I feel the pressure of his gaze, the way it lingers even after the car pulls away, like he is watching in his rearview.

The rhythm of the board returns, but it doesn't feel the same.

* * *

By the time I roll into town, Cedar Grove's square had come alive. The tables near the clock tower are decorated with streamers. A collage of photos catches sunlight like stained glass. Marie at every age, laughter frozen on glossy paper.

Mrs. Bloom stands near the cupcakes, eyes watering between smiles. She is setting another handful of missing person flyers out for guests.

Mr. Bloom shakes hands with familiar faces, and Dylan moves folding chairs with Willy and Adam; both still dressed like they just rolled out of a dorm party.

Billy hangs back near the bookstore, staring at the window as if it might talk.

Rene spots me on my way in and waves me over; eyeliner smudged, cheeks flushed from running between tables, coordinating cupcakes and candles with Mrs. Bloom. "Hey," she says, handing me a pen. "You're late."

I stare at the card. Already filled with messages. *Miss you every day. Happy 17th, Marie. Come home soon.* I add mine near the corner. *Still watching the stars. -L*

Kyle is wrestling with a strand of lights over the canopy, muttering like it had wronged him.

"You know it's not gonna listen, right?" I say as I walk by.

Kyle smirks. "Didn't ask for backtalk, Lennox."

Abby stands beside Maggie, arms folded. "This whole 'celebration' thing feels weird," she mutters. "Marie hated attention."

"She hated cheesy attention," Maggie corrects, handing a little girl with pigtails a cupcake iced with glitter frosting. "She didn't mind this kind."

Taz shows up a few minutes later, dragging a cardboard box full of glow sticks and paper lanterns.

"Fear not, Plan C is here!" he announces. "Don't ask about Plan A or B. Plan A involved raccoons, who ate plan B…"

Jason groans. "I told you not to bring glow sticks. It's a birthday, not a rave."

Taz used a glow stick as a middle finger and smirks.

They bicker, laugh, and bump shoulders. Marie would love it, all of it. Our friends and all our weird dynamics.

Then I notice her. The woman by the photo table with a volunteer tag, denim jacket, and soft eyes. I don't recognize her. She doesn't smile, doesn't cry. She just stands there, watching everyone with a camera in her hand, occasionally peering through the viewfinder, then examining the screen. When her lens tilts my way, I freeze. The camera clicks, yet there's no burst of light. Instead, I think I hear a soft hum, like static.

She lowers it, then scribbles something in a notebook. She glances at me for a second and gives a tight-lipped smile before looking away.

Rene passes by with a tray of punch cups. "You okay?" she asks.

I shrug. "I made my rounds."

"You sure?"

"Yeah."

She leans in. "You're allowed to leave, you know. Nobody's gonna hold it against you."

And with that, I chug my drink and duck out the back of the square, skateboard under my arm.

I skate through the alleys, climb the old tree behind the pizza shop, and haul myself onto the roof.

The square was still visible from up here, balloons bouncing, Taz's lantern light flickering like low stars. Voices drift up in fragments. Music, too. They'd switched to one of Marie's favorites, something acoustic.

Our town doesn't have any major chain stores. It's mostly family-owned places. Mike's market is one of the biggest stores on the street, and it always has a few people walking in and out. The barbershop with its revolving candy cane light.

Mr. Frank steps outside, lights a cigarette, and waves up at me. I wave back, then let my eyes wander.

Everywhere I look, there's a memory with her. The pizza shop. The bookstore. The tree we carve our initials into. I run my thumb over the groove of the M, remembering how she cut her hand, laughed through the blood, and insisted on finishing the B herself.

I never expect the small stuff to mean so much. A shared soda. A song hummed off-key. It all hits harder now, every fragment carrying more weight than it should.

I stay on that rooftop until the sun bleeds out of the sky, and the shadows grow long enough to swallow Main Street.

At some point, I end up flat on my back, staring up at the night sky. The stars are steady tonight. The moon hangs low, muted. Satellites cut across the dark like ribbons. Marie and I used to do this a hundred times over. Same roof. Same sky. Her finger would point out some make-believe constellation, like *"The Platypus Princess"* or *"The Lonely Spoon."* I never correct her. That grin she flashed was enough.

I scan the sky and wonder, is she doing the same right now? Watching these same satellites. Missing me the way I miss her.

I take a long breath and sit up, stretching against the chill that has settled into this November evening, and shove my hands into my pockets.

Below me, however, the birthday is still buzzing. Friend's laughter and chatting washes up to my rooftop perch; glow sticks dangle around kids' necks or are thrown through the night air.

Taz lights one lantern and sends it up. For a moment, I imagined Marie chasing it and smile. I watch it drift higher overhead, becoming one with those satellites.

Then I hear footsteps on the tree.

Rene pulls herself up, brushing grit from her hands. She settles in beside me, silent for a while.

"I figured you'd be here," she says. "I needed to be here too. To breathe."

I don't answer, just nod.

"Seventeen today," Rene adds. "Kinda surreal."

I nod again and then ask, "You holding it together?"

"No," she says. "But pretending is easier if I'm busy."

She leans against me. Her head resting on my shoulder, the way it used to when we were kids.

"She knows you care," Rene whispers.

"I didn't say it."

"She didn't need you to." She glances up at me. "You know none of this is your fault."

I swallow hard. My chest aches, ready to crack, like it's made of glass.

"I know."

"Seriously, Logan. It's not your fault."

"I miss her," I say.

"I know," Rene replies. "Me too."

We sit in silence; the town buzzing below. Another lantern drifts up, joining the stars.

That's when I see her again.

The volunteer in the denim jacket. Camera in hand. She wasn't taking pictures of the tables and guests anymore. She's standing at the edge of the square, lens tilted up. At me.

The camera clicks.

"Logan?" Rene asks, noticing my stare.

"It's nothing," I mutter, though my skin prickles.

I look back up, eyes on the stars, and for an instant, I thought I heard it again, hooves, distant but steady, like a horse running, just out of sight. I rub at my ear, and pretend not to hear it.

The lantern is gone now, swallowed up by the dark.

13

THE LIES IN THE TRUTH

Marie

Rat was right; the stone liked questions. Lucky for it, I had plenty. Its answers lacked clarity, and at times I questioned if it responded or narrated. It was hard to tell.

The only thing I was sure of was that this thing could think; it's sentient. So somehow, this thing's alive.

So far, the things it had shown me about this underground city were true. The eye had been leading me around via a dog's eye view from God knows when in time, but it wasn't current. My favorites were the random images of its inhabitants in the city's heyday.

Stores bustled, children played and laughed, street plays, and vendors sold goods. The elves were the primary residents, and the city reflected their belief structure and creativity in its very walls. Carvings and paintings, monoliths and structures set apart from the rest, suggesting chapels or schools.

This thought process brought me to my next thought. Why had the dogs attacked a city that was obviously wonderful, and seemingly on decent terms with the beasts?

I could not seem to get a straight answer from the eye, and honestly, I did not like what it showed me. It's terrifying and gruesome, and every part of me would have liked to avoid those visions like my life depended on it.

106

Instead, I was taking a different route in my search for answers. The eye showed me chaos, but the scrolls might speak with more care. That was the hope, anyway.

I had lit a couple of lanterns earlier, just enough to keep the shadows from swallowing the place. One sat on the crate-table beside me, another by the cookstove, and a few stubby candles flickered on the shelf. The fireplace was going too, more glow than heat, but it made the room feel less like a cave.

I pushed back from the table for a second, needing air even though the air down there never changed.

Stepping onto the balcony, I leaned on the stone railing and looked out. The cavern was so huge that the lanterns from the other dwellings barely made a dent in it; they were just scattered sparks floating in the dark.

Bridges stretched across the emptiness at different levels, some broken, some still holding on. And above it all, the ceiling glowed with a strange green bioluminescence, like ghost-stars drifting in slow motion. They sort of reminded me of the glow stars I stuck to Logan's ceiling as a kid, only now and then, one of the glowing creatures moved across the stone, reminding me that whatever they were, they were alive.

After a minute, I headed back inside and settled at my table again.

Chewing my lip in my *office*, I stared at the collection of words I'd managed to roughly translate by comparing the symbols with others I'd found around the city. Context clues, fragments, and guesses were what I had, but it was the best I could manage at the moment.

The office was nothing more than a small three-room dwelling with a cookstove that sat far up the side of the cave face. I'd claimed it as my own and had one of the Knockers help fashion me a door with a lock.

I groaned in frustration and sat back, my hands curled into fists and shoved into my eyes, trying to rub the fatigue from them; instead, the action turned into a stretch and a yawn.

"I wish I could ask the eye to just spell it out for me…"

"Can't it?" Rat said, slipping inside and clicking the door shut behind him.

He was the only one I'd given an extra key to. He paused for half a second after the lock clicked, head tilting as if listening for something behind him, and walked to my makeshift table.

"Find anything?"

He shook his head and set a loaf of bread on the crate table.

"Naa, just some bread." He broke it in half, steam whispered out, then handed me the crustier end without looking up.

He scanned the scrolls on the table while chewing and nodded at the parchment. Needing a break, and some food, I took a bite of the bread he handed me. His eyes flicked over the scrolls, pausing now and then on a symbol, brow pinching. I knew he couldn't read them any better than I could, but he liked feeling like he was helping.

Looking around at my little claim of the city, I was pleased with the space. It was modest, but comfortable.

The room with the cookstove was an old kitchen and dining area, it must have had wooden furniture and cabinets at one time, all of which had long since crumbled into dust, but after cleaning the place up I dragged a couple chairs and a large crate up here to use as a table.

The bedroom had shelves carved into the cave wall, and I had made a bed and pillow from some stitched together fabric, stuffed full of straw. It wasn't as nice as my bed at home, but good for what resources we had.

Both rooms had balconies; the one off the kitchen and dining area was the bigger of the two. Balconies lacked doors, a feature I presumed was deliberate. Curtains may have been enough for privacy reasons, or for decorative, or both. After all, we were underground; there was no exposure to weather down here.

I imagined the larger Balcony would have been used like a family room area, a place to gather and enjoy company, while the smaller balcony off the bedroom would have just been for relaxing and looking out at the city below.

Right now, the larger balcony had maps and scrolls and many of my own doodling laid out on its flagstone floor. I tried to organize the visions I received, along with the information I gathered from the city and local tales.

Rat was the only one who knew I found this eye. He was also the only one who knew I had been trying to make sense of what it showed me.

Rat flopped onto the crate table, causing it to wobble and the lantern to flicker, the last bite of bread still in his mouth as he glanced over my scroll pile.

"You'd love Nyltak… Mama said they have the most scrolls in all the realm."

He picked up the Lumo, turned it in his hands twice, admiring its glow, then set it down half on one scroll without looking.

"Yeah? You think they have scrolls on how to read scrolls?" I said, rubbing my temples.

Rat didn't answer, just shrugged, tilted his head again, and smiled.

I didn't notice at first, but after a few seconds, I saw that something was off. The symbols underneath the Lumo looked different.

I sat there chewing slower on my mouth full of bread, staring at the scroll like it had just winked at me.

I squinted at it and leaned in for a better look. It was clearer, not just clearer; it was changing. The symbols and lines were blurring and moving and reforming into… holy crap, I can read it; it's English! I removed the stone, blurry, shifting back into symbols.

I put it back.

Shift.

English.

"Rat, holy shit!" I said.

He raised his brows, mouth full. "Hmm?"

"You didn't… I mean, have you ever seen the Lumo do this?"

He shrugged. "Do what? It just… Glows up the night. You wanna use it?"

"No, I mean, look." I slid the Lumo across the scroll again. "Look what it does. When the light touches this part, the symbols change."

He leaned in but didn't seem impressed. "Still looks like scratches to me. But papas good at scratches." His eyes flicked to the corner of the scroll. "Kings mark." He mumbled.

"You can read them?"

"No. but papa can." He said.

I looked back at the scroll, lit under the lumo.

"This part… I don't know," I mutter. "History, a trade declaration, a treaty?"

It wasn't current English, but good enough. It was English, but with a lot of old-style words.

Rat hums and ate the breadcrumbs he'd caught on his shirt.

"Elves and Dogs," I say, skimming the text. "Dark elves. From this city. And the Cerberus who lived farther northeast, in a place called Hesiod, huge caverns. They traded along some massive underground road. A whole route that stretched from here all the way north."

Rat perks up. "Underground roads?"

"I guess so, and cities," I said, trailing my fingers over the text. "Only their cities weren't just for living in, they were built to hold back... Something bad."

Rat's chewing slows.

I pointed to the next section. This is a warning...

"Dest empire hold the lowest dark from rising, lest the slumbering gods, older than the realm's first breath, awaken. Disturb them not, for chaos and destruction follows in their wake."

Rat shivers a little, tucking his hands under his chin. "Old stories."

"They weren't just miners and masons," I said quietly. "They fought. Guarded the deep, it says they kept out things older than the realm."

Rat's chewing on a piece of straw now, forehead wrinkled. "Like... monsters?"

"Sure sounds like it. The scroll calls them 'buried gods.' Which, yeah, sounds like nightmare fuel to me. And apparently this entire city was built as a lid to keep them from crawling out."

I keep skimming the scroll until I found their undoing...

"Solrek, the devious didst offer up the eye of Ceyx, our ally, sovereign of the Cerberus, declaring him slain, one bestowed in mourning, the other vanquished by a foe. But lo, this token, given not in strife but in abiding, was but a mantle spun of deceits, veiling our sight from the dark shapes lurking aloft."

The Eye flickered, and suddenly I wasn't myself... I was running. Paws hit stone, my claws scraping, the scent of death thick in my throat. Ahead, elves kneeled in mourning, their hands pressed to a carved monolith. They weren't enemies. They were grieving...

The vision snapped away, leaving me staring at the scroll. The words blurred, then sharpened.

"Guard the eye, for our allies are fallen."

My stomach twisted. Both couldn't be true. Unless someone had made sure they weren't.

"They weren't ready for an attack from above." I sit back. "They believed Solrek's story."

Rat's brows pulled together as he unraveled his thoughts. "He gave them the eye; that's how you found it." He said with certainty.

I nod. "As a memorial; he told them the enemy had the other one, and that they had to guard this one until it could be recovered." I looked at him. "Do you know these stories?"

Rat frowns. "Cause he knew they were friends." His voice dips at friends, as if the idea was painful.

"Yeah..."

Rat nudges the Lumo closer. "So he tricked both sides?"

"Yeah, looks like it." I whispered.

I glance up at Rat, whose worried eyes looked back to mine. My thoughts tornado through my mind...

My throat tightened as the words and visions blurred together, unraveling the story.

"The scroll talked about 'dark shapes aloft,' but the Eye showed me something worse. It wasn't gods or monsters that destroyed Niren. It was Solrek, using the Cerberus like attack dogs on a leash."

Rat shook his head. "They knew these tunnels." He blurted.

I nodded.

"They'd practically lived in them, running through them for generations, side by side with the elves. No outside army could've hit harder or faster. Who better to tear the city apart than their friends?"

My stomach flipped as I spoke the word aloud. The elves hadn't just been betrayed. They'd been wiped out by the ones they trusted most.

I slide the Lumo along the edge of the next paragraph carefully, regardless of the spells used to keep the ink intact. The next line of symbols crept into focus again.

"In the days that follow'd the tribute, the tunnels lay in stillness. Trade wand, not by discord, but by bewilderment. Nary did the hounds of Cerberus send their scouts, nor came tidings from Hesoid. And we, simple in heart, took their hush for mourning."

Rat doesn't say much, just dismantles the straw he's been chewing and watches me from under his hair, the way he does when he knows something important is happening but isn't sure yet if it's safe to ask questions.

I read slower now, mouth dry. "They didn't even know the war had started," I said. "They just thought the dogs were… mourning. Taking time."

Rat's foot swings off the crate, and he frowns. "But they weren't?" A soft question, almost reluctant, like he's already guessed the answer but hates it.

I shake my head.

The next lines press harder, language tighter, less ceremonial, like someone wrote this part fast, maybe during the collapse or right before the city was sacked.

"Runners were dispatched unto the North, yet but one made his way back. He spoke of caverns laid waste, the very stone cloven as though it were but timber. The gates of Hesoid, lost beneath the earth's wrath, and the name of the king, consumed, naught but smoke and cinder remained to mark his reign."

Rat shifts closer, face pale. "He made them fight each other." His voice cracks with grief.

"Or made it look like the elves had done it," I said. "Or told them the elves were holding the Eye to use against them. I don't know."

I rub the side of my head, fingers pressed to my temple like that'll help me think through centuries of fallout, forgotten betrayals, and the terror that doesn't even have a word in my world.

"The lower halls were made fast, the chambers of prayer lock'd, in the passages 'round to the roots shut against intrusion. Stirring now in dread, the elder kind awakened from their slumber. We quail, lest they rise in the tumult, Drawn by the discord that spreads like flame."

My breath catches.

Rat whispers, "Who?"

"I don't know… The old ones…" I tapped a finger on the scroll. "The elves thought they were guarding against buried gods," I murmured. "But all the while, Solrek was the actual monster."

There's a knock; three short taps, one long, then the handle jiggles and Tessa pushes the door open with her boot, not waiting for permission. Rat scrambles upright like someone just sounded a fire drill. I straighten too, trying to look less like I've been talking to ancient paper all day.

She steps inside, locs swinging, and claws tucked. Her nostrils flare once, scanning the room, and she flicks an ear at the scroll spread across the floor.

"Yeh smell like ink and overthinking," she said, voice all low rhythm and sanded edge. "How long've yeh been holed up in here?"

"Not long," I lie immediately.

Tessa arches a brow. "Marie. You're wearin' yesterday's dirt and look like a ghost with scribes work."

Rat snorts. "She's learning history."

Tessa narrows her catlike eyes at the scroll, then crouches to look. "Dark Elvish, is it? I can't read it, not the old style, but I know enough symbols to guess. That mark there's used near warding texts. And that," she points with the curve of a claw, "means something's sealed. Or meant to be."

I blink. "Wait, you've seen this before?"

"Aye. Long time since I've seen these types of marks." She stands again, brushing off her knees, then looks me over from ragged old boots to collar. "None of that matters if yeh can't defend yourself."

"I'm working on translations," I say defensively.

Tessa's eyes track the room, noting the Lumo, the spread of symbols, the crumbs. Then she hooks a thumb toward the door. "Come on. Time yeh stopped squintin' at ghosts and learned to dodge somethin' solid."

I blink. "What?"

"Self-defense," she said, already halfway back through the door. "Ideas don't stop blades, lass. Yeh want to live? Yeh better learn to fight."

Rat smirks. "I told her the scrolls won't help when the Queen's guards show up." He rocks on his heels as he say it, like he's heard that warning before.

Tessa huffs a laugh. "Yeh not wrong, lad."

"I've never punched anyone," I admit, getting to my feet.

"Well, yeh won't today either," she said, already leading the way. "We start with stance, balance, stretching and defense. Punchin' comes after yeh learn not to fall over."

* * *

The corridor narrows before it opens, stone pressing close on either side, the ceiling low enough that even I have to duck, and then, without warning, it opens.

The room beyond is vast.

Not just large, but cathedral-vast, the kind of space that makes your breath catch before you remember to breathe. The ceiling stretches so high it disappears into shadow, lost in a haze of dust, smoke, and shadows from the large lit bowls of oil fed fire. Pillars rise like petrified trees, carved with spiraling runes that shimmer faintly when the torchlight brushes them, and the floor beneath my boots is smooth obsidian veined with silver, worn down in places by centuries of footwork and blood.

This wasn't a gathering hall. This was a crucible.

A training ground for warriors who no longer breathe, whose names are etched into the walls in a language I'm only beginning to decipher. The air hums with their memory, not warm or welcoming, but watchful, like the stone itself is waiting to see what we'll do with what's been left behind.

Tessa strides ahead like she belongs here, her boots silent on the stone, her shoulders loose, her claws tucked. Rat trails behind her, eyes wide, head craning back to take in the impossible height of the ceiling. For a moment he presses his hands to his ears, as if walking into a room full of talking people, or maybe just overwhelmed by the echoing space. He spins once, lowering his hands as quickly as he raised them, then trots forward to catch up. I follow slower, my fingers brushing the edge of a broken archway where a statue once stood. Only the feet remain, bare and in mid-step.

Above us, Jorrun circles once, wings outstretched, his silhouette cutting across the fractured dome like a hawk surveying prey below. He watches from above, feathers catching the light in flashes of bronze and rust. The space is enormous enough for him to fly. That alone says everything.

Caleen leans against a half-toppled column near the far wall, arms crossed, one horn catching the torchlight like a blade. She doesn't speak either, but her gaze tracks every movement, sharp and unblinking, like she's measuring the significance of our presence against the ghosts that still linger here.

Tessa stops in the ring's heart, a wide circle of worn stone, and gestures for me to join her.

I glance to a rack that's positioned to the side of the circle. "Don't we need weapons?"

Above us, Jorrun chuckles.

"Feet here," she said, ignoring my question. "Shoulder width. Knees soft. Don't lock 'em unless yeh want to eat the floor. My people like to say, "the sticks only as strong as the stance." Plant wrong, yeh fall."

My boots crunched on the dust in the cracks. It felt strange to stand where fighters had stood, stranger to think I might become one.

Tessa circles me once, slow and deliberate, her voice low. "This place trained killers. Not brutes. Not brawlers. Precision. Patience. Pain. That's what they taught."

I nod, throat dry.

She taps my elbow, nudges my ribs. "Hands up. Chin tucked. Don't blink."

"I'm trying not to."

Rat snickers from the edge. "She blinked six times."

"Seven," Caleen murmurs, not unkindly.

I sneer in her direction, and Tessa slaps me on the back of the head.

"Pay attention," she said.

"What was that for?" I asked, breath quickening.

"Surprise," she said. "Queen's guards won't warn yeh, love."

Then she stood before me, loose-limbed but ready. "Try to push me."

I hesitate.

"Push me," she said again, tone firmer.

I move forward, hands out, weight centered, and she's gone before I touch her. A twist, a pivot, a hook of her boot behind mine, and I stumble, catching myself with a grunt.

She grins, sharp and satisfied. "I don't block strength. I make it miss."

Rat claps once, delighted. "She pushed air!"

He bounces on his toes like he wants to try it himself, already mimicking the angle of Tessa's pivot with his shoulders.

I reset, cheeks burning, and try not to look at the watchers. Try not to think about the names carved into the walls or the way the statues seem to lean in, listening.

"So you're not going to teach me how to hit harder?" I ask.

Tessa's eyes shift, pupils narrowing, catching fire in the torchlight. "Why would I? You're human. You won't out-muscle a Bull. But you can learn to move like yeh mean it."

She moves again, fast and silent, and when she reappears behind me, I flinch.

"This isn't about strength," she said. "It's not about hitting, not yet. It's about using the world. Let it move, and move with it. Focus. It's about balance and control."

Tessa circled me like a predator sizing prey. "The Ember Path's trainin' rings have seen teeth and blood," she murmured, low so only I could hear. "We build from grief. From bones Queen Vaira'd rather we forgot. So, remember this: your stance ain't about strength. It's about sayin' you're not gonna be the one fallin'."

She moved again, a blur of dreadlocks and boots, then stood behind me like she'd teleported.

"Quick feet," she continued, "sharp eyes and sharper wit. That's how yeh survive. That's how yeh fight, dirty and smart."

I startled. "Seriously?"

"This isn't about being strong, Marie," she said again, voice low.

Rat rocked on his heels, still grinning. "You still blinked lots. I counted. Seven. Maybe eight." He holds up his fingers as if trying to count which finger he stopped on.

I narrowed my eyes. "You counted?"

"Yeah." He puffed up a little. "I can count good."

Tessa jerked her chin toward him. "Since yeh think yeh know better, your turn."

His smile faltered for half a breath. "Me?"

"You blink less than she does," Tessa said, deadpan. "Let's see if you're not just mouth."

I folded my arms. "Come on, brave boy. Show me."

Rat sauntered into the ring like he was born there, dusty boots skidding on the shale. He squared up, feet too wide, elbows sticking out like bent pipes, chin cocked like he'd seen fighters do.

"Chin down," Tessa warned. "Or I'll tap it with my boot."

He obeyed instantly. "That doesn't sound nice."

"It won't be."

He glanced toward me, lowering his voice. "I saw fighters do this. They got mean eyes." He furrowed his brow.

"Yours ain't mean," I teased.

He shrugged, serious now. "I'm not tryin' to scare. I'm tryin' to win."

Tessa moved first, fluid and low, like a striking cat, but Rat ducked fast, dropped into a crouch sharp enough that she had to pivot mid-lunge. She didn't hit him. He rolled, popped up behind her, and smacked her hip with the back of his hand before springing back with a cackle.

"See? Too slippery!"

Tessa spun, eyes narrow but not angry. "Good! Slippery's a start. Now let's see yeh do it again."

Rat darted forward again, confidence high, feet light.

This time, Tessa didn't pivot.

She waited just long enough for Rat to over commit, then shifted one boot sideways, subtle and fast, and tapped his heel with the toe of her boot.

Rat yelped, flailed, and landed with a soft grunt in the dirt.

Tessa folded her arms, gaze level. "Fast's good. But fast without your wits will put yeh face-first in a blade."

Rat blinked up at her, stunned. "You tripped me."

"I taught yeh."

He sat up, rubbing his elbow. "Was that a pretend hit or a real one?"

Tessa cracked a half-smile. "That was a lesson. Don't rush. Think."

Rat scowled for half a breath, then grinned again. "Okay. My turn again." He hopped to his feet with springy, animal quickness, dusting off his hands. "Alright, boy. Come on." Tessa nodded.

Rat nodded, breath huffing, little hands curled and ready. He darted again, less messy this time, spin low, hop right, and struck her wrist with a flat slap before falling back, wild-eyed and grinning like he'd stolen something precious.

Someone near the wall whistled. No cheers. Just respect.

Tessa blinked once, slow. "Well," she said. "Looks like someone's been listenin'."

Rat beamed, chest heaving. "I'm small. That's good. Big ones don't chase me 'cause I run weird. Makes 'em dizzy."

I laughed under my breath. "That was good, Rat."

He leaned into me. "Can I teach you next time?"

Tessa snorted. "No."

She crouched beside him, hand firm on his shoulder. "You listen close, boy. Yeh fast. Fast don't fix everything, but it'll keep you breathin'. Keep it sharp and yeh head on a swivel. Don't rush yeh thinking."

Rat nodded, solemn now. Then he turned to me with a crooked grin. "Your turn again. Try not to blink like a baby bird this time."

The sparring was only the beginning.

After that first bruising round, Tessa shifted focus. Less striking, more of every other hell I didn't know existed. She started each session with stretches that felt like punishment until I understood they were survival, slow, deliberate movements that pulled at tendons I hadn't known were tight, that made my spine crack and my breath catch in ways that reminded me I had a body worth keeping intact.

"Balance first," she said, crouching beside me as I tried to hold a low squat without tipping forward. "Yeh can't fight if yeh fall over every time the wind changes."

Rat mimicked her squat perfectly, arms out, heels flat, grinning like it was a game. "She's wobbly," he whispered, loud enough for Caleen to hear.

He held the squat with ridiculous ease, rocking heel to toe like he was testing how far he could push it before falling.

Caleen didn't laugh. She stood nearby, arms folded, horns catching the torchlight, her gaze sharp and unblinking. "She's learning, and so is her body." She said. "Every fighter starts unsteady. Balance is failing, then standing again. That's how muscle remembers."

Tessa nodded, adjusting my stance with a tap to the knee. "Aye. Some muscle be needed too."

I grimaced, shifting my weight, trying to hold the pose. "I'm working on it."

"That you are," she said, then pointed to the far wall. "Run to that column. Touch it. Run back. Then again. Ten times."

I blinked. "Seriously?"

"Yeh want to stand steady? Learn how to move first. Go."

I ran. Not fast. Not graceful. But I ran.

Jorrun watched from above. He had perched on a beam that had once held banners, his wings folded tight as he paced it. His boots send dust cascading below.

"She's slow," he said.

"Give her a week," Caleen murmured. "She'll stop tripping over her own thoughts."

Tessa barked a laugh. "If she don't collapse first."

After the runs came planks, elbows down, spine straight, breath steady. Then toe ups until my calves were knotted balls of fire. Then lunges deep and burning, until my thighs shook and my robe clung to my back with sweat. Rat did them beside me, counting aloud, skipping numbers when he got bored.

"Six... seven... eleven... twenty-hundred," he said, flopping onto his side. He kicked his legs like a beetle on its back, then popped up again the moment Tessa glared.

"Get up," Tessa snapped. "Yeh don't get to cheat just 'cause yeh small."

"I'm not cheating," he said, breathless. "I'm improvising."

Caleen snorted. "He's got your attitude."

Tessa grinned. "That's worse."

We moved into balance drills, standing on one foot, arms out and eyes closed. I wobbled. Fell. Tried again. Tessa didn't help me up. She just watched.

"Yeh learn to hold yehself," she said. "No one's gonna do it for yeh."

Jorrun dropped from the beam , wings flaring once before folding. He landed without a sound, his boots scuffing the stone in a whisper. "Try this," he said, stepping beside me. "Stand. Close your eyes. Keep your knees soft, never locked. Now breathe in through your nose, out through your mouth. Feel your weight settle in your hips, not your shoulders."

I did as he asked. Deep inhales, steady exhales. Focusing on my knees, my hips...

"Now shift your weight from one foot to the other, keeping your torso centered. Feel the floor under each foot. Let your weight flow like wings banking in the wind."

I did so again. My weight on my right foot, then my left. My wobbliness easing.

"Better," he said. "Balance isn't stillness. It's movement held at center.."

Tessa nodded. "See? Angel-boy knows."

"I'm not an angel," Jorrun said, deadpan.

"Yeh fly. Yeh practically glow in the sun. Close enough."

He rolled his eyes.

We ended with stretches again, long holds, deep breaths, the kind that made my ribs ache and my spine feel taller. Rat curled beside me, mimicking every pose, humming under his breath.

By the time we left the ring, my legs were sore, my ribs buzzing from one too many pivots, and the puzzles in the glyphs and scrolls felt heavier with all I hadn't yet understood.

Training sessions became part of my rhythm after that, symbols traced in my notebook at breakfast, sparring by midday, scrolls and sketches by lamplight. Between mapping the lower channels and piecing together the cracked histories scattered throughout the city and training, my days are long, but filled with purpose.

Stacks of new scrolls and maps, beside half-sketched diagrams of spiral tunnels and sealed vault doors, lay strewn about my quarters. I still didn't know what Solrek wanted or whether the Eye was leading me toward truth or simply showing me the wreckage of good intentions. But I knew now how to stand. I knew how to keep from blinking. And if there's more to uncover, more buried gods, more lies shaped like treaties, more angry bulls or tyrannical queens, I'd meet them with steadier footing.

Even if the past refused to answer me straight, the future was already yeeting me into its embrace, and I have no choice but to move with it.

14

THE DOOR

Marie

The Eye draws me in, not through a vision this time, but a palpable presence, almost a hum I can feel in my mind, as if urging me toward something it's seen before. The maps I've spent weeks creating are mirroring each other: routes intertwining, chambers folding upon themselves, and an odd draft where no air should be flowing.

Rat was the one who noticed it first, which was no surprise to me, or the eye. In fact, the eye seemed to like Rat. It sang into my bones whenever it knew he was near.

"Marie! Venn! I found something! You gotta come and see!" He exclaimed as he skids to a stop on the pebbled ground in front me.

I smile up at him from my map, and then look to Venn, whose brows are raised.

"Speak. What is it. We still have work." Venn said as she glances back down to her notes, comparing them to our latest map.

Rat pants between words, catching his breath. "It leads up." He said, his finger pointing upward.

"Up?" I ask. "What leads up?"

"A tunnel." He clarifies, then added. "It's all smashed and fallen in, but the air isn't old. Its new. Its breathing hard and sweet." His eyes are as wide as saucers as he spews the words out in a torrent of excitement. "It's what we need. Yea?"

"Slow down, Rat. Where'd you see this?"

"Over by tunnel five! Come, you gotta see!"

"Tunnel five is unstable," Venn said. "Another collapse, we cannot afford."

"But Venn…" Rat begged.

"You stay away." She said, cutting him off.

Rat's eyes met mine. "It breathes." He whispered.

I sent him a nod, and he smiled.

* * *

Evening settled in, and I followed Rat into tunnel five; the dry, old smell of the underground clung to the air. The faint glow of Rat's lumo and my lantern, a sputtering, oil-fed contraption I carried, cast dancing shadows of white and yellow on the rough-hewn walls, revealing the occasional glistening patch of some sort of crystallized stone.

We had been down here before, exploring the forgotten arteries of the ancient city, but tonight felt different. He was eager; the hushed urgency in Rat's stride, and the quickening of his breath against the silence, told me he was onto something, and the eye thought so too.

The air grew warmer, and the whisper quiet of the ruined city was replaced by the distant hum of insects somewhere in the tunnels ahead.

He pressed his cheek to the stone and whispered, "It's breathing. Here. Feel it?"

I nodded as I clapped my chalk dusted hands together. The dust swayed past us, pushed on a soft, warm breeze.

I pulled out my pocket sketchbook, marked the wall with ink, and began a new sketch, noting airflow, direction, distance, and pressure lines.

"Awesome job," I said, recording everything I could. "But we need to be careful, Rat. This definitely isn't stable."

We followed the draft through crumbling halls and down a corridor sealed with crumbled and broken Elven stone.

The markings we found throughout, were old trade glyphs and merchant sigils, markings I remembered Tessa saying predated the siege. I had rubbed them onto some papers to confirm them later.

"This is far enough." I said as I folded my papers and closed my notebook, which now held some alternative routes and symbols to translate. "We need to show these to Venn and Tess."

Rat nodded, smiling. "I found the door didn't I?"

"I sure hope so."

* * *

I brought the new map I'd spent most of the night drawing and my notes to Tessa.

By morning the weight of exhaustion still clung to me, a dull ache behind my eyes from the hours spent hunched over the table trying to decipher what symbols I could before I feel asleep.

I sat up, yawning and rubbed my face only to knock loose a pencil that had stuck to my forehead. I blinked down at the maps and scribbled annotations on the parchment, and a flicker of satisfaction ignited me. This map, a patchwork of terrain and pathways, was finally complete. It represented hours of painstaking effort, and was a cartographical gamble born from fragmented memories, thanks to Paxithra, and desperate hope for the rest of us.

Clutching the rolled map and my tattered notebook filled with cryptic observations and a potential route out of the city, Niren, I made my way to Tessa's quarters.

I found her already awake. It was time to lay it all out, to share the culmination of my sleepless nights with her, and to see if my efforts would guide us towards the answers we so desperately sought.

She stared at the maps, an intensity on her face that had me biting my lip.

"Has Venn seen these yet?" she asked, as she scanned the papers.

"Not yet."

Tessa closed the map in her hands as a smile played on her lips. "Best we get them to her then."

* * *

Venn studied my notes in silence, her lips shaping soft, clipped murmurs and gasps. She traced one glyph with a fingertip, and inhaled sharply.

"This… this is surface route," she said with certainty. "Old one."

Tessa leaned in over her shoulder, brows raised. "Your tellin' me this thing leads up top?"

Then nodded once. "Yes. It matches the trade sigils. This corridor… it went out." She said, tapping the map I'd drawn.

"So we found it?" I asked.

"Yes. But very old. I would like to see. Be sure."

Tessa straightened. "Right then. Up we go. Grab what ya need."

The three of us, plus 3 knockers already muttering excitedly, gathered clean parchment, charcoal pencils, chisels, axes, and lanterns. My hands shook a little as I packed my tools, but I told myself it was just the cold.

* * *

The passage was indeed a highway, or at least it had been. It once accommodated wagons and caravans, but now it has half collapsed, or near collapse.

Tessa lifted her Lantern. "Moons above… Look at the size of it. This was a proper road."

"Trade road, important one." Venn agreed.

The tunnel twisted upward, steep and serpentine, like we were climbing through the throat of something ancient. Which, yeah? I suppose it's that.

The walls had faint carvings, trade markers like the ones I copied, but also clan symbols and directional markers, both so faded that I missed them the first time.

I brushed my fingers over one. "People use this every day. They walked right here."

"Long, long time ago." Venn murmured.

Up ahead of us, the knockers studied the stone and old bracers.

"Here's a weak point," one said. "Ceiling's complainin' fierce."

Venn and I sketched every crack, and every shift in the stone that my first look through might have missed as the Knockers assessed the tunnel.

I snapped my pencil twice from pressing too hard, and Tessa noticed.

"Easy friend."

"Yeah, I'm just… it's been months and I wasn't sure I'd see the surface again."

She smiled and sat next to me, shoulder to shoulder, nudging me. "You done real good."

* * *

Ren stands over the map I've laid out, his fingers hovering over the lines I marked. He traces them, almost reverently; he doesn't speak right away. Just studied it all.

Venn stands beside me, hands clasped behind her back.

"It is true route," she says quietly. "Surface road. Very old."

Ren's jaw tightens. "This is where it all started. Mythborn and humans."

He stares a moment longer, then gives a curt nod. "Our priority is getting this path safe and operational again."

Tessa steps forward, arms folded. "We'll need Borun and Khett. And the Knockers'll want a look before we start makin' promises."

Ren's voice sharpens. "Send for them. Tunnel Five."

Rat bolts off like he's been launched.

* * *

Borun stomped into the corridor like it owed him coin he intended to collect. His boots ground against loose rubble as he squinted up at the slope, the fractured ceiling, the damp stone pressing in from all sides.

I braced myself.

He didn't even wait for context. "Too cursed, this stone," he spat. "Mother moon help us; I've seen better tunnels in Knocker latrines."

Rat grinned beside me, arms folded. "You say that about everything."

Borun snorted. "Because everything down here is trying to kill us."

Before Tessa could retort, Khett arrived, dragging a cart stacked high with salvaged beams and iron brackets. The metal clinked and rattled with every step. Three Knockers puffed behind him, trying to keep up.

Khett stopped, kneeled beside the old metal arch, and pressed his ear to the beams, like he'd been listening for a heartbeat.

"Ohhh," he whispered, delighted. "She's angry."

Tessa raised a brow. "Is she now?"

Khett nodded, eyes bright. "Mmm. Very. She remembers being a road. She remembers the weight of the wagons. The fresh air. And she does not like being forgotten."

Borun rolled his eyes. "The blasted tunnel doesn't remember anything."

Khett's head snapped up. "She remembers you, Borun. Every time you blow a hole in her ribs."

Borun scowled. "That's why I'm here ya coot. Blowing things to the mother is my job."

"But not today," Khett corrected. "And you're carrying black powder again." He gestured to the powder quills poking from the dwarf's pocket.

Borun covers them defensively. "It's for emergencies."

Tessa snorts. "Aye, and you're the emergency half the time."

Even Ren's mouth twitched at that.

Khett stood, brushing dust from his knees. "We'll brace it," he said. "But it'll fight us."

Borun grumbled, stepping closer, inspecting the ceiling. "Everything fights us. Even the damn stone."

Khett barked a laugh, sharp and delighted, but a little unhinged. "Aye, and that's why we don't ask the stone anything. We force it to behave." He tapped the arch with a knuckle. "See that?" he said, pointing at a hairline fracture. "She's not angry. She's lazy. Needs proper support. Iron brackets here, here, and here." He jabbed the air with quick, precise motions. "And a beam to take the load before Borun blows us all to the moons."

Borun bristled. "I don't blow things unless I mean to."

Tessa snorted. "That's not the comfort ya think it is."

Khett grinned wide, eyes bright. "Relax, Borun. If the tunnel collapses, we die. Then you won't have to fight anything."

Borun muttered something in Dwarvish that sounded like a prayer and a curse at the same time.

Ren stepped forward, his boots crunching over the loose stones. He studied the fracture Khett pointed out, then the slope rising into darkness. For a long moment, he said nothing.

"If this road truly leads out…" His voice was low and cautious. "Then this is the first real chance we've had."

Khett grinned like someone handed him a new hammer. "Aye. And she'll hold if we make her. I've more than enough iron in the forges."

Borun snorted. "If she doesn't kill us first."

Ren ignored him. He turned to Tessa. "I want a full assessment by nightfall. No shortcuts. No risks we can't afford."

Tessa nodded. "We'll get it done."

Then Ren looked at me, really looked at me, and tapped the map still rolled under my arm. "You found this," he said. "You and Rat. Good work."

My face heated as I nodded, and I hoped the lantern light hid it.

Ren nodded back, then straightened, the leader once again.

"This road changes everything. If it's stable enough to reopen, we could have a way out that Solrek never meant us to find."

The tunnel groaned somewhere above them, a long, low shift of ancient stone.

Everyone went still.

Khett tilted his head, listening with unnerving delight. "Ah. She's waking up."

Borun muttered another Dwarvish curse.

Ren lifted his lantern higher. "Then let's get to work."

* * *

By midday, the first wave of workers arrived, anyone able-bodied, pushing sleds of salvaged beams and carts heaped with rubble. Their boots dragged through the grit, but very few steps, someone glanced up at the ceiling, like they were waiting for it to fall.

Khett's torch hissed to life, its magic flame spitting blue against the damp stone. Each weld threw sharp light across the corridor, catching the sheen of moisture on the walls, the dust trembling with every strike.

Borun drove the beams into place; each impact sent a dull vibration through the floor, shaking loose a few grains of dust that pattered onto his shoulders.

One section near the midpoint was worse than the rest. The arch had folded inward, stone fractured in clean, deliberate lines, the kind left by people who wanted this passage sealed.

The ceiling sagged, and we braced it with iron ribs.

By the third night, just as the final bracket was being set, one support slipped. It didn't fall, but it shifted, just enough to drag the beam sideways with a grinding scrape. A low rumble, stone shifted against stone, and then dust burst from the ceiling in a thick cloud, swallowing the lamplight, and turning the air gritty.

Rat yelped and dived behind a pile of rubble, arms curled tight over his head before the dust even touched the ground.

Borun shouted. "Brace it! Brace it now!"

Khett, who was closest, didn't hesitate. He lunged forward, the sledge already in his hands, and drove the bracket into place with a force that rang through the tunnel like a warning bell. The stone groaned again, louder this time, then settled into a tense, waiting silence.

No one spoke.

Rat coughed, a dry rasp that broke the quiet.

Khett reached out without looking, his hand landing firm on Rat's back as his eyes fixed on the beam. "Still breathing?" he asked.

Rat nodded, eyes wide and rimmed in dust. "I think I swallowed half the ceiling."

Borun snorts, stepping closer and brushing grit from his beard. He jerks his chin toward Khett, who was already checking the weld. "That's one way to test your steel."

Khett doesn't glance up. "It'll hold."

* * *

By the fifth day, the corridor did indeed hold. It wasn't elegant or clean, but it was stable. Braced, mapped, and cleared by hands that understood the stakes for us all.

I watched Ren walk the path himself, his boots echoing off the stone as he studied the beams we'd set. He didn't speak until he reached the top, where the tunnel opened to a sliver of sky. When he turned to me, there was a faint smile on his face.

"Looks like you're making yourself matter."

The words landed like a stone dropped into still water. I heard them layered over that first day with the resistance: *Figure out how you want to matter.* He had said.

I nodded, the smile stretching across my face before I could stop it.

Ren added nothing more; he just nodded again, slower this time, and turned back toward the tunnel mouth.

"We have a door."

We stood at the mouth of the tunnel, the stone behind us braced and welded, the slope beneath our feet solid for the first time in thousands of years.

Above us, the sky stretched wide and dark, scattered with stars that felt too sharp to be real. Real stars. Not torchlight. Not painted ceilings. But sky.

I had forgotten what the open air smelled like. It was colder than expected, cleaner than it should have been, and the silence that settled over us all held meaning.

The silence hung so heavy, not even Borun dared break it.

Rat pressed against my side, his breath misting in the chill as Ren stepped forward, pulling a horn from beneath his cloak. It was etched with symbols that shimmered in the starlight.

He lifted it to his lips and blew. The sound wasn't loud. It was low and strange. It didn't bellow; it hummed into the air, into the bones of me, and then rose, rose into the trees, the sky. It's like a sound that I could hear in my mind but not with my ears. A strange resonance that I couldn't find the words for.

Then the scent came, wildflowers, crushed mint, something green and blooming that hadn't belonged in a place like that.

The air stirred, and then the light sound of wingbeats.

And they arrived.

They drifted down from the sky, slow-moving, each about a foot tall, their wings wide and patterned like butterflies. Their fur-covered bodies looked soft, mottled in earthy tones, bark brown, moss green, and stone gray.

Aside from their enormous eyes, a large, animal-like nose dominated their features.

I stared.

I didn't know what they were or what they wanted. I couldn't tell if I should feel terror or wonder, or maybe a combination of both. Though they were oddly adorable...

Rat tugged my sleeve,. "Astomi," he whispered. "They're messengers. They don't talk. They touch."

I blinked. "Touch?"

Tessa leaned in from the other side. "They send thoughts straight into your head, love... visions... memories. But if you're not trained, it can twist you sideways. Like trying to read someone else's dream while you're still half asleep."

Ren kneeled, not reverent, just ready, and extended his arm, palm open. One creature stepped forward and pressed its hand to his wrist.

Ren winced and then steadied himself.

"They'll carry the message," he said, voice rough. "To the Triune. To the outposts." He looks into the eyes of the Astomi. "Niren is the heart now. The others need to know."

The Astomi nods, releases Ren's wrist and lifts into the air, its wings catching the starlight as it rises, one by one flitting into the sky.

Rat exhales beside me. "They look like toys," he said. "But they're not."

I nod as I watch them disappear into the night. I don't know what Ren just did or how it works. But I know it matters. And I know I don't want one touching me; it looked painful…

Ren notices me watching. "Don't interfere," he says. "If the message isn't for you, or you don't know how to read it, it'll destroy you."

I nod again, not asking questions.

Ren turns to the group of us.

"This is where it begins."

* * *

Four days had passed since the Astomi disappeared into the sky, their silent journey carrying Ren's message.

Since their departure, the forge had remained smoldering; the corridor had held firm, and the tunnel entrance had been established as a checkpoint. Fighters, mixers, humans, and families had been trickling in. Niren was stirring to life.

I was with Venn, crouched by the door, sketching out potential ramparts to fortify the entrance by utilizing the natural terrain, when suddenly, an unsettling silence descended. It was a strange, heavy stillness that made you feel as though the entire world was holding its breath.

The wind stilled.

Even the Knockers ceased their humming.

I looked up, to find three figures who stood on the ridge beyond the tunnel mouth, walking in our direction. They had wings that shimmered like dragonfly's, translucent and twitching in the breeze.

They wore no shirts, just layered skirts of gray and brown fabric, tied with rope and twine. Their hair was wispy and pale blonde, almost white, and their faces were childlike and symmetrical. They were the size of toddlers, but they didn't move like children. Their pointed ears curved away from their heads, longer than any fae I'd seen, giving them a silhouette that felt… off.

Their eyes were gray blue, but seemed like they'd been hit with the thousand-yard stare, and they moved in perfect sync. Completely and eerily unified.

I lingered. Rat did too; his hand tightening around mine.

"What am I looking at?" I whispered.

He didn't answer. Just stared.

Tessa stepped up beside me, her voice low. "Triune," she said. "They've come the long way. Means they've never been here before."

I glanced at her. "Long way?"

"Aye. When they've no anchor to a place, they walk. They can't fold through the veil unless a place's been marked by them before."

The three figures reached the clearing. They stood silent, unmoving, unblinking.

Their voices came layered, low, resonant, pressing behind my ears like a chord struck too deep. It's pressure. Like music that didn't care if you understood it.

"The message?" They asked together.

Ren appeared behind us, slightly breathless, three heaving Knockers holding their knees, trying to catch their own breath. They must've fetched him.

He handed the Triune a scroll, rolled tight and sealed.

"Deliver to Embereth. Then Solvrae. Then Cintara's Grasp. No deviation."

The Triune nodded once, together, and took it. Their fingers brushed the parchment, and for a second the surrounding air rippled, like the world was trying to reshape itself.

There was no shaking ground or splitting sky. Yet something… opened.

It wasn't a door. It's more like a fold. Like a wormhole or a wrongness, a seam in the air that wasn't there before. Light bent and sound thinned. The space around them warped inward, swallowing color, swallowing motion, swallowing… them, until… they were gone.

Rat exhaled beside me, voice hushed. "Now they have an anchor here."

I didn't answer. I was still staring at the space they left behind. The air felt bent. Like it hadn't settled yet.

Tessa shifted beside me, her voice low, her lilted accent curling around the words like smoke. "They leave a taste in the air, don't they? Like thunder that… built up and never broke."

"Yeah, it was like some kinda wormhole," I said in a whisper.

Ren stepped forward, brushing dust from his coat like he was shaking off the last of the Triune's presence.

"Well," he said, voice dry. "That was only mildly horrifying."

Borun snorted. "Mildly?"

"I think they blinked sideways," Rat muttered.

"They didn't blink at all," I said.

Ren lifts a brow. "Which is exactly why we're going to pretend that was normal and move on." He turns to Caleen, who has slipped into our ranks. "I want a rotating watch on the ridge. If the Triune can just walk right up to our front door, so can anyone else. You're lead on defense. Pick your team."

Caleen nods, already scanning the slope. "I'll take the twins and that muted one with the scar. She moves like she's been hunted."

"Good." Ren nods. "Jorrun…"

The winged scout appeared from the shadows of the gate mouth, already stretching his wings, feathers catching the light. "Northern sweep?"

Ren gives a half-smile. "You read my mind. Take four. I want eyes on the Tearwood pass, and reports by dawn."

"Gladly," Jorrun said, and with a single beat of his wings, he's airborne.

Caleen smirks as Jorrun lifts off. "Try not to get distracted by the view, feather boy."

Jorrun grins at her mid-flight. "Too late."

"Borun," Ren said, already moving. "You've got the next intake. Prioritize builders and medics. We'll need both."

Borun grumbles, but he's already heading toward the tunnel. "If they can lift a hammer or stitch a wound, they're in. If not, they better be good at cooking and cleaning."

"Khett," Ren said, pausing. "How's the salvage?"

"Messy," Khett replies. "But promising. I'll start sorting tonight."

"Good. We'll need blades."

Ren finally turns back to us, to the small knot of people still standing in the Triune's wake of departure. His voice softens.

"We've got a foothold. Let's make it count."

He doesn't raise his voice or posture. He moves through us like gravity, quiet and constant, impossible to ignore. He doesn't command attention; he collects it. I watch how the others move around him, not out of fear, not even duty, but something steadier. Trust, maybe, or belief.

But tonight, there's something in his eyes. A flicker of hurt, as if he's counting his ghosts. He turns away before I can read it, brushing dust from his coat as if it's just habit. But I know better. That coat has seen more than dirt. Ren's gaze lifts to the stars, and for a moment, the weight he carries feels visible. Not in his stance, but in the silence.

* * *

Mythkeepers Log,

The ancient city of Niren, once a bastion of the dark elves and now cloaked in ruin, has been reclaimed and transformed into the pulsating heart of the Ember Path. This shift marks a pivotal turning point, heralding a new era of strategic realignment and burgeoning resistance.

From its shadowed depths, the currents of power are being irrevocably rerouted. Supply lines, once flowing outwards, now converge inward, feeding the burgeoning strength within. Fighters, their resolve hardened by adversity, are being marshaled and dispatched from this central nexus. Simultaneously, a clandestine operation unfolds beneath the city's broken facade, with prisoners being surreptitiously smuggled through its labyrinthine tunnels, a testament to the desperate measures taken by those seeking freedom.

For the fragmented remnants of resistance, Niren has become more than just a sanctuary; it is a burgeoning home. This haven was carefully constructed by those who were once the city's silent guardians, their intimate knowledge of its subterranean passages now repurposed for a new fight.

They, in turn, have refurbished these ancient spaces for those who now desperately seek refuge and a place to rally.

REALMBOUND

~J.L

136

15

THE TEARWOOD

Marie

Tessa waited just ahead, arms folded, weight sunk into one hip like she'd been trying to hide how tense she was. The door had opened there to the outside, above ground, yet not to the open. Massive rock formations formed a natural cattle chute, with old trees growing against the stones that wound a path until it opened. The entrance, the door itself, was concealed, and the rocks provided an ideal spot for guards.

Behind us, the fires at each station flickered in a line, a trail of orange points fading into the deeper dark, an *ember path* leading back into Niren.

Tessa's voice cut low through the hush.

"The veil breathes in the Tearwood. When it inhales, doors open, then they snap shut when they exhale."

I nodded as I gathered my courage.

Somewhere in this realm were gates. Gates set on top of mountains, gates that led home, and that mattered more than my unease. But I hadn't taken a step forward yet. Rat glanced sideways at me, like he'd been debating whether to speak.

"There's a library in Nyltak," he said. "Lots 'a stuff to read. If you found the city, someone there might know how to help figure things out."

Tessa adjusted the strap on my satchel. Her hands moved steadily, like she'd been trying not to show her concern.

"Most folk keep clear from Tearwood," she said. "They'd seen things in the forest. Heard things." Her eyes showed her worry. "If ye heard somethin' that donna belong, best not be answerin' it."

"I'll be careful, thank you."

I had laced the stone she gave me onto some twine that I wore like a pendant, which she noticed and smiled. The eye was nestled into my robe's pocket.

I had gained pants, a tunic, and boots for this journey, which were washed. Caleen had also gifted me a small dagger, which I sheathed into a rope belt. I'm ready for my journey home. Or as ready as I was gonna be…

"Keep yer feet, Marie. This friendship won't be turned to grief, yeh hear me?"

I nodded as she pulled me in for a hug, our arms wrapped Rat into the embrace without hesitation, and he was swept inside the circle.

"She doesn't come glowing." He stated from between us, wiping a fast tear.

"I don't know what that means." I said as I looked down at him and smiled.

"It's okay. Don't need to. I'll see you again." He said, straightening.

I had no intention of returning to this place, and that truth kicked me in the gut. I was going to miss him, both of them.

"That'd be nice." I said as I ruffled his shaggy hair. My attempt at lightening the feeling of finality.

I glanced in the door's direction and saw Ren there. Watching. He nodded, as if to say farewell, all stoic and mysterious looking in his red hood, standing in the stone's shadow.

Naturally, I had to ruin that for him. "See ya, red riding hood!" I called out obnoxiously, waving at him.

He cracked a smile. "Damn fools festival." He said, just loud enough.

I flicked him off as I turned into the Tearwood.

I carried more than I had expected, leaving this place, friendships, and allies, the scroll, my notes with the gates on them, the small tangible gift rock, and Paxithra the Witness, who sleeps nestled in my pocket.

I'm no warrior. But I have determination. It's time to leave the underground and step into the myth that had already begun to tell me its tales.

I was going to find my way home.

* * *

The fog thickened in places, thinned in others. I passed old barricades, half-consumed by vines. A human village, maybe. Long abandoned. The air tingled here, sending my hair standing on my arms. I moved widely around the ruins.

Three hours into the walk, something shifted. Not around me, but in me.

A thrum. Subtle. Like pressure behind my ears. Paxithra stirred faintly but didn't wake. I paused, crouched beneath a gnarled birch with bark like flaked bone. I pressed my hand to the eye.

"What is it?" I waited for a vision. Paxithra shifted but didn't answer.

The Tearwood, they called it, was twisted with history. An empire once stood here, one that practiced something called *veil-magic,* and the forest had swallowed their civilization because of it.

I froze; a figure loomed right past the treeline, where the fog curled low along the forest floor. It didn't move at first. Just stood there, tall and still, as if hewn from the forest itself.

Then it twitched.

A sharp, unnatural jerk of the head. One shoulder rolled, then snapped back into place. Its limbs were jointed like wood, but not made of it, something denser, darker, like petrified bone wrapped in bark. The movements weren't fluid, as though it was learning how to be a body.

Its face was a smooth plate of stone, engraved with symbols that flickered. It had no eyes, no mouth, no features at all, but I knew it saw me. I sensed it. The way its head tilted toward me, like I'd been marked.

I didn't move, and Paxithra shifted again, slower this time, like it was holding its breath.

It stood with its arms at its sides, twitching in small, sharp bursts. A shoulder. A knee. A clawed hand flexing and locking. Strange, long, vine-like tendrils jerked and flinched as they seemed to grow from the thing's

139

back. It didn't feel alive. It felt bound.

Then the veil tore open. No, not open. Not parted. It was freaking violated.

I whirled around in the tear's direction, my heart hammering.

The air didn't shimmer; it convulsed. A rupture split the space ahead, jagged and raw, like the world had been clawed open from the inside.

The tear didn't breathe.

It screamed.

Light bled from the wound in pulses, sharp and wrong, and the forest recoiled. Branches twisted away. The fog thinned like it didn't want to touch what had happened.

I felt it in my bones, a shudder that wasn't mine. The ground beneath me pulsed once, then held still, as if bracing for impact. Paxithra churned, then went silent, as if even it couldn't look.

Something came through.

It didn't step in; it forced its way in as if raping the realm itself.

A creature, also faceless, emerged, its body slick and jointless, moving like smoke. It didn't belong here. Not in Myth. Not in any realm that had rules. Its limbs were unnaturally extended and pliable, and its aura was akin to a scream contained within flesh. It didn't look at me. It entered me. Not physically, but through attention, through the way its presence pressed against my ribs, my throat, my thoughts.

I couldn't breathe.

The other creature moved, like a sentinel defending its ground. It twitched forward in lightning-fast bursts. Shoulder, knee, claw, vine, like it was being yanked by purpose. It didn't hesitate; it attacked.

The screech that tore from its body wasn't sound. It was a rupture of its own. A defense. A fury.

The wraithlike thing flared in response, limbs stretching wide, and the two collided like storms of grief and rage.

They didn't fight like creatures. They fought like forces. The sentinel clawed and slammed, its movements jerky and brutal. The wraith twisted and struck, smooth and merciless. The veil pulsed behind them, still torn, still bleeding into the realm, screaming in a way I could never recount with words.

I crawled backward, breath ragged, heart hammering.

The fight spilled sideways, deeper into the trees. The screeching faded, replaced by the sound of limbs breaking, of something ancient being tested and then…

Then they were gone.

Not vanished. Just… out of sight.

The tear hung there, flickering, then sealed itself with a sound like a gasp. The fog returned, and the forest exhaled, as if momentarily relieved of its torment.

I stayed on the ground, knees scraped, hands shaking, staring at the place where the sentinel had stood.

It hadn't come for me; it had come for that.

Paxithra hummed and pulsed as if in warning, and I scrambled to my feet.

"You don't have to tell me twice."

The eye hummed again in what felt like agreement.

I didn't wait. I moved, stumbling through underbrush, boots catching on roots and moss, my breath still uneven, my thoughts scattered like the leaves in the wind. The fog thinned, the trees seemed to pull back, and the air lightened, less heavy, less haunted.

I found a hollow.

A dip in the land, ringed by stone and low ferns, where the canopy broke just enough to let some clouded over sunlight spill through in a filtered haze. The ground was soft here, layered in thick moss and old leaves, but the silence didn't feel like a threat.

I dropped to my knees, then sat, legs stretched out, arms limp at my sides, and leaned against the rock. Paxithra throbbed, a heartbeat syncing with my own. I pulled it from my pocket, held it in both hands, and let its hum settle into my bones.

I listened to the sounds of the Tearwood as the two things battled in the distance until I no longer heard them, then crawled from our hiding place to make sure it was safe.

The sentinel was gone. The wraith was gone. The veil had sealed, so I settled back down into the hollow.

I pulled out my sketchbook.

The pages were warped from the damp air, but still usable. I flipped past maps and glyphs, past notes scribbled in haste, until I found a blank space. My fingers trembled as I drew, not well, not cleanly, but with urgency. The sentinel's shape. Its twitching limbs. The symbols carved into its face. The way it moved, like it was being yanked by something.

I didn't know why I needed to draw it. Only that I did.

When I finished, I stared at the page. It didn't look right. But it didn't look wrong either. Just, incomplete. The thing I had seen couldn't be captured in lines and on paper.

I leaned back against the stone, eyes half-lidded, and let the forest breathe around me. Paxithra pulsed once more, and I sighed.

"yeah ok, we should keep moving." I said to it before sliding the eye back into my pocket and rising to my feet again.

A few hours passed. I had no guide. Only the map I'd stitched from scrolls and glyphs, or Rat's stories and Tessa's overheard commentary, to keep me on what I hoped to be the right direction.

I kept low. Moved fast and, for once, Paxithra stayed silent.

Twigs snapped as something moved in the brush beside me.

My heartbeat leaped into my throat, the panic rushing back: sentinel, wraith, dogs.

"oh my." I mouthed as Wizard of Oz tumbled its way into my thoughts, and a smirked through my new and rising panic, just as a figure appeared, half-shadowed, riding something.

I exhaled, just a guy on horseback.

Relief trickled in. It even made me giggle.

He looked nineteen at most, built like a truck, broad, shirtless, wrapped in odd tribal ink that climbed over his arms and shoulders like vines. Handsome yet strange.

Why was he shirtless?

How was he steering a horse with his arms full of sticks?

What if this guy knows the way out of here?

He looked down at me, rigid but soft-eyed, like he wanted to speak but didn't know how.

"Hi," I blurted out loud, awkward, raising a hand like I was greeting a sitcom alien. I immediately regretted it and lowered my hand.

"Hello..?" he said, blinking as if he was unsettled. "You're not frightened?"

"Why, should I be?" I quipped, eyeing the weird shirtless rider and his sticks. Seriously, how was he steering?

"No," he drawled. "I presume you shouldn't be frightened. Not of me."

Do people from myth realm just casually ride horses shirtless through haunted forests? Because obviously, that makes sense. Marie logic, Cool.

But then I looked closer.

My gaze searched for the horse's head. I saw hooves. Legs. A belt strap. But the lines didn't track, not to a horse's neck, head, or bridle.

Just to him.

The realization froze me.

"What the...?"

His bare torso flowed right into the beast's chest. No separation.

He wasn't on a horse. He was one.

Chestnut fur. Stamping hooves. A body that didn't break between man and beast.

A centaur.

I backed away like my body was on autopilot.

He shifted his bundle awkwardly onto one arm, freeing the other, palm out.

"Easy now," he murmured.

But I was already gone. Spinning. Bolting. Scrambling like every bone in my body had decided to nope the fuck out.

Behind me, I heard the sticks hit the dirt, then hooves. Then, "Halt, human!"

Nope, nope, nope!

My lungs heaved as my ears began to ring. Every footfall sounded like doom. I slammed against a tree, gasping for air, stars clawing at my vision.

The forest shifted, and so did I, the world tilting sideways without moving at all. He stepped toward me, hooves cautious, hands raised, and I couldn't breathe.

Not because of him.

Because of then. Of the mine. Of the dark. Of the bulls and whips and being a slave.

My heart detonated inside my ribs. Not a thump, but a full collapse-and-rebuild, rapid-fire.

I didn't scream, didn't speak. Couldn't.

My tongue was thick and useless. My ears rang, drowning out thought, like someone had pressed a shrieking kettle to both sides of my skull. The sound was inside me.

My vision blurred at the edges. Black creeping in, stars bursting forward. He said something soft, maybe kind. But my body didn't care. It turned cold. Then hot. Then cold again. Sweat drenched me. My fingertips went numb.

I backed up into another tree; the bark scraping my spine, and tried to run, but my legs weren't working. They stuttered, buckled, hit every root and rock as if gravity was offended by my existence.

Am I dying?

Is this a heart attack?

No.

Just the mine, folded inside my chest like a knife.

I ran until my body crashed into yet another tree. Slid around it.

He was near now. Hands raised. Eyes gentle.

I retreated anyway. A reflexive learned behavior.

Every inch of me screamed to flee, and every inch had forgotten how.

I was panting like an animal, throat rasping, heartbeat deafening. The taste of dirt was sharp in my teeth and somehow familiar. Familiar in the worst way.

I needed out.

Out of this forest, out of this memory, out of whatever Myth had decided I belonged to. I wanted to go home.

He didn't chase or speak, just watched.

His hand hovered near my shoulder. I drew back and stumbled away again, legs shaking and deer-like. I jogged blindly, stupidly, heart hammering inside me like it wanted out.

I didn't trust Myth. Not its ruins. Not its queens. And definitely not some forest-born demigod looking creature who said "human" like it was a species label.

Behind me, he didn't chase, not really. Just kept pace. Effortless. Fluid. Observing me without pressure.

I glanced back once.

He stood framed in moss and setting sunlight, chestnut hair catching light in a way that made him look sculpted from bronzed stone. Mythic. Unreal.

He mouthed something I couldn't hear over the ringing in my ears.

And when I blinked, he was gone.

I spun, dizzy. Scanned the trees. Found nothing.

Then I tripped and face-planted into a sea of ferns, gasping like a dying bird and clawing at the ground for logic.

Was he real? Had I gone completely mad?

I lay there for a while, maybe minutes, maybe an eternity, waiting for my heart to settle. Hoping the world might make sense again, and then he spoke gently. Hesitant.

"Please… human. You have nothing to fear. Not of me."

I didn't move.

Another twig snapped nearby.

He was getting closer again. Not charging or stomping. Just…near.

I focused on the feel of the dirt beneath my hands, grasping it, twining the leaf litter between my fingers, trying to center myself.

The panic started to ease now; the ringing had nearly gone, and my breath more even.

With my head clearer, I bolted upright, out of the ferns and ran.

He followed gracefully and measured. Watching, yet never quite touching.

Why wasn't he attacking?

I could feel him beside me, his strides smooth, almost rhythmic, zigzagging through the trees with ease. He didn't crowd. He didn't speak. Just ran near enough that I could feel his gaze, steady and watching, like he was waiting for something I hadn't decided yet. His pace was deliberate, almost lazy. Mine was frantic. My lungs felt flayed from the inside, and the stabbing in my ribs grew sharper with every breath. I promised myself I'd never run again once I get home.

I staggered again, and he moved closer.

Not fast or invasive. Just near, hands out, poised like he meant to catch me if I collapsed.

I slowed to a stop; I couldn't do anything else. My knees shook beneath me as I bent forward, palms planted on them, choking on air like it was misbehaving.

He stopped when I did. Head tilted, arms still raised, ready but hesitant.

"Leave me alone!" I croaked, unable to lift my voice over the wheeze. "Can't you see? I'm trying to run away!"

He drew his hands back at once, straightened up, and stood staring.

I flapped a hand in his direction, a half-assed *shoo*.

His mouth twitched, fighting a smile.

"I'm not leaving you. There's danger in these woods," he said, voice low but urgent.

It's clear he meant no harm. If he'd wanted to hurt me, he could've done it already. My everything ached, and though fear had lost its grip, irritation had taken its place. I shook my head and raised my eyes, still breathless.

"Danger?" I scanned the forest. "Who are you? What are you?"

He dipped his head. "Traebhr, The Guardian. Bearer of Kabane."

That sounded rehearsed. Like he'd been waiting his whole life to announce it.

"May I ask your name?" he added. "Human."

"Marie," I said, dry-throated. "And don't call me human."

He repeated my name with slow deliberation, as if tasting it in his mouth.

"Marie, I'll accompany you to Nyltak," he said, watching me carefully. "We'll be safer behind its walls."

I blinked at the name.

Nyltak, Rat's city?

He squinted. "Were you truly trying to outrun me?"

"Yes," I answered, fast and flat.

Something gleamed in his eyes, not arrogance. Just disbelief.

And then, laughter.

It erupted from him, uncontained, a deep, ridiculous sound that echoed against bark and stone. I startled, took a half step back, unsure whether to bolt again or throw something at him. I decided I'd throw something.

A stick on the ground at my feet. I chucked it, but it whizzed by him, whirling through the air, missing its mark.

He covered his laugh with a half-smile as he watched it fly past him.

"Come. Let's get out of the Tearwood."

I nodded, unsure why. Somewhere between fatigue and surrender.

He led me to a small camp and rolled a fallen log toward me next to the encampment he'd been at before we stumbled into each other and gestured for me to sit. He reached into a pouch and pulled out a root, rough and spindly.

"Chew," he said, pointing to his forehead, then his chest. "It calms."

I turned it between my fingers. Debating my life choices.

Accepting unknown drugs from shirtless men in the woods with horse anatomy, what the heck has happened to your life, Marie?

I put the root in my mouth and bit down.

The texture was gritty, a little bitter, like chewing bark dipped in sand, but it worked. After a few moments, my mind had steadied. My breath evened, and the slight ringing in my ears disappeared. I felt, calmer.

I leaned to return the root, but he shook his head.

"Keep it," he said, tossing a small leather pouch to me. "In case."

I tucked it into my robe. As my stomach growled in protest, loud and ungraceful.

He raised an eyebrow, then handed me a strip of dried meat and a thin, cracker-like square of bread. As I ate, I watched him.

Traebhr was massive. Broad-shouldered and imposing, but not cruel. His tattoos were a dark red-brown color, worn like armor, full of runes I didn't recognize. His skin was smooth, golden-bronze, almost metallic in the light, and his eyes, amber and shadowed, held something unsure, yet familiar.

His hair was deep caramel, tied at the base of his neck, strands swinging freely around his jawline. When he moved, they danced. When he stood still, they settled against skin like brushstrokes.

He wore a carmine-red cloak; the hood folded back, the color deep against his complexion. A breastplate glinted beneath it, polished but scarred. When he tightened the straps, the metal caught the light, and so did something else. A quiet strength and a softness.

I stared at him, trying to make sense of the contradiction.

It felt like watching one of Granny's horses back on the farm. Big, gentle things, she swore could read hearts if you let them. Pop used to jokingly call the place "Bucking A Stables," as a contradiction to the very tame and sweet horses they had, and the name stuck.

"Traebhr," I began slowly, watching how he moved as he gathered his things with muted purpose, "you said you're the Guardian?"

He nodded, the gesture understated, as if the title was worn into him rather than worn on him. His back was still to me, broad and unwavering.

"Indeed, I am," he replied over his shoulder, while gently stamping out the last of his campfire with practiced ease.

I tilted my head, leaning to the side, hoping for a clearer glimpse of his expression, some cue, some flicker, but he remained partially turned away, his profile lit only by the fading glow.

"Who or what exactly are you a guardian of?" I asked.

My gaze flicked from the forest path to Traebhr himself. He stood like the trunk of an ancient tree, unshakable, immovable, and yet I couldn't help but picture him curled around something fragile.

His brow creased before he turned to face me.

"I believe your questions are best answered in Nyltak," he said with patient finality, motioning toward the direction we were headed.

He took the lead again, and I followed, brushing low branches aside and trying not to trip on gnarled roots. He hummed under his breath, a melody that didn't belong to any tune I knew, and every few steps he glanced back, not urgently, just a check-in, like a wolf keeping tabs on a younger member of the pack.

He was so much faster than I was, even when I jogged to catch up. Each time our eyes met, I felt something tug in my chest, curiosity, sure, but something else too. Familiarity. Magic. I tried to look away each time, but it lingered behind my ribs like an echo.

The forest thickened until the shadows outpaced the moonlight. I squinted into the dark, one arm outstretched, but everything ahead blurred together into one black wall. No path. No clearance. Just underbrush and silence.

"Are you sure you know where we're *goooing?*"

Before I could finish the thought, I felt myself lifted absurdly, over his shoulder like some bulky grain bag.

"Woe!" I yelped, flailing. "What the hell? Put me down!"

He let out a grunt as I squirmed, then set me down again with clear restraint, exhaling through his nose like he was trying not to laugh, or growl.

"You can't just go slinging people around like that," I snapped, brushing off my robes and trying to retain whatever dignity I had left.

He gestured to the woods ahead. "Can you see?"

I turned and stomped into the dark, only to become entangled in what must've been the world's most vengeful bush. I tripped, swore under my breath, and heard it, a low chuckle sliding out from him like smoke.

My face went hot. Anger or embarrassment, or both. "No, I can't see. But that doesn't mean you can pick me up like a sack of potatoes!"

His voice was mild, but far from serious. "May I carry you, Marie?"

I couldn't see the grin, but I didn't need to. It stretched through his voice, feathered with amusement.

I sighed. "Yeah, I guess."

He reached for me again, gentler this time, but I lifted a finger just before his arms closed around me.

"Not like a sack of potatoes, please."

16

NYLTAK

"Let the seal be lit; where it shines, no shadow reigns."
~Proverb of Kabane

Marie

"Almost there," he murmured, voice steady as the night folded closer around us.

His arms held me now, not slung over his shoulder but cradled, and though the forest remained pitch black, our momentum quickened. Branches whispered past us in rapid succession; the wind pressed along my spine.

Our pace surged forward, and though I couldn't see what lay ahead, Traebhr moved with precision, dodging low-hanging limbs, crossing uneven ground, leaping creek beds so seamlessly I barely felt the shifts beneath me. The moonlight was thin, carving out shallow pools of silver between branches. His face caught just enough of it to make me believe his eyes had met mine, but the shadows played tricks, and I glanced away, feeling the strange flush of being seen too clearly.

"How can you tell where you're going?" I asked, squinting into the dark. "Can you see anything at all?"

"I see everything," he replied. "The night steals color from the day but not shape. And shape is enough."

The way he said it, matter of fact, unboastful, made me pause.

I tilted my head upward. The stars winked at us, briefly visible through the canopy. It was the only way I could tell how fast we were moving. And we were moving fast.

Then he slowed to a stop.

His grip on me eased before lowering me to the ground. I turned to ask why, but he was already reaching for his blade. The weapon hissed free from its sheath and caught a fleeting ribbon of moonlight along the edge.

Paxithra pulled and twined, swirling angrily in my pocket. It doesn't physically move, but it feels that way.

"What's going on?" I whispered to both Traebhr and the eye.

His posture shifted, still and sharp. "Stay here. Stay quiet. Don't run."

I tried to follow his gaze, but all I saw was darkness. A snarl rolled through the silence like thunder. Traebhr stepped forward, positioning himself between me and the unseen creature, his blade spinning in his hand.

Then, the thing lunged.

The eye bellowed a silent roar in my mind.

Black fur split the shadows. Claws flashed, teeth bared. It blocked out the slivers of moonlight as it flew toward him, but flinched mid-air, as if it heard Paxithra, still barking in my mind.

I gasped, stumbling backward.

Traebhr surged upward, intercepting the beast mid-air, grabbing hold, twisting, and throwing. The weight of him alone sent it backward into the underbrush. His sword flashed once more, and then the two of them vanished into the treeline.

What followed was chaos, snapping limbs, guttural roars, the shriek of something struck deep. The eye quaked and thrummed, roaring. I dropped to the ground, hands over ears. The beast cried out in pain as Traebhr's hooves thundered back toward me within moments. He reached for me, hoisted me onto his back, and turned, blade still drawn, posture rigid.

"Quickly now," he said, "someone approaches."

His sword glimmered at the hilt, strands of soft blue light swirling like restless veins beneath the metal.

The eye snarled again, deafening and in rage. Again, I had to cover my ears.

"GET DOWN!"

A voice burst from the trees beside us, sharp and thunderous.

Traebhr recoiled, shielding me with his arm as an arrow sliced overhead. A yelp rang out behind us, followed by the heavy thud of a body hitting the earth.

Paxithra howled within my pocket. I felt its power thrumming through my bones; the vibrations of its growling rattled my skull. I squeezed my eyes shut, still holding my ears.

"Sheath your blade, Traebhr!" the voice boomed again, though this time with a curl of amusement.

"Eesym, by the gods, I thought you were scouting ahead." Traebhr replied, lowering his sword with reluctant ease. He stared into the shadows, where the speaker was obscured.

The eye settles. Something like mourning curls inside my chest, but also relief...

"I'm sorry." My whisper is as soft as a breath, and the eye seems to sigh within my mind.

I squinted into the gloom. A shape moved, leaner than Traebhr, more reserved, and when he stepped forward, I saw the equine lower half, unmistakable. Another centaur.

"I caught the scent of this one," the stranger explained, retrieving the arrow from the beast's heart. "Looks like you ran into it first. The Cerberus dogs are stirring again," he continued, his voice darker now. "They've been gathering in Hesiod. Large clusters, organized. If this one found you here, it wasn't by accident."

"They were chasing me before," I blurted out. "Same kind of thing, black fur, impossible speed."

He chuckled under his breath, casting a sideways glance. "Cerberus and wandering the Tear, and yet she lives. Remarkable."

"Glad you find it entertaining," I muttered.

"They're tracking her, Eesym." Traebhr said flatly. "Which means more will come. I take no pleasure in killing the dogs, not when their wills aren't their own."

"Tracking me?" I asked, as the eye seemed to send a somber tug at my mind.

Traebhr's mouth pulls taunt. "I'll explain later."

I started to interject, but the other centaur cut me off.

"Take her," the stranger said. "I'll sweep the perimeter. There are worse things than dogs in the Tearwood."

Traebhr took my hands, fastening them around his waist.

"Hold tight, Marie."

His body reared and pivoted, and the sudden gallop pulled the air from my lungs. I clung to him, pressed my cheek against his back as wind whipped past us. I kept my eyes shut, my fingers locked around his belt until finally, the rhythm slowed. The forest receded. The air grew warmer, less dense.

Then I felt it, his hand, resting against mine, caressing in slow circles.

"You're safe now, Marie," he said. "We've reached the moor. The dogs won't follow us here."

I opened my eyes.

The trees had vanished, swallowed by distance and shadow. The field ahead stretched wide, silver in the moonlight, tall grasses swaying in every direction. From my vantage point on his back, it looked like we were riding over the surface of a forgotten sea.

Above us, two moons shone. I had been in this Realm so long, but under the ground, I hadn't known. One shone pale, warm yellow; the other one bright and white, distant and cold. The larger had eclipsed the smaller, casting a ring across the sky like a worn circlet of light.

Beautiful.

"Two moons." I whispered.

Movement flickered in my peripheral.

The forest edge stood tall behind us, black and unwavering, and from its base, a figure approached, graceful, fast, silent. The second centaur, but moving like a ghost, the moonlight bending around him as if unwilling to land.

"About time, old friend," Traebhr called over his shoulder.

The figure slowed to a gentle canter at our side. He was smaller, built like he'd traded bulk for wisdom and stealth. As he approached, I noticed that the grass parted ahead of him, as if the moor was making way for his passage.

"You know I can't always be there to save you, Traebhr. You're getting much too old for a nursemaid."

Traebhr snorted but didn't argue.

They spoke like old friends, long worn in their friction, but rooted deeper than time.

"You're Eesym," I said, guessing without needing confirmation. I'd heard his name stated in the forest.

The centaur turned his gaze on me, eyes sharp but kind. "And you must be Marie."

He inclined his head, honoring without pretending servitude.

"The honor is mine," he said. "And should you ever need me, you have only to call."

Something shifted in me. No guards. No cold stone halls. Just open sky and the potential that maybe not everything in Myth wanted me broken.

Eesym was older, somewhere in his forties, but nothing about him felt spent. His hair was walnut, streaked with silver like frozen river water. It hung past his ears in uneven waves, strands whipping at his temples as he moved.

His skin bore the life he'd lived, deep brown, hardened from sun and long campaigns. Across one shoulder, a leather sash hung, decorated with metal beads and rings that clinked as he moved. A large dagger rode low at his hip, and behind him, a quiver of arrows feathered neatly in place.

His fur was a rich brown, scattered with snow-colored spots across his flanks and hindquarters. White sock-markings wrapped each leg above the hooves, and his tail swayed, striped brown and ivory.

If I hadn't known better, I'd have called him an Appaloosa, only this one had a heartbeat too human for that.

"Can you see the lights up ahead yet?" Traebhr asked as we cantered through the tall grass. I stared out into the night, trying to find what he saw. After a few seconds, I could see them, small points of light set into the skyline.

The moon cast enough light for me to see that the lights were atop a high, long wall of stone that glistened like granite, stretching in both directions. The stones were cut with precision, fitting together seamlessly to form an imposing barrier. Ancient runes glowed along its surface; deep magic embedded into its surface.

We slowed to a stop, gazing upon the massive city walls, awe-struck by their sheer size and grandeur.

"The seal of Nyltak," he said. He then pointed toward the open door. Awaiting our entrance. "Once the seal is lit, it cannot be broken."

I stared in silence for a moment. My face must have conveyed my confusion. "Magic?"

"It's late," Eesym said quietly. "We should get her settled for the night. There's much to do tomorrow."

Traebhr agreed, and we start on our way, the enormous doors slowly closing behind us, their magic sealing it, as it lit the seams and seal.

We walked down one large cobblestone road to the next. The light from the moons reflected off the road's surface and glimmered in the night. The air was cool and carried a faint hint of jasmine. It was silent on these streets, and I couldn't help but notice the rhythmic sound of my two guides' hooves on the hard surface.

Clip clop, clip clop.

I giggled at the sound, catching a glance my way.

At the end of the road, we turned left down a smaller, yet better-lit road. It reminded me of a mix between the main street in my town, and a scene from a wizarding movie.

Interesting stores and homes lined the main road, their lights casting warm shadows on the ground at our feet. I could hear laughter and glasses clinking inside a place called Elok's Pub. The large window revealed a well-lit place filled with tables of friends and smiling faces.

Up the street, the sound of cantering hooves ricocheted off the stone. Two young centaur men barreled out of a side street and slowed to a trot as they entered the pub. Inside, voices greeted them with joyous cheers.

We moved on through the city, turning from one road to the next. The layout was maze-like and confusing.

The city center opened onto a sizable courtyard. Several streets connected here, and I imagined this would be the place for city gatherings, fairs, and public markets. The courtyard was adorned with lanterns that twinkled, creating a dance of light and shadows. A fountain stood at the center, its water glistening under the moonlight, adding a calming murmur to the night. Several temporary structures stood at its edges, undoubtedly for selling goods and food during the day.

On the other side of the courtyard, arose a building that contrasted with its surroundings. Its long, deep staircase ascended to a grand entrance flanked by massive, fluted pillars. Tall, elegant windows were arched, filled with stained glass that glowed softly with interior light, casting colorful patterns on the steps below.

Decorative statues of mythical creatures lined the staircase, each one crafted with such detail that it seemed almost lifelike. To my surprise, two of them did snap to life as they watched us, slamming the butts of their spears onto the stone steps as we made our way up to the massive doors, seeming to command them to open.

When Traebhr set me onto the stone floor inside the palace, I felt it, that tremor in the air, a whispering hum that shivered through my body. It wasn't a sound, not quite. More like echoes of something speaking between moments, between worlds, their voices slipping through unseen cracks in reality itself.

"Oh my, oh my, oh my!"

The chorus surrounded me, layered in an unsettling harmony that seemed to come from everywhere and nowhere at once. I turn in confusion but saw nothing, only space, dim shadows flickering in the light.

Then, as if the world itself folded to their will, they manifested into being.

Three tiny figures bloomed into existence before my eyes, their bodies forming as though stitched together from fragments of forgotten light.

Wings shimmering with iridescence, catching the glow of the chamber. The sheen of their skin seemed almost ephemeral, as if they weren't here, not yet.

"These are the Triune Faye," Traebhr's voice grounded me. "Lyris, Aeris, Tyris. They will ensure you are made comfortable." He spoke to them not as individuals, but as one entity. "Triune, this is Marie, our guest."

And there it was, that flicker of recognition.

The terrifying messengers that help my friends, and now here they are, right here, right in front of me, radiant and strange. Lyris. Aeris. Tyris. The Triune Faye.

"Holy shit." I whisper to myself.

"Marie, human guest, yes. How wonderful! Yes, we will show her to her room; it's a lovely room, yes."

Their chorus wove through the air like enchantment, words tumbling in perfect unison even as their mismatched voices layered over one another. They're identical in stature: small, stout, their extra-long-pointed ears twitching with excitement. Their childlike round noses and youthful features should have been endearing, but something about them, about the way they speak, as if many and one, all at once, kept me rooted in an uneasy wonder.

Their gender is un-placeable. Nothing about their physical appearance gave that away, and their voices, both male and female at once, resonating from somewhere beyond human speech. Although their presence is unmistakable, I could still feel them lingering somewhere beyond the edges of my perception. As if still having one foot in another world.

A whisper where there should be silence, or a flicker where the world should be still.

The Triune Faye were marvels, odd and radiant, wondrous and unsettling.

And they watched me with delighted, knowing eyes. *We've seen you before,* they seem to say.

They guided me through wide hallways lined with doors, up a staircase so broad it felt ceremonial. The carved oak doors swung easily, perfectly balanced. Everything here was enormous, doors, halls, rooms, streets, buildings.

My room was warm. Rustic, yes, but not crude. The bed looked like something stitched together from fairy tales, heaped with feathered down pillows. In the corner, an ornate wardrobe, covered in carvings of flora and fauna, so fine I could see dew etched into each petal. A marble table waited by a wide arched window, holding a vase of wildflowers stirring beneath the fall breeze. A shelf of books rested beside it.

I linger in the doorway, staring.

I couldn't remember the last time a room didn't feel like a threat.

The Triune flitted past me, opening a second door opposite the window, revealing a bronze clawfoot tub, lined with engraved vines and flowers. Two of them filled it with steaming water and fragrant oils while the third laid out a silk nightgown across the bed, hands folded as they waited.

One, I thought it was Aeris, twined his fingers together near his belly, and the other two mirrored the motion exactly.

"A bath, Marie, yes. Nice, warm, and soothing. Yes?"

Their chorus landed softly and patterned, like someone singing bedtime instructions across a veil.

I nodded. "Thank you."

They didn't react beyond a smile and slipped out the door to give me privacy.

The bath was lovely in a way that felt almost unfair. Like I hadn't earned it, but it welcomed me anyway. The oils smelled like lavender; the scented steam curled around my face, softening everything. I ran the sponge along my arms, slow and deliberate, letting the soapy warmth settle into my skin, the warmth of the water settling into my bones. The bath calmed me in places I hadn't realized were tense.

I leaned back, letting my hair float, letting the ache in my shoulders dissolve. Dirt lifted from me in ribbons. I sat in that bath until the water went cool and my fingertips shriveled. Until the silence felt earned.

The nightgown slipped over my shoulders like mist poured into fabric. It fit without tugging.

The fall night air was cool, but a fire had been lit in the hearth, and it crackled, low and steady. I hadn't noticed it before, but now, clean and dressed, it felt like the right kind of warmth.

The kind that lets things go.

I crossed the room and picked up my robes. My fingers curling into the fabric as I stared at the flames. A tear slid down my cheek as the feel of the rough fabric bit into my fingers.

I fed them to the fire.

The fabric curled and blackened, threads unraveling, vanishing into smoke. I watched until the robes were gone. Until nothing was left of them but heat and ash.

I took a deep breath in and released it, allowing my shoulders to fall, my jaw to relax, and the crease in my brow to smooth. Releasing the girl within the Maw.

Tonight, in this moment, she would be free.

On the marble table by the window, lay my satchel. I walked to the table, flipped open the notebook and wrote about my crossing of the Tearwood, about Traebhr and Eesym, about Nyltak and its magical glowing rampart, the triune faye, and my burned robes.

Once finished my writing, I placed my notebook back inside; the Eye glinted to me from within, so I took it, and stood, looking out at the gardens below.

"It's beautiful here, Paxithra." The eye flickered as if in agreement.

Was it safe to sleep, though? I checked the door.

The Triune hadn't locked it. There were no chains. No screams from other rooms. I opened the door, only a crack, and peered down the hall. Empty, so I slipped back inside the room, closing the door and leaning my back against it.

I look down at the eye, at the depths of its blue. "Are we safe? Can we sleep?"

The eye hums, not an audible sound, but more of an exchange of energy, one that feels like, *yes, sleep.*

I walked to the bed, climbed in, and slid the eye beneath my pillow. The moment my spine met the mattress, my chest unraveled yet again. I hadn't realized how tightly I'd been holding everything in place, how much my breath was still shaped by months spent in straw and stone, half-listening for the scream that would follow someone else's punishment.

The pillow under my head didn't scratch. The air didn't smell like rot or blood or piss.

The window stayed open, a clean, cool breeze meeting the warmth of the fire. I closed my eyes and listened to the gentle crackle of the fire, and just like that, sleep wasn't something I earned through exhaustion. It came on its own, curled into me like a soft creature claiming space.

I slept.

17

QUEST FOR ANSWERS

Marie

I woke up before sunrise. The silence here was palpable, a tangible thing, not emptiness, but a hush I hadn't experienced since Earth. Since home, freedom, and safety.

My lungs hesitated, unsure if I should expand them. I savored the scent, testing it. The air wasn't heavy, thankfully; it lacked the awful smell of the prison mines. So I drew in a breath, which turned to a yawn and a stretch.

As I lay there, I gazed at the place where the wall met the ceiling. Watching it change color. A gentle gold. A soft pink. Shades I hadn't witnessed in months. Not the gray of stone, or the glare of a torch in the dark. Just… light.

Then I noticed the ceiling wasn't blank. Something was painted there, soft shapes, shadows, hints of green and stone. In the dim light, it looked almost real. Like a place I might've dreamed once.

I didn't linger before sitting up, my bare feet hitting the floor as I swung them off the bed and onto the rug. The calm, the peace, felt strange. Like something I wasn't sure I could still have.

I pulled the blanket around me and walked to the window.

The room was elevated, and I could see beyond the garden, past Nyltak's inner walls, past watchtowers and sloping roofs and wide arches, into the world, into this realm. Into a world that had dawned, I realized.

The pale light of dawn crept across the distant rolling mountains, turning the dew on their peaks to silver. Mist unfurled from the valleys, like silent sighs.

Pressing my fingers against the cold glass, I remembered the sun again. In the mines, the day offered nothing new. Labor never ceased. Light didn't penetrate, and time lost all meaning. Only pain, fear, and death remained.

Then came the hum, like bees. The Triune Faye buzz into the room, around me, their wings beating in a rhythm too fast to track.

I dashed to the bed, reached under the pillow and pulled Paxithra free. The Eye is cool in my hand, quiet and watching.

The Triune laid the dress across the bed, shimmering like something from a story I didn't believe in.

I stared at it, then at the eye.

"I'm not leaving you," I whispered.

There're no pockets on the dress. No place for secrets. But I found a fold in the bodice, a seam stitched with silver thread. Once dressed, I slid Paxithra inside it, pressing it flat against my ribs.

"I never wear dresses…" I muttered, backing up.

But anything was better than the robes. Those stinking, scratchy, slave-mine robes I'd burned the night before. Their ashes still clung to the edges of the fireplace.

The Faye paid little attention to my bellyaching regarding my attire, and together, they had helped to dress me. They had guided my arms through the delicate sleeves of the dress, directing my limbs like gentle stagehands. Ensuring the fabric settles perfectly on my shoulders. I had let them guide my arms through gossamer sleeves. The fabric whispering against my skin.

This dress is exquisite. It's silk skimmed over me like water, and it caught the light, shimmering emerald. The bodice, embroidered with small silver threads, formed intricate patterns of leaves and flowers. The skirt flowed gracefully to the floor; its layers of gossamer-thin fabric reminding me of the Faye's wings. Lyris adjusts the gown's flowing skirt, ensuring each layer cascades while the other two fix my hair. They place a delicate matching shawl over my open shoulders.

They pulled back, eyes gleaming.

"Enchanting, lovely, human. Lovely, beautiful Marie. Yes. Ready for the king. Yes, lovely."

The word lodged deep in my chest. The King. I cringed. No more royals.

"The King?" I gasped.

Before I could gather my thoughts, a knock echoed through the chamber. Tyris darted to the door.

"Are you ready?" Traebhr asked.

I stood. Mechanically. My hands smoothing the dress, a gesture more grounding than graceful.

"We're going to see the King? Are we coming back here after?"

Traebhr nodded. His expression softening.

"Yes, this is your room now. And yes, King Larrek... You look lovely, Marie."

I smiled weakly. My mouth could fake normalcy; my stomach couldn't.

A bundle of nerves gathered like a knot in my gut, but I joined Traebhr into the hallway. Together we strode. Doors loomed wide, tall enough to swallow horses whole. Centaur-sized, I realized.

Centaur people stood in a few of those open doors as we passed by. One of whom turned, saw us, reentered his room, and whispered to his companions with excitement. Like I was a museum piece. Or a ghost. Telling its occupants that there's a human in the hallway with Traebhr. The inhabitants within buzzed with whispered enthusiasm.

Every door felt like a checkpoint. My skin prickled as we passed each one.

Rooms appeared, libraries, studies, plant-filled chambers, tables covered with jars of herbs, scrolls, mechanisms I couldn't name. I wanted to look; I really did. But part of me stayed braced for a shout, a reprimand, or a closed fist.

Nyltak's people aren't just centaurs, though they are the majority. The creatures... such an array of creatures. Green, blue, scaled, bark-skinned, winged, tailed, animal-legged, and sprite-eyed.

Across what appeared to be an open foyer was an immense wooden double door. Two sentries, dressed for battle and holding polished halberds, stand on either side of it.

As we crossed the foyer toward those doors, a long line of open floor to ceiling windows loomed to our left. Tiny gray and brown fairies with iridescent dragonfly wings danced and flitted, weaving in and out and around the room, chasing one another in a playful airborne game of tag. Their tiny bodies had no hair or clothing, which didn't seem to matter as they didn't appear to have sexes. They weren't at all what I'd expect fairies to look like, no magic dust following them like in popular cartoons; the only brightness was the glint of sun that reflected off their wings.

I could stay to watch them for hours, the way they danced and played, teasing each other. Their tiny giggles and tittering just barely tickling my ears as we passed by them. I gawked at them as they flew and chased overhead. One stopped mid-flight, eyeing me. Then another collided into him, sending him spiraling down.

Too fast. Too sudden.

My hands reacted before my mind did, catching him instinctively.

It landed on its bottom and stared at me from his seat in my palms. His large, dark eyes were like looking into a distant galaxy. Black or deep blue, and filled with flecks of silver, looking a lot like stars. Unnamed constellations stare back at me.

I'm holding a damn fairy...

I didn't move, and he didn't fly away.

Traebhr looked down at me and raised a brow at the creature that now sat in my hands. Shaking his head, amused.

"First day and already catching fairies?"

I stammered, unsure of the protocol. "I umm..."

The creature climbed up my arm and burrowed beneath my shawl. I couldn't help but huff a laugh at the fairy, who was now making a hiding place in the fabric.

As we crossed the open foyer, the grand double doors rose ahead. Closer now, I noticed the carved wood, golden inlays, centaur kings etched into their faces. As Traebhr and I approached the doors, the two Elven sentries snapped to attention and moved together, taking hold of the doors. My heart pounded, my stomach tied in knots as my attention was drawn towards the opening of those colossal doors, and whatever awaited us beyond them.

Don't collapse, don't run, just breathe. A new mantra on repeat in my mind.

"Traebhr, The Guardian. Bearer of Kabane." A powerful voice announced his presence as we entered the great hall.

Traebhr strode into the grand hall with his chin held high. I rushed along beside him, my focus everywhere at once. The tiny fairy peaking from under the fabric on my shoulder.

Nervously, I bit at my lower lip.

The hall had a long walkway through its center. The ceiling arched like a cathedral; fluted pillars line the path; colorful banners fluttered above. Statues and artifacts and history staring down from every wall.

The platform ahead bore the throne, not a chair, but a structure. A space built wide, deep, and cushioned, the tall back reaches up the wall, to the ceiling. A place to settle a legacy, who walked like a horse.

A regal, massive Centaur stood before us, cloaked in deep blue with gold trim, wearing an embroidered tunic and a pendant. His crown of woven gold rests on his head, while his white fur and matching tail complemented his appearance. Blonde, wavy hair framed sharp blue eyes that reflect both authority and wisdom.

I blanched when those eyes met mine. Not because they looked cruel, but because they were looking at me.

We approached, and Traebhr halted before the platform, bowed his head as his right fist slammed onto his chest in salute. I watched him, unsure of what I was supposed to do, and the fairy on my shoulder moaned and shuttered as it balled up the fabric of my shawl to hide, which I suddenly wished I could do as well.

"Traebhr, your return to Nyltak is a momentous occasion. I see you have not returned to us empty handed." The King regarded me.

"Your majesty, King Lerrek, I'm honored to introduce Marie of…" His voice wavered. Hesitation and silence. I filled it.

"Earth! I'm… I'm from Earth. Your majesty."

The king lingered on the name. "Marie of Earth."

The crowd shifted behind us; murmurs filled the hall. Reverence or shock, maybe both?

A small smile pulled at Traebhr's lips, glancing at me, before returning to his stoney features.

"Traebhr, your unwavering dedication has brought us a guest of great significance."

The king's gaze shifted between us.

"Marie of Earth, though you may feel like a stranger in our midst, know that your presence here is highly valued and deeply respected. You are now a member of this kingdom, Nyltak, and as such you will have our protection, and guidance. Learn our ways and your purpose here."

I nodded woodenly. Protection, guidance, citizenship?

"Traebhr will oversee such things."

Traebhr saluted once more, his fist pounding his chest as he thanks his king, and we're ushered out. I moved because I had to, not because my legs believed this yet or because I knew what the crown saw when it regarded me. But because for now, I was still standing, not gagged and accused of theft.

Eesym met us outside the Hall, leaning casually against a wall.

"I've scheduled a meeting inside the temple with Litharn while you two got through the formalities." He spoke.

"Who's Litharn?" I asked, hearing the tiny fairy chirp at our plan as it peaked from the fabric of my shawl.

"He's the tomes keeper, at the temple." Traebhr answered.

Eesym eyed the creature on my shoulder. "Blast the gods, she's caught a fairy?!"

"Seems so." Traebhr's mouth pulled thin.

"I didn't mean to. It fell into my hands." I said, voice taut in ways I didn't expect. "Is that bad?"

Both centaurs chuckled, eyeing the creature that held the fabric over its head like a hooded cape on my shoulder.

"Catching one of those little bastards is an arduous task, but they're supposed to bring you luck if you do." Traebhr said.

"As long as you don't mind it clinging to you like an ailment." Eesym said.

The fairy seemed to hear and understand the words, and it sent teeth chattering noises and waved a fist from under my shawl at them.

"Or the occasional bite; feral little things." He continued.

The fairy zoomed out from under my shawl and into Eesym's face, still waving a fist, its tiny teeth chattering just inches from his nose. Eesym let out a huff of air at the fairy, and the little creature flew away, clinging to a nearby buttress. Watching us as we passed by.

I watched him perch himself on the wall like he belonged there forever. "Oh Eesym! I like him." But at this point, maybe I just liked anything that hadn't tried to hurt me.

"You won't be rid of him that easily." Traebhr said, eyeing the fairy.

We made our way to the back of the palace, which opened to a lush green courtyard filled with gardens, statues, fountains, and flowers. A peacock strutted past, unphased by any of us. A few centaur children played with a ball, tossing it into the air to a winged Faye who giggled as he caught it and tossed it back.

On its opposite side was a lofty and beautiful building. Banners hung from the upper reaches, emblazoned with symbols. The exterior walls were adorned with intricate carvings and reliefs, ornate and wonderful. The sight of it took my breath for an instant, as I stopped to allow my mind to take a mental snapshot of what I saw.

"Woe…" I said in a breath.

"Answers. As promised. All your questions can be answered in the temple." Traebhr turned to me as he spoke, extending his hand towards the building.

I nodded and followed his lead, in awe.

* * *

Inside, the temple opened to a vast room with vaulted ceilings that seemed to soar, reminding me of the heavens. The pillars lining either side were covered in intricate carvings of their deities, each one a creature I had never seen.

One creature just inside the door stood like a man, but with owl-like talons for feet. He was covered in feathers, robed, and his head bowed, eyes peering into a crystal he held in his clawed hands at his navel. Each of my centaur companions touched the crystal with two outstretched fingers, kissed the knuckles of those fingers, and then dabbed their foreheads as they continued into the temple. From the looks of the dulled edge of the crystal, I'd guess that this was a regularly practiced ritual here.

The detailed work in the stone brought the creature-deities that lined the temple to life, their eyes appearing to watch over the room's visitors. Between them were shelves, which housed delicately placed scrolls, books, and artifacts.

The temple floors were covered in large flagstones, and two long granite tables ran parallel on either side of the room. These tables, carved from single slabs of granite, were polished to a mirror-like finish, reflecting the dim light of the lanterns hanging from the ceiling. Interestingly, the tables stood bare, with very few chairs around them, revealing that the main inhabitants, centaurs, didn't require seating.

Between the tables, a woven carpet ran the length of the room, its deep blues and golds contrasting with the gray stone. At the far end of the room stood a large altar, made of the same granite as the tables, and adorned with offerings. Flowers, small tokens, and candles that had piles of wax from burning down and being replaced many times over. Small spiraling rings of smoke, both on the altar and in small hanging burners, had the scent of incense lingering in the air, adding to the sacred atmosphere. Glowing symbols and runes were etched into the walls, casting a gentle, ethereal light throughout the room.

I found myself overwhelmed by its beauty. Beauty wasn't the right word though. It was like walking into something so old, so powerful and inspiring that the place itself got stuck in my chest.

At one table, two centaur males, hooded in gray mage robes, were deep in conversation. As we walked by them, one glanced up from a scroll he was examining and had to do a double take. His eyes never left me as he patted his friend's chest for his attention.

Apparently, I already had it; he was gawking at me while he blindly pushed the patting hand away. Embarrassed by their stares, I quickly changed my pace to hide behind Traebhr's massive figure.

Traebhr wasn't blind as to what I was escaping, and he put his arm behind me and his hand came to rest gently on my right shoulder blade, hiding me from view.

A much younger centaur, maybe twelve, approached with the solemnity of someone auditioning for adulthood in a sacred space, still unsure which way to bow. His crimson robe, stitched with gold trim meant to signal reverence and rank, engulfed him, appearing as though he'd stolen a circus tent. The hem dragged, and I half expected it to trip him and demand a tribute.

He moved with ceremony, or at least the desperate approximation of one, his legs mimicking the deliberate stride of temple elders while the robe clung to him and refused to cooperate with his sense of balance.

His eyes darted from me to Traebhr to Eesym and back to me again, settling with palpable suspicion, as if the towering warriors beside me were standard issue, and I was the glitch here.

"What business brings you here?" he asked, summoning every ounce of rehearsed authority from his still-developing voice. It almost worked, too, until his voice cracked at "business," and a sliver of childhood escaped through the sentence.

Eesym's eyes locked onto the boy like twin ballistae. The stare wasn't cruel; it was weighty, like he was measuring the boy for ceremonial armor he hadn't yet earned. The boy wilted under the pressure, shoulders sinking and fingers twitching around his scroll, clearly wondering if he was about to be excommunicated by glare alone.

I tensed.

Then, Eesym's face cracked into a slow smile. "I remember when Traebhr used to shy from my gaze in that manner." He stated to both me and the boy. "Nearly fell over his own hooves striving not to make eye contact."

Traebhr snorted. "Please. I wasn't shying, I was avoiding glare burn. On the previous occasion you looked towards me in that manner, the temple's ivy caught fire."

Eesym looked skeptical. "The ivy caught fire because you tried to flirt with the firekeeper while she was literally aflame."

"She smiled!"

"She was shouting."

"And yet, that was still a warmer reception than your mentorship speeches."

I coughed a laugh and quickly covered my mouth.

The boy blinked, the tension slipping from his shoulders as he watched the two banter like old warhorses bickering over grooming techniques. I hadn't expected the ease and laughter in a space carved by reverence. Their quips danced through the sacred air, absurd and oddly welcoming. Something heavy inside me shifted, just a little.

Traebhr leaned slightly toward the boy. "He's all steely stares and silence until the teas lukewarm. Then he talks your ears off about his glory days and the wear pattern on his hooves."

Eesym snorted. "Those wear patterns are a testament to centuries of service."

Traebhr nodded solemnly. "Yes. Also, to your complete inability to walk around puddles."

"They disrupt the sacred alignment of my stride."

"Oh, of course. Nothing says 'battle-tested warrior' like pirouetting over a shallow splash."

The boy's eyebrows lifted, lips twitching. I was trying not to smile, too. This wasn't the type of warmth I expected from warriors who looked carved from history, but it was the kind I desperately needed after so many stiff silences and wary eyes.

Humor had a way of making things more comfortable.

Traebhr gave him a wink.

"Don't worry," Traebhr whispered. "Once you survive your first Eesym glare, you're one of the herd. He only squints at people he's quietly rooting for."

Eesym, already turning away, muttered over his shoulder, "I do not squint. I scrutinize."

"See?" Traebhr said, patting the boy's arm. "Practically a hug."

"Who is your tutor, boy?" asked Eesym, half smiling.

"I am the boy's tutor," a voice, deep and resonate approached. He placed one blue hand on the boy's shoulder and whispered something into his ear. The boy smiled and ran off. This creature was also robed in gray, but with beautiful copper-colored patterns along his sleeves and hood. Not a centaur, something else.

"Eesym, Traebhr, it good to see you again!" His arms spread wide in a welcoming embrace. Then, his two large yellow eyes settled on me, and I abruptly felt nervous again. "I see you have brought a guest. Please, join me." He gestured for us to accompany him at a table.

The boy returned with a single chair, so I could sit. A young female fay, also robed, lit candles with a flame that sparked from her fingertips. I gawked at her as I lowered into my seat. She smiled, and the pair of them walked down a corridor to our right, out of sight.

Traebhr offered a brief nod. "Marie, this is Litharn, the tome keeper," then gestured to me. "And this is Marie of Earth."

I stood as he approached, slow and composed. It wasn't just uncertainty; I was calculating. Teeth, yellow eyes, proximity, escape routes.

His skin was the shade of cobalt under deep water, and his hair, some fiery cascade of red fell out from under his hood. The pointed teeth didn't help.

I smiled, but a small voice inside my head whispered, 'If this goes sideways, I'm stabbing him with his own scroll.'

"It is an honor to meet you," he said smoothly. "Marie of Earth."

He smiled, revealing each one of those fangs. *Great. He's courteous and could bite through chain mail. Love that for me.*

Then, with a flick of his wrist and the snap of two fingers, half a dozen scrolls shimmered into existence mid-air and landed softly on the table.

I jumped. A tiny yelp escaped before I could trap it behind polite Earth-girl composure.

Litharn's golden eyes slid toward me, mildly amused. "Forgive me, Marie. We dryads have a natural affinity for magic."

"Dryad?" I asked, trying to sound cool but probably sounding like someone who'd just seen Thor materialize at a PTA meeting.

"We may need more scrolls," Eesym quipped without looking up, his tone dry and effortless.

Litharn sighed, eyebrows lifting into his hood's shadow. "A tree nymph," he explained. "My life-force is tied to a very old tree. We are creatures of nature and magic. You'll find that many lives here differ from those on Earth."

How do they know about Earth? I pondered.

He reached up and tugged his hood back, and I stared.

Two magnificent horns curved over his head, ram-like and perfectly symmetrical, wrapped in copper bands that glinted when he moved. His pointed ears twitched, and he reached for a scroll like this was just another Tuesday.

I blinked, brain stuttering.

He looked like the kind of person-creature who should woo mortal women into a fated mate narrative while lightning strikes behind him, shirtless, with dramatic wind and existential monolog.

"Of course you're a tree nymph," I muttered, torn between awe and the creeping suspicion that he could bench press my entire moral compass. I shook my head. I need to stop reading romantasy novels…

Litharn met my gaze and smirked. "Indeed."

He then turned to Traebhr and Eesym with something approaching concern. "Did you encounter trouble? Has the King had an audience with her yet?"

"We ran into Cerberus dogs," Traebhr said, not bothering to dress it up. "They were tracking her."

Litharn's jaw tightened. "The Vexed…" he murmured, gaze sliding back to me and then to the tabletop. "Tell me everything."

They recounted the encounter in clipped detail. Cerberus. The chase. The meeting with the king. When the last word fell, I leaned forward.

"Who is the Vexed?" I asked.

All eyes turned toward me with a hesitation that made me wish I hadn't asked. Litharn considered. "A Mythborn male. A tyrant of old blood and bitter purpose. His name is known. But not spoken."

Eesym didn't look up. "His path was predicted. So was yours."

I blinked. "Mine? Why is Traebhr called a Guardian?" I blurted, trying to redirect my brain before it unraveled.

Litharn gave a soft nod. "Because he carries Kabane."

Traebhr stepped forward, voice steady. "The sword chose me when I came of age. It responds to the truth of one's heart." He regarded me with no falter in his gaze. "It's the prophecy."

"Wait... Kabane?" I echoed.

Litharn reached for a scroll laced in gold filigree and smoky thread that pulsed like lightning trapped under glass. He didn't open it yet, just held it with reverence.

"Kabane was the savior of our Realms," he breathed. "Long ago. His sacrifice broke a magic that nearly devoured everything."

My voice lowered. "The prophecy?"

Litharn's fingers traced the scroll's edge. "It speaks of two, the girl from Earth, and her protector. A Centaur born beneath the Seven Stars and twin moons. If they meet, they may stand against the darkness rising. If they do not..." He let the sentence hang.

Eesym leaned in, voice gentler. "She would arrive nineteen years after the protector's birth."

I looked to Traebhr. I didn't need to ask.

"And here you are, and from earth realm."

"Happy belated birthday... You think I'm her?" I asked, trying to keep the laugh from cracking through my words.

"You are Marie," Traebhr said. "And I am your Guardian."

I wasn't sure if I wanted to throw one of these floating scrolls at his head, or crawl inside one so the dryad could make it disappear.

"You don't understand," I said, trying to force it out. "I got lost in my backyard. I'm not brave. I panicked once when I choked on my milk! I ate cereal dry for two days!"

Traebhr blinked. "What is cereal?"

Litharn raised a calming hand before I could spiral. "Assuming you are not" he said gently, "then who is?"

I opened my mouth... nothing came out.

Rat's crooked grin flashed across my thoughts. Tessa's quiet shoulder in the night. The Eye, humming with a voice I couldn't explain.

I just wanted to go home...

18

BE BLESSED, BE GRATEFUL

Marie

Stepping out of the temple felt like I had climbed out of the mud; the weight of everything within seemed to have had me stuck. Swamped by all the responsibility they were dumping on me, my thoughts were a jumble, and for a moment, I just stood there, trying to collect myself as the weight of what I'd just learned settled heavy in my chest.

They think I'm part of a prophecy, a main part.

Think positive, Marie, at least they aren't throwing you in prison. I thought to myself.

Outside, the air smelled of flowers and incense. The city's sounds drifted our way; a gentle swell of voices that rose and fell as people went about their daily lives.

Traebhr and Eesym moved a little further ahead, their hushed voices mixing with the city sounds beyond the gardens. I couldn't understand what they were saying, but I noticed how carefully they spoke, as if aware that my thoughts were still caught up in the whole saving worlds prophecy story I was apparently supposed to be part of. And Litharn's look… yeah, that was still messing with my head.

Eesym glanced back once, studying me with that unreadable calm of his. "You're quiet," he observed, not unkind.

"I'm thinking," I said.

Except it wasn't thinking — it was more like my mind was a tornado that I couldn't shut off. Prophecy. Getting home. The Gates. Everything circling at once. It made me nauseous.

Traebhr slowed his pace until he walked beside me. "The city will help," he said, his voice steady. "Nyltak has a way of easing the mind."

I was not sure any city could do that, but I nodded anyway, grateful for the attempt.

The courtyard opened into a broad walkway that led toward the heart of Nyltak, and as we stepped onto the cobblestones, I noticed lanterns being hung from balconies and long ribbons of colored fabric drifting in the breeze, and something inside me loosened at the sight because it was the first time since arriving here that I saw people, just being people. They were preparing for something fun.

Children ran past with painted faces, laughing as petals slipped from their baskets and drifted across the road. It looked like the whole street was being dusted in color. Human-sized Faye hovered near rooftops and terraces, their large wings catching the light as they worked with streamers and ribbons that lifted and twisted in the breeze.

A delicate flutter stirred the air beside me. Before I could turn, the tiny luck fairy I'd caught earlier darted into sight. It circled my head with a joyful chirp, then perched on my shoulder, as if it had been looking for me all along.

Traebhr noticed and shook his head with a faint smile. "He returns; seems you have made a friend of him."

"I think he made that decision for me," I said, watching the little creature settle onto my shoulder and bat his hands at loose strands of my hair.

"They often do," Eesym replied, his tone dry. "Pray he does not chew your hair."

I moved ahead, pulled in by the city noise and the chaos of the market stalls. Traebhr caught my eye and nodded, basically saying, *Go on, you're fine. The inner ring's safe.*

The thought sat in my chest in this weird mix of comfort and unease. I really was a stranger in a strange land. Even so, I kept moving, letting

Nyltak's colors and sounds surround me while I tried to figure out how to belong in a place that felt so big and new.

"The festival will begin at dusk," Traebhr said behind me. "The city prepares to honor the Seal."

Eesym added, "A blessing of gratitude. A light touch. Nothing more."

I knew the Seal already. I'd seen it carved into the towering gates when we first entered the city, and now I noticed its symbol everywhere, painted on banners and etched into stone fountains.

The street curved to the left, and the noise of the festival preparations faded beneath a sudden burst of shouting from somewhere nearby, a sharp voice rising above the crowded bustle, and curiosity tugged me forward.

I moved toward the sound, listening as something crashed inside a shop just ahead. A flash of bright light flickered behind the window, followed by another shout that made me stop in my tracks. The luck fairy on my shoulder perked up, wings trembling with interest.

"That sounds like trouble," Eesym remarked, though there was a hint of amusement in his voice.

"Or entertainment," Traebhr said with a grin.

I stepped closer, pulled in by the noise and the chaos spilling into the street. Something wild and playful was practically vibrating out of the shop, and before I could decide if this was a terrible idea, the door flew open and a swarm of tiny creatures blasted into the air.

I gasped and ducked as one zipped past my face with a triumphant squeal, clutching a ribbon of something sticky and amber that dripped onto the cobblestones in a thin line of glittering syrup. Another spiraled upward with a handful of candied nuts, while a third tumbled through the air with a jar twice its size, wobbling like a drunk bee before righting itself and darting away with a shrill, delighted chirp.

A book flew out after them and hit the ground with a heavy thud, its pages fluttering like a startled bird trying to escape its own binding.

"AND STAY OUT, YOU LITTLE MENACES!" a voice roared from inside, rich and sharp and absolutely done with the world.

The shopkeeper stormed into the doorway, a stout woman with pointed ears and a braid that coiled into a bun. Her apron was dusted with shimmering powder, and her sleeves were rolled up to reveal forearms inked with faint runic markings that danced in the light. She planted her fists on her hips, chest rising and falling as she glared at the sky where the fairies vanished in a giggling cloud.

"Filthy little pests," she muttered, though there was something almost affectionate buried under the frustration. "Every blasted morning. Every blasted one. They're lucky its festival tonight."

I hovered a few feet away, unsure if approaching was wise, but she spotted me and pointed at the fallen book.

"You there, sweetheart, do me a kindness and hand that over before it decides to sprout legs and run off to join the circus," she said, her voice brisk and commanding in the way of someone who had spent a lifetime giving orders to both people and objects that didn't always listen.

I scrambled to pick it up, startled by the faint hum beneath my fingers. "It's warm," I said before I could stop myself.

"Of course it is warm," she replied, snatching it with a huff that softened when she saw my expression. "It is temperamental. Like me before tea. Don't worry, it only bites if you insult its binding."

"I'll keep that in mind," I said, unsure if she was joking.

She sighed and wiped her brow with the back of her hand. "Luck fairies. Mischief incarnate. They smell sugar from three streets away and think everything belongs to them. And naturally they hit my shop first because the gods enjoy watching me suffer."

Her eye fell on the luck fairy, who was now wearing my hair as a disguise, allowing it to hide him like a curtain. "And that goes for that one as well." She pointed the book towards him, and he chattered his teeth at her from behind my neck. She nodded as if she understood him. "Good then, the rest of your brethren should have the same manors."

Traebhr and Eesym had caught up, and the shopkeeper's eyes flicked over them with the quick assessment of someone who had seen every kind of customer and troublemaker in her long career.

"Oh, Guardians," she said, her tone shifting into something like professional courtesy mixed with mild annoyance. "Lovely. If you are here to tell me the fairies are a protected nuisance, save your breath. I have already filed three complaints this week."

"We are not here for that," Traebhr said, his voice steady.

"Good," she replied, already turning back toward the chaos inside. "Because if the Guild expects me to keep replacing stolen goods without compensation, they can come sweep the floors themselves."

I glanced past her into the shop and felt my breath catch. Shelves lined the walls, overflowing with trinkets and enchanted objects that glowed or floated or hummed, jars of shimmering powders stacked beside tiny mechanical birds that clicked their wings in restless anticipation, ribbons that curled and uncurled like living things, and a lantern that hovered near the ceiling without a chain.

"What is this place," I asked, unable to hide the awe in my voice.

Her chest puffed with pride. "Thistleton Arcane Provisions," she declared. "Finest practical enchantments in Nyltak, approved by the Mage's Guild and maintained by yours truly, Brena Thistleton, graduate of the Guild's twenty-year program, survivor of vow trials, and the only woman in this city foolish enough to run a shop where half the merchandise has opinions."

Eesym lifted a brow. "You took the vow of sacrifice."

"I took all the vows," she said, waving a hand as if brushing away a memory. "Some of them twice because the examiners were in a mood. Now come in, all of you, and watch your step. The fairies knocked over half my inventory and I'm in no state to pretend I'm not furious about it."

I stepped inside, the air smelling of cinnamon and old books, while an enchanted broom swept the floor by itself, shivering its bristles like it resented the extra work. A jar on the counter quaked as if something inside was trying to escape, and a quill scribbled on a floating notepad next to me. I stepped closer, and the writing looked suspiciously like a complaint letter addressed to the fairies.

Brena stomped past it. "Oh hush, you were not even the one stolen."

I laughed, a real, startled sound that felt strange and warm in my chest.

Brena glanced at me, eyebrows lifting. "First time in a Guild shop?"

"First time in any of this," I admitted.

Her expression softened. "Well then, welcome, girl. Try not to touch anything that glows red, hums, or whispers your name. If it whispers twice, call for me."

I watched the quill furiously write its complaint, angered by the command to silence, and smirked.

I ventured deeper into the shop, mindful of anything that looked volatile. The luck fairy perched on my shoulder, chirped at a floating ribbon, which danced playfully in its direction.

"Now then, what brings a human girl into my shop on a festival day. Curiosity or chaos." Brena asked.

"Curiosity," I said, though chaos sparked my curiosity. "You said you trained in the Mage's Guild. What is that exactly?"

Brena's expression shifted, pride blooming across her features. She set the temperamental book on the counter and folded her arms, the runes on her arms twisting as she spoke.

"The Guild," she said, her voice shifting into something practiced and almost reverent, "is where magic-users of the Realms go to become more than they are. With discipline. Sacrifice. Study. Twenty years of it if you want the right to call yourself a mage. Longer if you're slow or easily distracted, which many are." She gave a pointed look at the broom, which had stopped sweeping to eavesdrop. "You learn to shape magic, not with wild instinct like the Faye or the dryads, but with intention and structure. It is a craft, not a simple gift."

Traebhr nodded. "The Guild helps keep the city running. Their enchantments hold the wards, maintain the archives, and support the Seal."

Brena lifted her chin. "And we do it well. Even if half the city forgets how much work it takes."

I hesitated, then asked, "Do you ever regret taking the vows."

She laughed, a short, bright sound that filled the room. "Regret. No. Complain. Constantly. But the Guild is family. It is purpose. It's one reason this city stands as it does. And tonight, during the festival, you will see exactly what we protect."

Her eyes softened as she looked at me, and for a moment the sharp edges of her voice gentled. "You should go, girl. The festival is not something to miss. The Seal shines brightest on this night, and the city becomes something beautiful. Even the fairies behave for a few hours."

The luck fairy on my shoulder chattered, and Brena pointed at him with a knowing smirk. "Yes, even you."

Eesym stepped forward. "We should let her see the city before the crowds gather."

Traebhr nodded. "The festival is indeed, a sight to see."

Brena waved us toward the door with a brisk flick of her hand. "Go on then. I have a shop to salvage and I won't get many customers with you two taking up the room with your horses asses. Enjoy the night, human girl. Let the Seal hear your gratitude. It listens more closely than you think."

I smiled. "It was nice to meet you, Brena. Your shop is amazing." I said as I stepped back into the sunlight.

* * *

The city sounds swelled around me, warm and loud, and the luck fairy plopped onto my shoulder again like it had claimed the spot.

Paper lanterns swayed, music drifted through the streets, and the whole place buzzed with festival energy.

The first thing that caught my eye was the long row of food stalls lighting up the square, packed with people trying whatever the vendors were stirring, roasting, or handing out.

The air was thick with the scent of sweet fruit simmering in copper pots and spiced meats turning slowly over enchanted flames.

A woman with bright paint across her cheeks handed me a small pastry filled with something warm and fragrant.

Before I could protest, her smile widened. "It's tradition to share food with a stranger on festival night. Be blessed and be grateful!" she said as she trotted off to hand another treat to a passerby who greeted her with a smile and the same words. *"Be blessed and be grateful."*

I bit into the pastry and groaned at its flavor, the sweetness melting across my tongue in a way that loosened my chest, and Traebhr chuckled beside me as if pleased to see me enjoy something so simple.

The luck fairy chirped at the pastry until I tore off a tiny piece for him, and he devoured it with such enthusiasm that a nearby vendor cackled and declared him a creature of excellent taste, as he displayed a small sharing basket of the sweets.

"They're wonderful!" I said as Eesym paid the man for a small sack of them and Traebhr ushered me past the vendors.

I took one from the sack and handed it to Traebhr, "Be blessed." I started.

"And be grateful." He finished, with a smile.

We moved on, drawn by the sound of drums echoing through the square, and I stood at the edge of a performers' circle where dancers spun in wide arcs, their skirts flaring, ribbon wands curling like banners as they moved in perfect rhythm with the beat.

A pair of acrobats leaped over each other with impossible grace, their bodies twisting through the air as if gravity was only a concept, and the crowd clapped in time, their cheers rising with every impossible flip.

Traebhr passed me a pipe as we watched the performers, his eyes bright with the firelight.

"It's fairy spice," he said, smiling as he exhaled a slow spiral of smoke that smelled warm and sweet, almost spicy. "It warms the spirit."

I hesitated for half a second, then took a small drag.

The taste hit me first, like apple pie and allspice and something bright I couldn't name, and then the warmth spread through my chest and up to my cheeks.

My whole body felt lighter, like someone had turned down the gravity just a little.

I giggled before I could stop myself, which only made me giggle more, and Traebhr laughed with me, the sound rolling through the air like it belonged to the festival.

The colors around us seemed a little brighter, the music a little deeper, and the luck fairy on my shoulder chirped in approval.

I was instantly warm, floaty, and a tiny bit sparkly inside, like the world had softened its edges for me.

My small luck fairy laughed and flew from my shoulder to dance in the air with the performers.

Farther ahead, a burst of heat brushed my face, and I turned to see fire-breathers performing near a fountain, their bodies moving in this steady, hypnotic rhythm as they exhaled long streams of flame that folded into winged shapes; birds, beasts, things I didn't have names for, before unraveling into drifting sparks. The firelight reflected in their eyes, and the crowd watched in awed amazement as the flames rose higher, shifting from gold to blue to a deep violet that shimmered like starlight.

I'd never seen anything like it.

The musicians' platform stood just beyond the center of the square, raised just enough for the sound to carry, and a group of players stood in a loose circle.

The melody was warm and steady, a song that felt older than the city itself, and people swayed to it without even thinking, their bodies moving with the beat. I let myself sway with them, my cheeks flush and warm, a smile that seemed to settle into me with the rhythm, and when I glanced at Traebhr, he smiled in a way that made something inside me flutter.

Beyond the platform, a small line had formed, spiraling toward the Seal mosaic in the center of the square, and it took me a second to realize where everyone was heading. As we got closer, the whole vibe of the crowd shifted. The laughter faded into something softer, peaceful.

People stepped up one at a time, kneeling at the edge of the mosaic and touching their fingers to the center. The Seal glowed beneath each person's hand, a soft light that pulsed once before fading.

Traebhr and Eesym stopped a respectful distance away, giving me space, saying nothing, and I inched forward, my breath catching as I took in the mosaic up close. The carved lines shimmered beneath the lantern light. The people ahead of me touched the Seal with such devotion that I felt almost intrusive, but no one hurried me, and when it was my turn, I kneeled and touched its surface.

The stone was cool beneath my palm, smooth, though a light danced within its stones. I closed my eyes because everyone else had, and because it felt right. I tried to think of something to offer, something the Seal would accept, and for a moment my mind was empty, too full of fear and confusion and everything I had lost.

But then, without meaning to, I started thinking about everything that had brought me here. Traebhr leading me out of Tearwood with that steady kindness of his. Eesym speaking to me with respect, even when I understood absolutely nothing and was completely lost. The luck fairy curled against my neck, warm and alive and not even a little afraid of me. Rat, tiny, stubborn, impossibly brave. Tessa, who became my first real anchor in this strange new world. The resistance members, who had somehow turned into friends. Venn, who gave me purpose. Lyren, strong and sure in a way that made everyone feel safer.

And then… home.

My family. My friends.

Earth.

All of it drifted through me in this soft, peaceful way, like the magic wanted me to remember every piece of my life at once.

I thought of wanting to live and to see this through.

The warmth that spread beneath my hand was soft at first, like a breath, then deeper, settling into my chest in a way that made my throat tighten. It felt like acceptance, like the Seal had taken what I offered and held it, not demanding more, not judging, only acknowledging the truth of it.

"Chosen one." I heard the voices in my mind, *"I accept."*

When I opened my eyes, the glow beneath my hand faded, and the surrounding crowd moved on with reverence, as if nothing unusual had happened. I was startled, but also relieved somehow. I felt different, lighter in a way that made my breath catch. As if I had given it all away to a higher power.

Traebhr stepped beside me, his voice low. "You did well."

I didn't know what he meant, but I felt it, a shift inside me that was small and fragile but real.

I nodded, unsure what to say and still processing the experience.

The music swelled as we stepped away from the seal, the crowd danced freely, and I was swept up in the energy, the laughter, and the warmth of the night.

For the first time since I'd arrived, I knew I wanted to stay, to understand this place, myself, and the people who'd become my companions. That realization settled over me, a silent promise I hadn't realized I was ready to make, even if I wasn't ready to say it out loud.

19

SECOND GUESSING

Marie

I've spent the last few weeks here in Nyltak and find myself second guessing going home.

I'm going to miss this place…

The stores bustled with customers; their facades dressed in intricate carvings and wooden signs that swayed on their hooks. There's so much color and life to the city; the people are a veritable melting pot of culture and warmth.

The citizens had all been more than kind to me, and Traebhr had become my closest friend here, hardly leaving my side. There's something about him that was comforting, something that reminded me of home. Still, I wanted to go home; I missed my family and friends, and I wanted to see Logan again. I had never thought I would miss him this much.

They had seemed to understand that I couldn't stay here; after all, I wasn't chosen one material. Traebhr, however, begged to differ. He was insufferable with his determination to convince me otherwise.

They're bringing me to Shay tomorrow to retrieve the key for the Ayrah gates, which will lead me home. King Larrek is opposed to my going outside the city walls. He worries for my safety, but after a long council meeting, they seemed to have talked him into it; I suspect that they have an alternative motive, but as long as it gets me closer to those gates, I don't care what their

186

motives are. I'm just stoked they're letting me go. Though I'm not letting my guard down until I have that key.

Eesym had shown me some of the history, art, and statues displayed around the temple. One of the stained-glass windows depicted two Nymphs, a male and female, holding hands. The male is called Genic, the king of the Nymphs; Einah is his queen. They were ethereal, shimmering from the sun lighting their glass likenesses. Eesym said they're divinities of the elements, spirits of nature. Apparently, they harness unique elements, wielding naturalistic magic.

In the window, Genic looked like an onyx god, his polished form melding with twilight, while Einah appeared as if she were cut from diamonds, her form sparkling and radiating with an inner light. Eesym explained that Genic controlled the shadows and night, embodying its power, while Einah was the elemental of sunlight and day. I walked by that window every day on the way in or out of my room, and each time, I couldn't help but stop and marvel at it.

It's by far my favorite.

* * *

Nyltak was covered with images of Myth's tales, literally built into the city. The fountains looked like they were made of liquid diamonds, and the gardens never stopped blooming with bright colors and amazing smells. There was intricate art all along the cobblestone roads, and the city was packed with history; you could almost hear the ancient stories in every stone. Discovering all its secrets would have taken forever, but I'd only had one more night to soak it all in.

It was late, and I couldn't sleep. I was nervous about leaving the city the next day. Traebhr had warned me that leaving would be dangerous; I still had a target on my back, regardless of whether or not I was the chosen one.

I was eager to go home, but I couldn't wait to go to Shay and meet the Nymphs; I wondered if Genic and Einah looked anything like my favorite window.

As I lay on my bed, I stared up at the dark ceiling; the beautiful mural stretched across its surface. The dim light made it look so real, drawing me in like Alice into the rabbit hole. It was a painting of a lush, thick forest, with a small winding trail leading to what was left of some ancient ruins. The buildings and statues had all been overgrown, and only the shells were left standing, covered in lush ivy. Laying there entranced by the picture, I imagined myself walking down the path into the ruins, feeling the weight of time and the whispers of history all around me. The mural's detail was so vivid that I could almost smell the damp earth and hear the rustling leaves.

A noise yanked me out of my daydream. I heard something or someone tapping on my door. I sat up, straining to listen for it again. My door cracked open, and Traebhr's voice whispered through the opening.

"Marie, are you awake?" Traebhr's voice, soft yet rich, floated through the door as he peered in, seeing me sitting up in bed. He darted his head back out. "Forgive me, I didn't mean to disturb your rest."

I jumped out of bed and went to the door. "It's alright, Trey, I wasn't sleeping." I stood there in a nightgown, holding the door open. Traebhr averted his gaze as he spoke.

"I had thought perhaps you might like to venture out tonight. There is someone I would be honored to introduce you to."

"Yes! I've been going stir-crazy in here. Just a minute, let me get dressed." I closed the door and scrambled into my clothes. In no time, I was back at the door. When I opened it, he peeked at me from under his brow. Now dressed, he wasn't afraid to meet my gaze.

"Me too," he said with a gentle smile.

"Me too what?" I asked, confused.

"Stir-crazy," he replied, his eyes twinkling with a hint of mischief. "It seems we both yearn for a breath of fresh air and perhaps, an adventure?"

I nodded as Traebhr took my hand and led me quietly through the temple's halls and corridors flickering with torchlight. The little fairy that I'd caught, Pipwhistle, I named him, was curled up on the shoulder of a statue. I gave him a little nudge as we passed. He yawned and blinked at me, then eyed us both. I smiled at him and gestured to come along with us, and he sprang onto my shoulder.

We approached the front door, only to see a guard stationed there. Traebhr pulled me back before we were seen.

"We're not allowed to leave? Are you trying to sneak me out?" I whispered, my heart pounding with a mix of excitement and fear.

"Yes. Is that all right, or do you not wish to go?" Traebhr's face was full of concern.

"Are you allowed to leave?" I asked. He dawdled, not quite understanding my question. "Do you think I can fit under there without the guard noticing?" I pointed to his cloak.

A mischievous smile spread across Traebhr's face as he wiggled his eyebrows. "What do you think I brought it for?"

I bit my lip and smiled back. This was thrilling; it reminded me of Logan, and I suddenly felt a pang of guilt for going on an adventure without him.

"Where are we going anyway?" I asked.

Traebhr's eyes glowed with excitement as he kneeled and took off his cloak. He cradled my wrists as I climbed onto his back, his voice pitched low and conspiratorial.

"It's a surprise," he said, grinning.

He draped the cloak over us both, just enough to let me know this wasn't his first smuggling operation. I imagined a young Traebhr sneaking centaur wine under festival banners or racing the moons for bragging rights.

Pip popped his head out from a fold near Traebhr's shoulder, peeped, then zipped ahead like an impatient bee. He reached the door before us and began performing tiny aerial loops, his version of "hurry up, you fools!"

I tried to press close, tucking myself low and breathing in the scent of pine.

Traebhr muttered, "stay silent," as he stepped toward the guard.

The exchange was brief, something about a routine moonlit patrol, nothing suspicious here, just a majestic centaur out for a stretch, certainly not harboring any stowaways with bright eyes and questionable curfews.

Then the door creaked open.

We bolted.

Down the temple steps we flew. Traebhr let out a laugh, raw and joyful, and broke into a full gallop. His cloak whipped behind us like a banner of rebellion, revealing flashes of my face, my legs, Pip's silver wings as he spun beside us like a miniature outrider.

We streaked across the cobbled street beneath the stars and two beautiful moons, a blur of hoof-beats and wild heartbeats. Somewhere, an owl tooted. Somewhere, a bell tolled. And somewhere, in some ancient book nobody had written yet, this moment was going to be titled, How Not to Contain a Girl Named Marie.

I flung my arms out from beneath the cloak, allowing the cool air to rush past my fingertips. Tipping my head back, from under the now bannered cloak, I laughed. Trey's laughter joined my own. For the first time since the mines, the sense of freedom overwhelmed my heart. A tear welled in my eye, and before it could run over, it was blown dry in the cool night air. Through a smile cracked wide, I shrieked again, delighted.

I reclaimed my hold around Trey's torso, as the night's chill slowly made its way into my core. But Trey was warm and solid beneath me, so I pressed my cheek to his back and squeezed tighter. He tucked the ends of his cloak around me mid-run, never missing a step.

"Better?" he asked, breathless but still smiling.

I nodded against him and gave a gentle squeeze around his ribs. His hands found mine at his stomach and returned the pressure; comfort passed back, unspoken.

As we neared our destination, Traebhr slowed to a stop and reached back to help lower me down. It's Elok's pub, the little bar that we had passed on my first night here. He held the door for me and Pip, and I stepped inside.

The pub was a cozy, dimly lit establishment with a tall, long wooden bar stretching across the back of the room. Shelves behind the bar were lined with bottles of various shapes and sizes. A drape covered a passage into a back room beyond the shelves, and round tables with small lamps on each one dotted the pub. In the corner, an enormous stone fireplace crackled; its flames danced and cast a warm glow that filled the room. The rich scents of hops and honey filled the air, mingling with the aroma of ale, pipes, and smoked meats.

Pip hurried to the bar, where he began diving into a small bowl of peanuts. I giggled at him as his body disappeared into the bowl, first his head, arms, and torso, until only his little butt and kicking legs were visible. Then he was gone, lost among the peanuts. An empty shell launched from the bowl and spun, hollowed and halved, on the bar top.

Two elderly gentlemen stood at the table in the back. It's late, and they were the only patrons left. They were smoking pipes, their eyes sharp and suspicious as they followed us across the room. One man took a long drag from his pipe, and the smoke swirled and spiraled around his bearded face. I wondered if I would be told to leave for being underage.

Traebhr strode to the bar and slammed his fist onto the counter, rattling the peanut bowl and sending Pipwhistle yelping behind the antlers of a mounted stag. The crack of it echoed through the quiet pub like a warning shot.

I flinched.

The two elderly gentlemen turned slowly, but my focus landed on the massive silhouette behind the backlit drape. The voice that answered wasn't just gruff; it's heavy, animalistic, deep enough to stir memories I wasn't ready for.

"We're closed, get out, four-legger!"

I could feel the air change. My skin prickled. Traebhr shouted something back, joking maybe, but all I heard was the bellow. The curtain burst open, and a giant form charged out, dagger in hand, horns gleaming.

I reacted instinctively, heart racing, the stool overturned behind me. I couldn't breathe. The clanging of weapons slammed into me like the sound of chains. My vision tunneled, and I wasn't in Nyltak anymore; I was back in the mines. I didn't register the clanging of blades so much as feel it in my bones. A tremor in my hands, a knot behind my ribs. The flash of steel, the bellow, memories that clawed their way out from places I'd buried deep.

I swayed.

That's when Pip moved.

Pip was already fluttering next to me, his dragonfly wings beating in tight pulses. He circled once, inspecting me, then landed softly on my shoulder, legs curled beneath him in a perfect crouch. His gray skin shimmered faintly in the lantern light as he pressed a tiny hand to my cheek.

"Ch-chit Ch-chit." His chitter was low and rhythmic, timed to my breathing. Calming.

He leaned in and tucked himself against the curve of my neck. Like he knew the exact pressure to apply to remind me where I was, and who I was. A luck fairy's version of an embrace, his tiny chest puffing with little affirmations of presence.

Traebhr and the beast, no, the Minotaur, were laughing, clapping each other on the back like old friends. But my body wouldn't understand the joke. I remained frozen, fists clenched, unable to move.

Traebhr's smile faded as he turned to me. "Marie…" His voice softened. "I didn't mean to scare you. This is Elok, the King of the Minotaur."

Elok scoffed. "King my tail," he muttered, noticing the broken stool behind me. "I'll get her another chair."

He moved kindly, slowly, and that helped. I studied him warily. Seven feet of mass, horn, and scar, built to terrify, yet his brown eyes held something tender.

Pip's wings fluttered, evaluating. His eyes narrowed, and he let out a long, musical trill that made the bull slow.

Traebhr glanced at him and muttered, "Easy now, Pip. He's a friend."

"Didn't mean to frighten you." The bull positioned the chair with caution beneath me. I let my body lower, not because I trusted him yet, but because standing felt impossible.

"Would you like me to take you back to the temple?" Traebhr whispered.

Elok cut in, voice low and deliberate. "She'll be fine. What can I get for you two tonight?" He asked me.

It took me a moment to answer. My throat felt dry, but the words came. "Beer?" I said more of a question than a request. My nerves eased.

"Ale," Elok grinned. "My personal brew."

He turned to the barrel that was tapped behind him, filling a couple of glasses with a rush of liquid. The smell hit first; earthy, herbal, a little sweet.

He lowered them, sliding one to me like he was offering something crafted, not served.

I stared at the glass for a long moment. Then muttered, "I can't, can I? I'm not twenty-one yet."

They looked at one another, all three of them. Faces perplexed. Then broke into laughter. Too loudly. It shook me again, but not in the same way. Traebhr teased, and Elok guffawed like laughter was its own language. I didn't get the joke, but their joy made space.

I frowned at both of them, arms crossed, unsure if I felt mocked or safe, or both.

Then, I picked up the glass and drank, then slammed the mug down and belched louder than I meant to. "Excuse me," I said stiffly.

They both stared in disbelief.

"I like her!" Elok said, blinking at me, grinning like my burp had made me a legend.

Eventually, the mood settled. I sat listening. The stories they told were loud, clumsy, and beautiful. Tales of love, war, long-dead friends, old laughter. Pipwhistle drank from an acorn-sized mug like he belonged here all along, chirping nonsense at the mounted stag.

I kept watching Elok. His voice was thunder, but his words were poetry.

I learned about Ira, his late wife. He spoke of her the way some men speak of summer: warm, golden, impossible to hold for long. She'd been beautiful by minotaur standards, all sweeping horns, and soft eyes, her laughter bright enough to shake dust from the rafters. Graceful, he said, in a way that made you forget how strong she was.

When she died, Bullforge lost its queen, and Elok lost his world to grief. I learned that he once ruled Bullforge alongside her, but now he brewed beer and tended bar, and laughed from the belly.

Elok leaned toward me across the counter. "Does this look like the face of a king?" he asked, licking his nostril with an obscene sweep of tongue.

I wrinkled my nose and shook my head. "Not even close. King of the brew, maybe!" I added, surprising myself.

He raised his mug in triumph, froth clinging to his whiskers. "King of the brew she said!"

Trey laughed and raised his mug. "Long live the King!"

They drank to that, and I found myself smiling into my own glass. The tension in my shoulders eased; the tavern felt smaller, safer, like we'd carved out a pocket of warmth in the night.

Elok took that comfort as permission to talk, and once he started, the stories flowed. He was halfway through an embarrassing tale about Traebhr when Eesym walked in the door.

He stood in the doorway, looking like a father who had just caught his son skipping school. Eesym, looking angry, crossed his arms over his chest and exhaled loudly.

Trey and Elok lowered their heads in shame, like two scolded children. You could cut the tension in the room with a knife. I decided that this might be the one and only time I get to save Traebhr.

"Aww, c'mon Eesym, sit down and have a drink with me." I gave him the best pitiful girl face I had. "I'll be going home soon; this is my last night in Nyltak." Now I was in full pout, lip out and all. "Please…" My hands were folded in front of me, begging.

His face softened as he let out a huff. He dropped his folded arms.

As he approached the bar, he smacked Trey on the back of the head. "You could have at least told me you were taking her out for drinks!" Trey was in the middle of taking a swig when he was smacked and spilled some down the front of himself. "And to meet with the majestic Minotaur king." He mocked while gesturing to Elok, who proceeded to dig deeply at his ear with his finger.

Elok guffawed at Eesym's comment and poured another mug. "King of the brew my old friend." He corrected as he slid the mug to Eesym, and then winked at me, a smile tugging his lips.

"See Marie, you are the chosen one." Trey said, smiling. "Only a truly exceptional being could persuade Eesym out for a night on the town; it is usually like pulling fangs from a living basilisk!"

I giggled and picked up my drink.

Eesym smiled crookedly at Trey as he took a spot at the bar. "Was Elok telling you stories about us, my lady?" He asked.

"Mhm." I hummed into my mug. I was taking a sip when he asked.

Eesym lifted his mug and smirked. "Has anyone told you about the famous apple-groping tragedy of Mele's arboriculture class?"

Traebhr groaned audibly. "I was fourteen! FOURTEEN!"

"Mele," Eesym continued without mercy, "was demonstrating how a Nymph can accelerate fruit growth with a little love, sunlight, and magic. She held out an apple, gleaming, ripe, absolutely radiant."

Traebhr buried his face in his hands. Groaning.

"So young Traebhr, seeing this glowing orb of fruity perfection, decides he must impress a young classmate by gifting these beautiful apples to her. He saunters up, all swagger, puts one hand dramatically on the tree trunk, Mele herself, of course, and reaches for what he assumes is an apple…"

Eesym paused, letting the silence simmer.

"…and grabs her left breast."

The pub erupted. I had covered my mouth, hoping it'd help my grin from hurting my face. Elok choked on his ale. Pip tumbled backward mid-air with a high-pitched peep of disbelief. Even the mounted stag seemed to tilt with a frown.

"She yelps," Eesym went on between snorts, "snaps a branch across his backside, uproots herself with full nymph vengeance, and starts chasing him around the courtyard like a wrathful willow."

Traebhr's ears were red now. "It was an accident!"

"She was shouting 'Not fruit! NOT FRUIT!' while pelting him with actual apples," Elok added helpfully.

"And now," Eesym said, raising his mug with mock solemnity, "every time Mele visits, she brings him a basket of apples and wares a vine-woven bra. Just to be safe."

"I'm amazed she still speaks to me," Traebhr muttered, half laughing, half mortified.

"I'm amazed she doesn't photosynthesize a restraining order," Elok quipped.

I was laughing so hard that I had spilled half my drink.

"You know, I don't flirt with destiny." Traebhr said, watching me laugh, his smile going straight to his amber eyes. "But if fate had a laugh like yours, I might reconsider."

I narrowed my eyes at him. "Was that smooth-talking or damage control?"

Traebhr gave a mock gasp. "Madam! I am offended. That was pure poetry."

Elok snorted. "It rhymed with hornswoggled, if you squint."

I laughed again, light and buzzing. It wasn't just the ale. For a flicker of a second, I felt seen, not the healed version I was trying to wear, but the cracked one beneath. I wasn't ready to show it, so I just grinned and wiped ale off the table with the rag Elok had been using.

"Careful, Trey. Laughs can be addictive." I warned, smiling.

He leaned in, voice low. "Then I'll be your worst habit, Marie of earth."

Before the heat could settle, Eesym clapped Traebhr on the back, almost spilling both their mugs.

"Easy there, silver tongue," he drawled. "You're one metaphor away from composing love songs about moonslight and mashed fruit."

I grinned into my drink, cheeks warm.

Traebhr chuckled and raised his mug toward me, all open-hearted mischief.

"To friendship," he said simply. "The kind that forgives fruit-related mishaps and laughs along."

If friendship had a sound, it was the collective wheeze of four slightly tipsy idiots, reliving adolescent shame while toasting to friendship and laughs.

But through it all, I held onto something quiet inside me.

I hadn't told them about the mines. About the things I still see when I blink too long or hear a snort too close. And maybe I wouldn't. Not yet.

But I could sit here with them, drink with them, laugh with them.

And maybe that was enough. For tonight.

20

LEAVING NYLTAK

Marie

The candle beside my bed had burned itself into a puddle of wax. I must've watched it die, though I couldn't remember when. My eyes felt grainy, like I'd slept with sand beneath my lids, but I knew I hadn't slept at all. Every time I closed them, someone's face flickered behind them; Trey, Eesym, Pip, Rat, Tessa, each one tugging me in a different direction.

I pushed myself upright and rubbed the sleep from my eyes, yawning.

My gaze drifted to the pack on the floor next to the bed, half-open where I'd left it. I'd checked it twice already, maybe three times, but my fingers still reached for it, tugging at a strap that didn't need fixing. The Lumo's light brushed the wall like a whisper. I found myself staring; the warmth of it softening the sharp edges of my thoughts.

Going home. Staying. The words kept circling, yet never landing.

My hand found my journal, thumb tracing the worn spine. The leather was tattered from use.

The soft swirl of golden light drifts closer beside me, casting faint shadows across the messy sprawl of my belongings. I blink at it and wonder if I can take it with me. It would be one hell of a souvenir. Like a tether to everything I'm about to walk away from. Rat would lose his mind if I showed up with this thing back in Niren. His tiny sliver barely lit a corner of a tunnel; this one could illuminate a whole cavern.

I smiled as I thought of taking it home; at the image of Rene's face when she saw it, her eyes bulging, her voice shooting up an octave. "You got what from who, where?!" She'd absolutely combust.

The orb drifted, floating in air, a miniature dragon weaving through clouds inside a stormy amber sky. The sight tugged a memory to the surface, the old Faye scholar who'd found me squinting at temple script I couldn't hope to decipher. I'd asked him what the markings meant, embarrassed by how little I understood. His entire face brightened at the question, the creases around his eyes folding like pages of a well-read book. "Ah," he'd said, as if I'd offered him a gift instead of a problem.

He coaxed the Lumo toward me with a slight gesture; the orb drifting from his side to hover in front of me. Its light had seemed to warm the air between us. "For you," he'd said, as if offering something alive. When I hesitated, the orb dipped closer, as if understanding the exchange.

He lifted my hand beneath the floating sphere, and it followed my every movement. Its glow washed over the text. The painted symbols had shifted under its light, reshaping themselves into words I could finally understand.

"Zhuyin," he whispered, nodding toward the tiny dragon gliding through the orb's sky. The way he said the name made the temple feel different. "Knowledge is a gift. We honor it by sharing it."

I should've gone with him when he invited me to see the academy. I can still hear the way he described it; halls lined with scrolls that hummed with old magic, students bent over illuminated pages, ink staining their fingertips. Domed ceilings painted with histories older than the city. A place where learning and magic wasn't locked away or guarded, but offered to anyone willing to seek it.

This Lumo had carried that spirit with it. It had helped me read everything from Myth's crumbling scrolls to the prophecy Litharn dropped into my lap, turning impossible text into something I could finally understand.

Rat's sliver had barely glowed in comparison, a broken shard of what this one held. But even this intact orb, with its dragon weaving through its own pocket of sky, couldn't give me the answers I needed.

Every truth it revealed only split into more questions, each one tugging me in different directions.

"If I stayed here, it wasn't just about saving the world, was it?" I said to the miniature dragon, whose long, snake-like body twisted and rolled through its painted clouds.

It wasn't sentient; more like a magic screensaver inside the orb. I stared at it for a moment.

"It was about taking on an enormous responsibility that I never asked for." I said. My lips pressed together as the weight of it settled.

They kept saying I was the Chosen One, like that meant something. But no one ever explained how. Was there some handbook I missed? Some cheat-sheet for chosen saviors? Because so far, all I've seen is this vague hope that Trey will guide me, protect me, and I'll miraculously know what to do to save a realm from some unknown darkness.

"Hard pass…" I murmured to myself.

I thumbed through my new leather-bound journal and let its weight settle in my hands. I'd written about every wild thing I'd seen, drawn maps of Nyltak, cataloged creatures I did not understand, and tried my hand at sketching. It's messy. Imperfect. But it's mine. There was no camera roll or cloud storage here, just graphite, paper, and me trying to capture something I'd never see again.

I never thought journaling could feel so grounding. Putting pencil to paper made things real, my fears, my trauma, my triumphs, the pain of leaving behind Trey, Eesym, Elok, Pip, Rat, Tessa, and Ren, the echoing laughter and hope in Niren's underground halls, the silent way Rat offered me food when I forgot to eat, how Pip curled up next to me when dreams turned bad.

These weren't just moments. They were lifelines. These Mythborn idiots were real, and they were my friends… and now, I was supposed to walk away from all of it like it was the end of a chapter?

I missed Logan and Rene. I missed my friends back home; I missed my parents, my family, school, my life. But there's an ache for people I never knew existed until a few months ago. What happened when I went back, and no one believed me? How did I explain meeting centaurs, Faye, mixers, and dragon lights called Lumo? How did I explain the tiny amulet in my pocket that sent me visions of past, and present, from an entire pack of Cerberus dogs? How did I tell people who thought all these creatures were just stories, that it's all real, and that was where I had been?

I gathered my things and cinched the bedroll tight. The clothes they made for me; a green cloak with a deep hood, a soft linen tunic, the lightweight armor corset, reinforced pants and sturdy leather boots, all of it felt like it came from someone who cared, who saw me, and not just my chosen one title.

Even though the fit said, *"chosen one,"* I didn't feel like it. I felt like a girl playing dress-up in someone else's story, like I'm getting ready for some cosplay fest.

I was still struggling with the clasp on the cloak when Trey knocked on my open door. He stepped into the room and closed the distance in three easy strides.

"Let me help," he offered, his voice quieter than usual. He fingered the broach, fussing with the metal as I stood rigid under his touch. My eyes met his, and I blushed, because his gaze was too open, too full. Logan used to look at me like that sometimes, different color eyes, same weight.

"The clothes suit you," Trey said. "Almost like you belong here." There's something in his tone, underneath the certainty in his words; sadness buried in admiration.

I know that look…

"I'm not the chosen one," I said, slinging my pack over my shoulder. "I'm just Marie. A regular girl from earth, and I'm going home."

His jaw tightened. "Why do you run from who you are?"

The softness in his voice made it worse. I felt heat rise under my skin. "Don't start with that again. You think I haven't torn myself apart over this? You think I haven't thought through every step of this decision?"

"You have doubts." His eyes narrowed, searching my face. "Then why not stay?"

"Because I can't. I can't do this."

"I don't understand you, Marie." His voice thinned, as if holding back.

"Why is it so hard for you to see what's obvious? You're clever, brave, stronger than you think. Every single one of us sees it in you."

I stepped back, Arms crossing before I could stop them. "What you see is a prophecy. You're all seeing some cosmic riddle instead of *me*! You think I'm your good-luck charm. Is that all I am to you?"

"If that's what saves both our worlds? Yes." The words landed sharp, too sharp, like he hadn't meant them to cut, but they did anyway. "If it means survival, I'll take that trade."

"Then go find a rabbit's foot!" I snapped.

Trey's brows knit. "This isn't just about you, Marie. Our homes, our families, our futures depend on this. I'd give my life for this cause… for you. I lost my brother in this fight, and I won't lose again."

He turned and left before I could answer; his hooves struck the stone in a rhythm that felt like an angry heartbeat.

I stood there, arms locked across my chest; my shoulders ached, the words I wanted to say crowded my throat, yet none emerged. I wanted to chase after him, to scream, to cry, to say something that makes sense of it all… but the words scattered like startled birds.

A soft knock broke the silence.

Eesym stood in the doorway, eyes flicking from me to the hall. "Everything alright?"

"Yeah, Eesym. I'm fine," I muttered. My lie scraped on the way out, thin and unconvincing.

I tried to shift my body sideways in the doorway, looking past him down the hall, but Traebhr was already gone, the thud of his hoofbeats long faded.

He stepped inside, careful, like approaching a wounded animal. "I heard arguing,"

I nodded once, chewing the inside of my cheek. "He said something about losing a brother… I didn't know he had one."

"He has a brother," Eesym replied, and the way he said it made me pause, present tense, not past.

"What do you mean has?" I asked, brow furrowing. "I thought he said–"

"He no longer sees him as such," Eesym interrupted, his voice low. He stepped further into the room, arms folded, the weight of a memory settling into his features. "Do you remember the tale Litharn told you? About the two equally matched students? The ones who trained for Kabane's blade?"

I squinted and then nodded. The memory seemed far away, muddled with prophecy, confusion, countless scrolls, and stories, too much to recall.

"Remind me?"

"The other student was Kaedhr," Eesym said. "Traebhr's twin."

I blinked as I let that sink in. I'd never met his brother. Hadn't even known he existed.

"They were the best," Eesym continued, walking to the edge of the bed and resting a hand on its tall bedpost. "Kaedhr might've been stronger in some ways, fierce, brilliant in battle, but there was a hunger in him that Traebhr lacked. Not for knowledge or honor. For glory. For recognition."

I leaned forward. "He was jealous?"

Eesym's mouth pressed into a thin line. "When Kabane chose Traebhr, Kaedhr didn't take it as a disappointment. He took it as a betrayal. Traebhr, ever compassionate, tried to pass the blade to him anyway. But Kabane choses a pure heart, and the sword knew Kaedhr's wasn't worthy."

A shiver crawled up my spine. "What does that mean, exactly?"

"It means Kabane doesn't just grant power freely. It reflects the soul." Eesym's gaze dropped, shadows gathering beneath his lashes. "When Kaedhr grasped the hilt, the sword burned him. Not just his skin. It opened his mind to the darkest parts of himself. Showing him his own truth."

"His flaws?" I asked.

Eesym nodded. "Flaws yes. Madness, some say. Rage given form. He thought Traebhr was mocking him by offering the blade, thought Traebhr knew it would burn him. So he ran."

My spine straightened. "So why doesn't Trey talk about him? Why act like he never existed?"

"Because he saw Kaedhr," Eesym said slowly, "not as his brother that day, but as someone who would sacrifice temples, lives, innocents, just to carve out his own legend. When Traebhr followed him to the Cyclops temples, he hoped to stop the bloodshed. He hoped to reason with his brother and bring him home. Get him help. Instead, Kaedhr turned on him."

I swallowed hard. "He had to fight his own brother?"

"No." Eesym's eyes drifted past me, as if replaying something he wished he could forget. "He refused. Even when the blade urged him, even when Kaedhr would've killed him, Traebhr couldn't raise his sword against his own blood. I intervened. Dragged them both home. It was ugly. And in the end, Kaedhr's punishment was death. But Traebhr begged the council for mercy. Pled for his brother's life. So Kaedhr was exiled instead."

"And now?"

"Now, Traebhr grieves in silence. For the brother he lost, for the friend he couldn't save."

I leaned back against the wall, fingers curling around my journal like I needed something solid to hold on to. "I didn't know."

Eesym placed his hand gently on my shoulder. "He doesn't want you to do this for him. He wants you to do this for yourself. That's why he pushes. Not because he doubts you, but because he sees something in you you're not ready to see."

A breath escaped me, thin and uneven. "Is that supposed to help?"

Pip popped over Eesym's shoulder, his wings fluttering, giving a tiny nod like he was adding his vote.

Eesym chuckled faintly. "We're all conspiring," he said with a wink. "Hoping you will see it for yourself."

I rolled my eyes, letting the exhale stretch. "So unfair."

Eesym stepped toward the door. "It's a long road to Shay. Longer still to Ayrah." He glanced back at me. "Maybe you'll believe by the time you reach the gates. Maybe you won't. But even if you don't, we will still believe in you."

As he left, I blew my hair out of my face with a sharp puff of air. They're impossible. All of them.

Pip hovered in front of me, still nodding like his vote was final. "I guess I better talk to him, huh?" I muttered.

Pip zipped into the hallway like that was already obvious.

I followed Pip down the hall to Traebhr's room. The door was ajar. "Trey, are you here?"

His voice drifted in from the veranda, low and distant. "I'm here. Come in."

The light hadn't fully arrived yet, just that soft, tentative bloom that precedes a true sunrise. Pale gold stretched thin across the treetops, and mist drifted like the remnants of breath. The stone under my boots was cool, damp from dew, and as I stepped onto the veranda, the door clicked shut behind me.

Traebhr rested his hands on the stone railing. This posture looked carved from something older than the morning.

"I spoke to Eesym," I said quietly. "He told me about Kaedhr."

Traebhr didn't move at first. The silence between us seemed to stretch with the light, patient and unwilling to be rushed.

"Kaedhr hasn't been gone long enough for us to forget the hurt he caused," he said at last. "But he's been gone so long, there's no chance he'll return as the person he once was."

I stepped closer, the chill in the air brushing against my arms. "Why didn't you tell me before?"

He angled his head, enough that I saw the edge of his expression. Not guarded, just worn. "Because speaking his name means unearthing everything I buried with it."

A breeze lifted strands of my hair across my cheek. Traebhr didn't look at me; His gaze stayed fixed on the horizon, as if the rising sun might soften something inside of him.

"You tried to help him," I said. "You offered him Kabane."

"I did." His voice thinned. "And the sword refused. Not because he lacked strength. Kaedhr was…" he hesitated, searching for a word that didn't wound. "Brilliant. Terrifyingly so. But Kabane doesn't answer to brilliance. It answers to heart. And when it burned him, it didn't just reject his ambition. It showed him the truth of it."

"And he turned against you."

"He turned against everyone who wouldn't kneel to his power lust." He finally looked at me then, eyes shadowed by something deeper than anger.

"The council. The temples. The people and ideals we were raised to protect. But me most of all."

A tightness coiled low in my chest. I leaned against the railing beside him, the stone cold through my sleeves. "You could've killed him," I said. "The blade would have let you."

Traebhr shook his head slowly. "I stood in front of him. I didn't raise Kabane to strike. Not once. Even when he nearly took my life. Kaedhr may have been dangerous, but he was mine to mourn. Mine to love. My brother, my blood. I couldn't reconcile killing someone I spent my whole life believing in."

The sun crept higher, light stretching across the hills, casting long shadows over the veranda floor.

"Is that why you push me?" I asked.

He hesitated, breath catching. "I push you because I recognize your heart. Because I see you, even when you don't."

I swallowed, throat tight. "So, you believe I can carry it. This prophecy. All of it."

"Yes," No emphasis. No flourish. Just certainty, raw and unadorned.

I looked back towards the waking city, the mist thinning, the rooftops catching the firelight of the sun. "Why didn't you tell me?" I whispered, though I wasn't sure which truth I meant.

"I didn't think it would change anything," he admitted. "And I was afraid that if I said his name aloud again, I'd start looking for him in every shadow."

I turned toward him, not expecting an apology, but hoping for some crack in the armor he wore so effortlessly. "He's still alive. And you grieve?"

"Yes," he said, voice hoarse. "And I will. Because losing someone doesn't require their death. Sometimes, it only takes their choice."

The early morning sky above Nyltak was unlike anything I'd known back home. The air had still been crisp, edged in silence, and the city below us had lain tucked beneath a gauzy veil of sunrise mist, rooftops glinting like scattered coins across a velvet cloth. There had been no streetlights, no buzzing wires, no pollution to blur the edges, just sky, stretched wide and impossibly clear. Even the shadows had felt gentle here.

From the veranda, I could see the domed spires of the inner quarter catching first light, their ridged stone halos glowing amber, as if touched by a painter's brush. The merchant streets had still slept, tucked between structures, though the wind had teased a few banners loose from their bindings, sending them fluttering across half-shuttered windows. It had been too early for movement. Too early for noise. But the light had been stirring, and with it, something inside me.

Two moons still hung stubbornly in the sky, refusing to relinquish their place even as dawn broke around them. One large and swollen with light, bore the same gentle familiarity as Earth's, though here, it felt ancient, more sovereign than celestial. The other was tucked just next to it, shy and soft, like a child peeking around a parent.

"What are their names?" I asked, my voice low, as if speaking might disturb the rhythm of the waking city.

Traebhr followed my gaze and nodded toward the moons. "Selene," he said. "She is the mother. And the smaller moon is Elera, her child. You won't often see them together like this."

"They're beautiful," I murmured, the ache in my chest tightening, not painful but deep. I watched the halos that circled each moon flicker as the light shifted. "I don't think I'll ever forget this sky."

He said nothing, but I could feel his thoughts pressing close behind mine.

I tilted my head back, breathing in the moment, and without meaning to, let my mind drift to Logan. I wondered if he missed me the way I missed him, like a song stuck at the edge of my mind... he'd have loved this view. We used to lie out under the stars at night and imagine worlds beyond our own. I don't think either of us believed they could be real. But now I'm leaving one.

"It's almost time," Traebhr said, and I turned to find him watching me with that same look, equal parts patience and inevitability. "We need to reach the harbor before the sun clears the ridge."

"I have everything packed," I said. But I didn't move.

Instead, I gazed back once more at the city, at the cobbled streets I'd wandered, the places where I'd listened to strange music that spoke in riddles, and magic, the taverns where laughter gushed and embarrassment was worn like armor. I thought of Elok. Of Pip. Of the long, peaceful walks through temple gardens. I thought of Rat's jokes that played out in my mind, even if he wasn't there, and Tessa's fierce loyalty. And the way their warmth had wedged itself into places I hadn't known were hollow.

I stepped back into my room to grab my bag, pausing in the doorway as if the walls themselves were asking me to stay.

The mural and the arched ceiling; my second sky. I tried to take it all in at once, knowing I couldn't.

I slung the pack over my shoulder just as Traebhr appeared in the doorway, one hand braced against the frame.

"Ready?" he asked.

I nodded, then glanced towards the lumo still drifting near my bed.

"Can I keep the Lumo?" I asked. I hadn't meant for the question to sound so hopeful, but I couldn't help it.

"Of course," he said. "It was gifted to you. It belongs with you."

I smiled and plucked it from the air. As my fingers closed around it, it shrank as if it knew it needed to fit someplace small. I tucked it into the side pocket of my pack, and it flickered once, an amber farewell across the ceiling.

As I shifted the pack on my shoulder, something else stirred, a faint pulse against my hip, subtle as a second heartbeat. Paxithra. I slipped a hand into the pocket and brushed my fingers over its surface. The stone was cool, but alive beneath my touch, a soft thrum rising as if it recognized the moment. For weeks in Nyltak it had been still, almost sleeping, but now a flicker. Not light, or sound, but something like a memory brushing the edge of my mind: a crown of fractured metal, a voice calling from far below the earth, a sense of unfinished purpose.

I swallowed. "Not now," I whispered, though I wasn't sure who I was speaking to.

The pulse faded, but not entirely. As if it wanted to be certain I'd felt it.

"Shall we?" Traebhr offered, holding out his hand.

I took it, chuckling under my breath. "Yes, we shall," I said, mocking his formality with just enough reverence to make the teasing fond.

Before we crossed the threshold, I turned toward my favorite window. The colored glass, once vivid with sunbeam kaleidoscope magic, now looked faded, washed in dim gold and shadow. It wasn't the same without full daylight. I wanted to remember it the way it had been, radiant, fractured light pouring onto stone like spilled paint. Instead, it stood with muted colors. Regal still. But just waking from sleep.

We walked down the hall together. At the end, the king waited.

He folded his arms around my shoulders, firm and warm, the embrace that didn't need words. "We will miss you, Marie," he said, voice thick with truth. "Stay close to Traebhr," he added with a crooked grin. "He's reliable, in his own way."

A laugh escaped me, soft and unsteady.

"May the gods watch over you," he finished, Pressing a kiss to my forehead like I'd been a part of this place for longer than I had.

"Thank you," I managed. "I won't forget you."

He stepped back, eyes warm. "Nor I you."

21

MAY MYTH BURN CLEAN

He did not kneel for crown nor coin, but for reckoning. His oath, once spoken, did not serve Myth. It served her.
~Mythkeeper Scribe J.L.

Marie

The market gentled that morning; Nyltak's sun cast bronze light over jars of honey and spices stacked like sand art.

I walked beside Trey, our pace unhurried as we passed baskets woven tight with dried fruit and candied roots. Eesym trailed a pace behind us, his gaze flicking across pottery and bundles of pressed herbs, while Pip flitted overhead, circling a laughing vendor who tossed roasted chestnuts into the air to the fairy.

He caught them and balanced them in his arms, so overloaded he seemed to defy gravity.

"I swear he'd shake someone down, if anyone told him, *No*." Trey muttered, grinning as Pip let out a triumphant trill and landed squarely on my pack.

He stuffed the hoarded chestnuts into the flap of my pack before cracking open a nut to eat.

"They gave it to him willingly," I smiled, looking over my shoulder at Pip, who took a massive bite of chestnut.

"Probably afraid of what he'd take if they didn't." Trey teased.

Eesym laughed under his breath.

It was easy here, easy in the way warmth pooled in a mug of hot chocolate. Those moments, filled with small joys and simple talk, didn't feel like survival anymore. They felt like something brighter.

At a stall shaded by saffron cloth, I paused. Beautiful pressed glass pendants strung on braided twine, shaped like feathers, or river stones, or curling leaves, caught my eye.

The vendor offered one in soft blue. "Protection for travelers," she said, "and luck."

"Luck, huh?" I glanced back at the fairy, who's stuffing the rest of the chestnut into his too full mouth.

My fingers move over the cool glass.

Pip glanced up, alarm on his face, and chattered as if to say, how dare you cheat on my luck. I'm the luckiest luck you'll ever luck!

"Okay, okay..." I said and carefully set the pendant back on the display.

Behind me, Trey bartered for dried citrus slices and hardtack bread, while Eesym tried not to look impressed by a puppet show staged between crates of tubers.

Pip chirped and pointed at a child holding a sugar stick shaped like a fox.

Then it happened.

A commotion.

Too loud and too sharp for the morning's fragile rhythm.

At first, I didn't understand what I was hearing, just a loud thump of boots and hooves, the sudden scrape of a cart shoved off balance, voices rising too fast. I turned toward the sound, expecting some heated haggling or a scuffle over the spilled spice jars, but what I saw stopped everything inside me.

He lurched between two guards, limbs thrashing, his robe ripped and stained, gripping a half-eaten loaf of bread as if it's his lifeline. His skin was powdered with a dust I knew too well; that pale gray grit that embedded itself into your pores until scrubbing doesn't help. Mine-dust. Maw-dust.

And his voice, God, his voice, it wasn't loud for attention. It fractured. Breathless. Spitting syllables that came too fast, too hot, words he wasn't choosing and couldn't hold in.

"She eats the light!" he shouted. "She eats it, feeds off it, feeds off us! Vaira is the root, the rot, she's got teeth everywhere!"

People recoiled. Vendors frowned. A child whimpered and buried her face in her mother's skirts.

The guards laughed, told him to shut it, called him cracked, called him a thief. They pushed him harder, down onto the cobbles, and he sobbed through it, clinging to the loaf with fingers curled like claws.

But I couldn't move.

Because those robes, tattered and stained and hanging on by a thread, I'd worn them. I'd felt them against my skin as I curled around pain and tried to disappear. That dust, they think it made him dirty, but I know it marked him as one who survived hell, and no one asked how deep he went to crawl out.

He could've been me. I could've been him.

If I didn't have Tessa's voice whispering hope in the darkest tunnels. If I didn't have Rat silently slipping food beside me when no one was looking. If I hadn't found purpose in Niren, hadn't felt warmth in Elok's laughter, hadn't breathed light again in Nyltak beneath Pip's trills and Eesym's calm, Trey's stubborn belief and friendship, I wouldn't be standing here. I'd be curled up next to a market stall, gripping bread and screaming truths no one would listen to.

He never had that. He's been forgotten and lost in the maw inside his mind. The same maw that yawned open for me occasionally.

I stepped forward before my brain gave me permission.

"Wait," I said, too loudly, too sharply, my voice scraping through the rising tension.

The guards didn't look at me right away, but others did. Trey did. Eesym shifted, sensing a shift in me.

"He's not lying," I said, my voice less steady now. "He's not a drunk. Leave him be, can't you see he's been broken?"

They blinked, scoffing, half amused, half annoyed. "You know him?"

"No," I said. "But I do, *know* him."

And I realized suddenly that I wasn't speaking for him; I was speaking for myself.

Trey moved first, his hand brushing my arm, firm but careful, the way you'd grip someone who might fall without showing you're worried they will.

"Marie," he breathed. Not a command, but a question wrapped in my name. His gaze flicked to the man still caged between the guards. Then back to me. "Are you sure?"

Eesym's expression tilted into unease. His mouth parted like he might speak, then closed again. His fingers tightened on the satchel at his hip, retrieving coin to pay for the loaf. He didn't understand, not really, but he trusted me. That trust held him still, waiting for my approval.

Pip moved from my pack to my shoulder, with no grace whatsoever. His wings thudded against my cheek before he leaned in, radiating heat, his little noises, and worry. He whistled low, a sound I knew, the way he sings to me through nightmares. It was grounding. It was a lifeline.

The guards laughed again, one shaking his head. "You want to speak for him, girl? He's mad."

"Yes," I said, stepping closer. "He's not mad, he needs help. He's… fractured."

Trey didn't baulk, but I could feel him watching me like he was seeing something new in me. Something terrible. Something he'd never known he should fear for me. "Fractured," he repeated quietly, trying the word out like it might explain me, too.

"I want him released," I said.

"You want to claim him?" the second guard asked, incredulous.

The word stung. Claim. Like possession. Like ownership. A slave… my world tilted for a moment, then came into focus again. They understood that language. So, I nodded.

"I do."

Eesym finally spoke, voice solid with authority.

"She's Chosen. That is her right." He tossed a coin to the vendor for the loaf. "This settles the debt." He declared it as law. Like it would settle everything.

And it did.

The guards hesitated. One muttered something in astonishment about *'the chosen.'* The other just stepped back from the man as the man stumbled toward me. His eyes on me and my friends. Trey's hand never left my arm.

The robed, tired man collapsed at my feet, fingers still curled around the crust of his loaf, whispering the same words he'd screamed before. "She eats the light. She eats the light. She–"

I kneeled to console the man.

"Not anymore," I whispered, more to myself than to him. "She doesn't get to. I won't allow her to."

He looked at me like I was a hallucination. Like he wasn't sure he'd survived long enough to reach kindness again.

His face was stained with tears that had spilled over dust, time and time again. Blood was caked in his long, unkept hair with that same dust. I could smell the Maw on him. It wasn't something you could forget, and I felt the Maw within me, as it clawed its way back to the surface.

I took a long, steady breath and focused on the feel of Pip, his weight on my shoulder, and the vibrations of his flitting wings. The long, low song he sang.

He grounded me.

The market watched, hushed.

"Not anymore." I repeated.

Trey stayed close to us as Eesym kept his eyes on the crowd, who were murmuring about *'the chosen'* now. Pip touched a hand to my cheek, still humming his calming tune.

They didn't question me; they were my support, my stability, my safety.

They followed my lead, protected me… and waited, because if I needed to save a madman of Myth, raving nonsense on the streets of Nyltak, then they knew that was no accident.

That was the truth, evolving into prophecy.

* * *

Traebhr

I didn't take my eyes off her, not even as the guards stepped back and the man collapsed onto the road at her feet. Marie's kneeling implied their shared space, as truth electrified the air.

I didn't understand it, not fully. But I discerned her face; it lacked pity. It instead represented recognition. Pain mirrored in flesh, and that scared me more than the man's ramblings.

We coaxed him up gently, with Pip flitting ahead to guide the way, chirping like a beacon. Eesym exchanged discreet words with one of the city officers posted near the lower east archway, giving a name I knew well: Chalis of the Broadstone Clinic. A healer who didn't just tend wounds, she tended people.

I helped carry the man there, his limbs slouched with exhaustion, his loaf still clutched like something holy. Marie stayed near him, but not too close. There was a line she understood, a boundary that belonged to the broken. She crossed it when he needed her and stepped back when he couldn't handle anyone or anything else.

Chalis didn't ask questions when we arrived. She saw his eyes and knew; I noticed. Her hands were steady, and she told us we'd done right. As soon as Chalis signaled her assistants forward, I sensed something was amiss. It wasn't the man's suffering that unsettled me; that was plain enough, but the way Chalis reacted to him, as if she'd seen too many like him lately.

Her assistants hoisted him up, and a grimace flickered across her lips when mine-dust smeared their sleeves. Not in disgust, but again, in recognition.

"Set him near the back," she said.

But when I looked, there was no back left to set him in.

The clinic was packed.

Cots crammed against the walls. Bedrolls filling the corners. A child curled against their mother, an arm crudely splinted with wood. A man lay with a bandage across his ribs, the bruising beneath it the color of a coming storm. A woman's wrists bore the raw, angry marks of restraints.

Pip went silent on Marie's shoulder. Even he felt the weight of the room.

Chalis sighed and drew Eesym aside; he was known and trusted here. I followed at a respectful distance, close enough to hear without intruding.

"Another one," she murmured. "Eesym… we're drowning."

Eesym's brows drew together. "I thought the last shipment–"

"Never arrived." Her voice cut like a blade. "That's three in a row. Herbs, bandages, grain. All *'delayed'* or *'mis-routed.'*"

My spine stiffened.

Chalis rubbed a hand over her face. "And the people coming in? Humans. Mixers. Families of them. Injuries that don't match their stories… they're afraid. They're being pushed out of somewhere. Hard."

Behind me, I heard Marie's breath catch as she took in the room.

"We've sent reports to the council," Chalis said. "Three. No response."

Eesym shook his head. "That shouldn't be possible."

"It is," she said bitterly.

She lowered her voice further. "Supplies cut. Shipments lost. Borders tightening. And now this." She gestured toward the man we'd brought. "Another human. Another one running from something no one will name."

Her gaze flicked to Marie.

"Do you need something, girl?"

Marie's eyes snapped up to meet her gaze.

"She's with us," I said before she could answer.

"I see…" Chalis studied Marie again. "You're traveling with them?"

Marie nodded once.

Chalis sighed. "The roads aren't safe for your kind anymore." Then her eyes shifted to me. "Something is amiss out there, guardian. Be mindful."

Marie's fingers curled at her sides. I stepped closer to her, hoping to provide some silent comfort and support.

"She is under my protection," I said.

Eesym looked between us all, realization dawning slow and heavy. "This isn't border trouble."

"No," Chalis said. "It's something worse. And it's getting closer."

I met Marie's eyes. She didn't need to speak; I understood. Her past wasn't a solitary horror; it was a cycle repeating and expanding, reaching into kingdoms that believed themselves secure, even here it would seem.

I exhaled, grounding myself.

But Marie didn't stay long. Before exiting the building, she turned to me, calm and decisive.

"I need Elok," she said.

There's no tremble in her voice, but I saw it behind her eyes. The flicker of dread. The pressure of truth pressing too long against her silence.

"I'll find him," I said.

She nodded and stepped outside.

* * *

Elok arrived promptly. The city was already stirring, word trickling through the outer circles about the chosen one, about the madman in robes, and about the girl with the fairy on her shoulder, who speaks for the downtrodden.

But Elok didn't come out of curiosity; he came because Marie had asked for him.

When he arrived, Marie stood straighter; she was holding herself together, not hiding, not shrinking, just bracing.

Eesym and I lingered close while Pip curled into her pack.

She looked at Elok, then looked at all of us.

"If I'm going to say this," she said quietly, "I'm going to say it once."

I nodded, already feeling the shift. She was about to hand us something that could not be given twice.

We gathered behind the clinic, a private area surrounded by tall stone walls. The sunlight met the stone in the small courtyard, where vines climbed its carved walls, and the wind carried the scent of citrus from the upper terraces.

Marie began.

And I listened.

What she shared wasn't a story. It was a reckoning. The mines weren't tunnels filled with miners. They were cages carved in cruelty. They ate the light, as the man had said, but worse, they ate names, identity, hope, and lives. She described the darkness not as an absence, but as presence, thick, malicious and clawing. Every sentence felt like a blow that landed deep in my chest.

Her voice shook when she spoke the word genocide. And again, when she said the queen aimed to exterminate humans from myth. I couldn't breathe for an instant after that.

I longed to stand. Wanted to stop it. Wanted to seek out the Queen and rip the lies from her mouth, stomp them into the dirt, show them to my king and my council, and force them to see what we let fester in the corners of Myth which we'd refused to look.

But Marie didn't need fury.

She needed witness.

So, I sat, and I absorbed.

Each of us did.

Pip curled close to her, his wings flicking faster with every word, trembling. Eesym's knuckles blanched where his fingers gripped his sash. Elok didn't interrupt once, his brow lowered, his eyes shadowed, but his presence steady.

And I stayed near Marie, not for what I could do, but for what I could hold, her story, and offer some unspoken solidarity if she felt herself in need of it.

After she finally fell silent, the breeze filled the space she'd left behind.

None spoke.

I did not weep. But I crumbled as I let her story into the places of my mind and heart that ached to protect.

If she asked for war, I would bring it.

If she asked for silence, I would keep it.

If she asked for truth to be heard, I would see it shouted from the gates of Ayrah themselves.

The look that plagued Elok's face was like watching wind shear through a cliffside.

Elok didn't move at first. Didn't blink, didn't even breathe as Marie told her story. I'd never seen him so still before; his stillness was a paralysis.

Marie had stopped speaking several breaths ago. Her voice no longer filled the space, but her words still did, staining the air like oil. Slavery. Prison mines. Genocide. Vaira's hands soaked in the blood of the innocent.

The courtyard held its breath.

I stepped forward, my hand resting on Marie's arm. To allow her a tether to me. To whatever protection and promise I could give.

"I found you," I said. "I don't know how, but I did. And I'm not leaving. Not now. Not ever."

She looked at me, puzzled for a moment, her brows pulled together slightly, as a tear slid down her face. I wiped it away with my thumb.

"It's gonna be ok." I said.

I glanced back to Elok and nodded once. I know what hell swarmed my bull friend's mind. Ira's death… the crown left empty… and Elok walking from it like his grief deserved his silence more than justice.

He hadn't looked away from Marie. Not once. And now, now he was breaking.

"I should've stayed," he said. His voice was low, and sharp around the edges. "I should've…" He stopped. Something broke behind his eyes.

Eesym shifted uncomfortably but stayed silent. Pip had gone still beside Marie, wings drawn tight. And Marie… she didn't blanch. She didn't interrupt him. She just met Elok's gaze with something between forgiveness and fire; tears lined her face, but her eyes were a storm, building strength, a tempest in the making.

Elok lifted a hand and pressed it to his jaw, grounding himself.

"Bullforge was sacred. She… Ira… she made it sacred. It was hers. Her people. Her forge. Her light." His eyes turned glassy. "I let it fall."

"You mourned her," Eesym said quietly.

"I abandoned them," he snapped. His voice cracked like iron splitting. "I should've looked closer. I should've seen the change. Vaira's hunger. Her icy disdain. She hated Ira's warmth, notably towards the humans, and I missed it. I missed everything."

Elok stood so fast he stumbled, then steadied himself with a hand to the stone wall. "I thought my grief was the worst truth. But this… this is rotting. The mines. The unchecked hatred. And I…" He closed his eyes. "I let it happen."

Marie rose slowly. Her gaze didn't soften, but it steadied. "You didn't do this," she said. "You let the world convince you that breaking meant quitting. That loss meant silence. But you didn't do this."

"But I left," Elok said. "I let her take the throne. Look what she done to it!"

The courtyard held its breath around him.

"Ira would never have let this pass," he said. "She would've bled for them. For you." His eyes found Marie again. "She believed in the old prophecy. The one that said the Chosen would not be born into glory, but into ruin. That strength would rise from soot."

"She believed," Elok whispered. "And I stopped believing when she passed."

Silence swelled again, painful and holy.

Elok sank to one knee in front of Marie.

"I failed this realm," he said. "But I will not fail you. If Vaira is hiding genocide behind fire-lit forges and golden trade, then Myth is not free. Not until you are."

Marie blinked back tears. Surprise marked her face.

He looked up at her like a knight unmaking his sword, with nothing left but an oath.

"You say it once," Elok said, voice hoarse, "and I'll carry it every day after. You speak it into air, and I'll speak it into kings. You have my devotion, my sword, my horns, and my life. I swear it by Ira's name. I swear it by mine– Elok, true King of Bullforge."

I hadn't seen Elok's strength in a long time.

But it was here now.

And it belonged to Marie.

I clapped my fist into my chest in salute of his proclamation.

Marie didn't speak. She wiped away her tears and gripped his shoulders, a nod of gratitude. Firm. Resolute.

So, I spoke.

"Then let the fire rise," I declared softly. "And may Myth burn clean."

<h1 style="text-align:center">22</h1>

FISTS AND VISIONS

Logan

I didn't plan to stop. I also didn't plan on hitting him. But the moment didn't care, and frankly, neither did I.

I walk past the lockers, trying to keep my head down, trying to get through the day without unraveling. The dreams, flashes, and shadows do not stop. I don't sleep over three hours in a day.

Every time I close my eyes, I see her, but not the way I remember her. Not the way she looked in the school courtyard, or at the diner, or curled up on the couch with Rene. These visions are different, too distant. Like I am watching her from far away, but she's not quite herself. Sometimes she's walking through a forest, her eyes focused, wearing weird clothes. Sometimes she is speaking to someone I can't see, her voice low and urgent, but never directed at me. And sometimes, most unsettling of all, I see her resting, curled against something massive and quiet, something that feels protective but not human.

I don't know what to make of it. They aren't like dreams exactly. They don't feel like memories. They feel like intrusions, like someone else's life bleeding into mine. None of it makes sense.

I wonder if I am losing my mind as I head to class, but then I hear Charlie's voice. Smooth and pouring on the charm, he leans against the lockers, talking to a girl I don't recognize, one of the newer juniors, maybe. Pretty and wide-eyed. The sort of girl who hasn't learned yet what kind of guy Charlie truly is.

"Yeah, it's been rough," he says, his tone low and dramatic. "I mean, Marie and I were close. I tried to help her, you know? But she was always kind of… off. I guess I saw it coming."

The girl tilts her head, sympathetic. "You think she ran away?"

Charlie sighs, like the weight of the world is on his shoulders. "I don't know. I just wish I could've done more. I mean, I was probably the last person she really talked to. It's messed me up pretty bad."

I stop walking. My fists clench before I even know what I am doing. He is using her. Twisting Marie's disappearance into some noble bullshit story. He acts like her savior. He hasn't been, never was. The fucker cheated on her, humiliated her, and then uses her to gain sympathy from this unsuspecting girl.

He isn't grieving. This asshole's performing.

I turn before I even know I am moving. My fist connects with his nose, and the sound is immediate, bone cracks, cartilage splits, blood sprays across his face. He staggers, eyes wide and stunned, as I drive my left hand into his side. He folds like paper and drops to the floor.

The hallway freezes. Only muttered gasps from the few students around us, and the sound of Charlie groaning.

"What the hell?!" The girl, Becka, I think her name is, drops to the floor to help him, but her eyes kept flashing to me with a mixture of disbelief and disgust.

I stand over him, fists still clenched, the pain in my knuckles sharp. My eyes meet hers, and I loosen my fists, my mind flashing to how my father looked to me when he was on a rampage.

For her, I am sorry, but for him… No regrets.

Taz, Kyle, and Jay haul me away. Their grips are tight, voices strained, like they are miles away. I'm in such a haze that I barely notice them.

Charlie is bleeding, holding his face, and I couldn't care less. He has earned every bit of it. Each word he speaks is a lie, and each lie twists the knife in Marie's memory.

We run down the English stairwell, the echo of our footsteps chasing us. At the bottom, I pace like a caged animal, the adrenaline still burning through me. My hand throbs, and I run it through my hair, trying to breathe, trying to think. The guys stand nearby, watching me.

Taz breaks the silence first, his voice dry, his usual sarcasm tempered by something heavier.

"Well," he says, "that was… exciting."

Jay lets out a low breath. Kyle leans against the wall, arms crossed, eyes narrowed.

"Logan," Kyle says, "what the hell, bruh?"

I don't answer right away. My hand throbs, and my head buzzes.

"He was running his mouth," I mutter. "Trying to impress some girl. Talking about Marie like he was a lovesick hero."

Jay nods. "We heard. He's a piece of shit. But you–"

"I'm fine," I say too fast. "Just needed to shut him up."

Taz smirks. "Mission accomplished." Then adds, raising his brow. "You sure your good? You've been… off lately."

I shrug. "Just tired."

Kyle just looks at me for a long moment, then says, "I think you broke his nose."

"Good." I say flatly.

"You gonna turn yourself in, or..?"

"Yeah," I said. "Might as well get it over with."

Jay frowns. "You *want* to be suspended?"

"No… but I want out," I say. "Just for a while. Gotta get my head right."

Taz gives me a crooked grin. "Well if you are crazy, you're our kind of crazy."

I laugh once, short and sharp.

"Thanks."

They all go back in, one after the other. I stay in the stairwell, staring up at the ceiling, and question my sanity. Perhaps I've already lost it and just don't know.

I stand there for a few minutes, trying to figure out how to deal with the situation. Rene looks up to me more than the others. She always has. She was nine when it happened. I swing one punch, wild and stupid, and it was enough to make him turn on me. Our dad. I don't remember the impact as much as the sound; his snarl, my breath leaving my lungs, Renee screaming my name before she bolts. He thrashed me until I couldn't stand, until the floor felt like it had tilted and all I could taste was blood.

They said I was brave... But I don't remember bravery.

I remember blood in my mouth, the thud of his boots, Renee's sobs muffled behind the bathroom door, and my mom begging from the basement stairs that he'd thrown her down.

He's in prison now, and I've spent years trying to unlearn every piece of him that got stuck under my skin.

I look down at my hand. It's swollen and split and trembling from the hit I just threw.

Same fist. Same heat in my chest. For a second, I swear I can smell the old trailer again. The beer, whiskey, the sweat, and stale smoke.

"Some example," I mutter.

Will Renee see the difference, or will she look at me and see the beginnings of the man we both fought to escape?

The thought makes my stomach twist, and I curl my hand tight, letting the pain throb around my knuckles. I step back into the school, the air inside somehow heavier than it is, as if the building itself has absorbed the violence, and is holding it up in my face, daring me to pretend I am not becoming him.

The fluorescent lights buzz overhead, casting a sterile glow that makes everything feel too sharp, too exposed. I keep my head down, but I can feel the eyes on me; students pausing mid-conversation, turning just enough to watch me pass.

Word had spread fast.

As I move through the hallway, I pass a cluster of Charlie's friends. They don't speak or laugh, but they don't pretend not to notice me either. They just watch, their gazes trailing after me.

Somewhere behind me, a voice speaks, low and muffled. I turn, expecting someone to be right there, right behind me, maybe trying to get my attention. But no one is there…

One of Charlie's friends steps forward, misreading the gesture, assuming I turn to confront him. His posture shifts, ready for something. I shake my head and turn away, but the unease doesn't leave with the motion. Something is off.

The voice hadn't sounded external; it had felt closer than that, like it had come from inside my head.

I clench my jaw, trying to push the thought away. What the fuck is wrong with me? Why does everything feel like it's slipping sideways?

"Yeah, that's it," the guy calls after me. "Keep on walking, freak!"

I stop. Turning, locking eyes with him from beneath furrowed brows, my jaw clenches hard enough to crack my teeth.

I march toward him, in no mood for his bullshit. His friend's shift backward, the bravado draining from their faces.

"I'm sorry," I say, voice low and steady. "What was that?" My fists curl again without me noticing, and the pain in my right-hand pulses in time with my heartbeat to remind me.

It's a sharp, familiar, and strangely grounding feeling, like a tether to reality in a moment that feels anything but real.

He looks like a lamb tossed into a den of wolves, wide-eyed and frozen, unsure whether to run or beg. I shake my head, not out of pity, but because the fear in his face makes it clear he isn't worth it.

"You're not worth the trouble," I say, voice flat, and turn away without waiting for a response. As I walk, I hear one of them mutter something behind me.

"Crazy."

A word like that wouldn't bug me before, but now, it hits differently. Now, it feels like a diagnosis.

Maybe I am crazy; maybe they're right.

I keep my head down as I make my way toward the office, trying to piece together what to say, how I explain myself without sounding like I've lost my grip.

But mostly, I try not to think about Marie. Every time my thoughts drift to her, reality seems to bend, voices that aren't there, visions that vanish, sensations that don't belong to me.

When I finally look up, I am just outside the office. Mr. Meckler stands waiting, arms crossed, his expression furrowed and taunt.

Behind the glass, a few underclassmen sit on the bench, their detention delayed by something far more interesting: me.

They stare at me like I'm a ghost, or maybe something worse. I walk past them without a word and step into his office, sinking into the chair across from his desk. He follows, closing the door behind him.

"What in God's name were you thinking, Mr. Lennox?" He barks, his voice sharp enough to cut. "Do you have any idea what you've done? You broke that boy's nose!"

"Yes, sir," I say, rubbing the bruise blooming across my knuckles.

The pain was steady now, a dull throb that reminds me I'm still here, still real.

"What do you have to say for yourself?"

I shrug. "He had it coming, sir."

The calmness in my voice surprises both of us.

Meckler opens his mouth, then closes it again, as if the words he wanted had slipped away.

"Your mother's been called. She's on her way."

He lingers for a moment, hovering like he wasn't sure whether to lecture me or leave. Then the front desk buzzed, and he steps out.

* * *

My mom picks me up from school, and aside from the initial burst of yelling, sharp, clipped, more fear than fury, we don't speak.

She grips the steering wheel like it might anchor her, and I stare out the passenger window, letting the silence stretch between us like a thread pulled too tight.

I lean my head against the glass, the chill biting through my skin. Outside, the forest blurs past in streaks of amber, rust, and gold. The trees are thinning now, late November in Pennsylvania, leaves still clinging to branches but falling faster each day, carpeting the ground in a patchwork of color.

It's a twenty-minute drive home, but it feels longer, like time slows just enough to let my thoughts catch up and start clawing at me again.

Then I see her.

Marie.

She strolls through the woods, not hiding, just moving, steady and deliberate, a long green cloak trailing behind her like ivy against the fall blaze.

Her head dips; her hair catches the light, making my chest seize.

"Marie!" I sit up so fast my seatbelt locks, twisting to get a better look.

"Mom, stop the car!"

She blinks, startled. "Logan…?"

"Stop the car! I saw her, I saw Marie!"

Confusion flickers across her face, but she eases the car onto the gravel shoulder, tires crunching slowly as we roll to a stop.

"Logan! Where are you going? Logan."

I didn't wait.

Before the car stops, I dash out the door and run.

I run down the embankment, boots skidding on damp leaves, and crash into a patch of tall, yellowing grass.

The air smells like wood smoke and cold earth, and my breath comes out in clouds as I scan the trees with frantic precision.

She has to be here.

I saw her.

Not my imagination. Not a dream. I saw her.

But the forest is still.

Just trees and wind and the rustle of leaves shifting underfoot.

I climb back up, heart pounding, and jog along the shoulder, eyes darting between the trunks, searching for movement, for color, for her.

"Marie!" I shout, voice raw.

I stop, cup my hands around my mouth, and call again. Nothing.

The silence presses in, thick and unforgiving, like the woods themselves have swallowed her whole.

I stand there, throat tight, trying to breathe past the ache rising in my chest. Why doesn't she answer? Why does it feel like I am chasing ghosts?

I hear footsteps behind me, slow and hesitant, crunching through the gravel. My mom.

"Logan…" she says, barely above a whisper.

Her hand lands gently on my shoulder, and I don't pull away.

"Logan, honey. Are you alright?"

Her voice trembles, and I realize she's on the edge of tears.

I don't answer.

I just keep staring into the trees, hoping for movement, for proof, for something that would make sense of the moment I'm already starting to doubt.

I turn to face her; the wind tugging at my sleeves, the forest still whispering behind me.

"Let's just go home," I say, voice low, and start walking back up the road toward the car.

We get back in the car, and not a word is spoken. Silence drifts between us, a soft but heavy blanket. Mom sits there, the car keys in her hand, flipping them over and over, a small clicking sound each time.

She opens her mouth like she's going to say something, then closes it, her lips pressed together.

Finally, she puts the key in the ignition, and the little hybrid hums to life. Whatever's on her mind, she keeps it to herself. We don't speak for the rest of the ride.

When we pull into the driveway, I step out and walk straight into the trailer, right down the hall to my bedroom, without looking back.

"Logan, are you going to be alright?" She calls after me, her voice catching slightly.

I stop halfway and look back at her.

Her eyes are wide, rimmed with worry, and I hate that I'd put that look there.

"I'll be fine, Mom. I just haven't been sleeping. I'm sorry if I scared you today, with Charlie, and with the Marie thing…"

I trail off, unsure how to explain something I barely understand myself.

"I'm going to try to get some rest now, okay?"

She nods but says nothing else.

I close my bedroom door behind me and collapse onto the bed, burying my face in the pillow.

I'm bone-tired, the kind of exhaustion that settles in your chest and makes everything feel heavy.

Sleep had been elusive all week, and now it feels like my body is finally giving in.

I roll onto my back and stare at the ceiling, then sit up and look down at my hands.

A fresh bruise already blooms across my knuckles, deep blue, and tender. I hold them out in front of me, examining the damage, band-aids on my left, bruises on my right.

The guitar strings finally broke through the calluses I spent years building. Lenore is always my outlet, but she doesn't work in school. Not when the halls feel haunted, and the air is too thick to breathe.

Yesterday, I thought I saw Marie's shadow walking beside me again. Just a flicker. But when I turned, there wasn't anyone there.

I hope I get suspended. At least then I won't have to sit in classrooms pretending I am okay, pretending I am not unraveling.

I put my earbuds in and close my eyes.

I don't remember falling asleep. One minute I stare at the ceiling, earbuds in, some lo-fi beat looping like a heartbeat I cannot sync to, and the next, I am somewhere else. Not dreaming, not exactly. It feels more like being dropped into someone else's memory mid-sentence, like I walk into a movie halfway through and cannot find the exit.

There's light, golden and soft, but not warm. It filters through vines climbing the stone walls, and the air smells like citrus and dust, like someone spilled orange juice on a library floor. I stand in a courtyard I don't recognize, surrounded by people I don't know, but I am not afraid or confused. I just… am.

And then I see her.

Marie.

This is not the Marie from my phone wallpaper, nor the one I replay in old videos, chuckling at some silly thing I said. This Marie stands tall, shoulders back, her voice steady despite trembling hands. She does not just speak; she testifies. Her words land like blows, each one a gut punch that echoes the bruises forming on my knuckles. "Genocide," she says, as if she lived through one. "Prison mines."

Her voice falters, and I want to shout, to grab her, shake her, urge her home. But I'm frozen, detached, unsure if I even possess a body.

There are others here, although it's so foggy in this dream that it's hard to tell how many. They don't speak or interrupt her; they just listen.

One, a centaur, paws at the ground across from me. I stand there, watching her break open and pour out everything, and I feel it all.

Then something shifts.

I step forward.

My hand reaches out and rests on her arm, and I feel her pulse under my thumb, fast and fragile.

I'm not supposed to be here. I'm not supposed to touch her. But I do. I need to know she's real.

I need this tether between us.

I need her to know that I see her. I'm here.

And then I speak.

"I found you," I say. "I don't know how, but I did. And I'm not leaving. Not now. Not ever."

The words come out of someone else's mouth. Deeper than my own. But they are mine. I felt them rise from my chest like a scream I'd been holding in for months, maybe years. Marie looks at me, at him, and her brows pulls together like she'd heard something she wasn't expecting.

I wipe a tear from her cheek.

"It's gonna be okay."

And then I'm gone.

Ripped out of the moment like a line pulled from a fishing pole. I wake up gasping, fists clenched, heart pounding like I'd just run a mile uphill.

My earbuds are still playing. My phone buzzes with some notification I don't care about.

I just know.

I know I saw her, not in a dream, but in real time, through someone else's eyes, Traebhr's.

I heard her say his name before, but this time I know it, or rather, I feel it. Like it is *my* name resonating deep within my chest, a name that vibrates with a significance I can't explain.

The feeling is visceral, an undeniable connection that transcends the boundaries of my consciousness. Traebhr... Traebhr, a name that now feels inextricably linked to my existence, a stranger's reality that has somehow become my own.

The implications are crazy, a labyrinth of questions swirling within the newfound awareness.

Who the hell is Traebhr? And why in the fuck am I, of all people, the only one experiencing this?

I don't know how or why, but I am there, wherever that is.

I feel her; I speak to her, and she's alive.

She's not on Earth. She's somewhere else... somewhere with monsters, and I'm going to find her.

I swear it.

TAP, TAP, TAP. TAP, TAP.

I look up, startled, when something taps against the window. Not the glass, but the metal siding just next to it.

I push the curtain aside and see Renee standing in the narrow strip of yard which dips down into a drainage ditch, between our trailer and the neighbors, a handful of pebbles ready to launch.

"Jesus! Watch it!" I hiss as another pebble pings off the aluminum.

"Sorry..." she whispers back, grinning like she isn't sorry at all.

"What are you doing? How did you get here?" I ask, glancing at the clock, 12:13 pm; she should still be at school.

"Let me in," she says simply.

I slide the window up, then lean out and reach down. She steps onto the cinder block under the window, the one Darius keeps meaning to move, and grabs my forearm.

I haul her up the rest of the way, and she swings her leg over the sill with practiced ease.

"I'm cutting school," she says, brushing dirt off her jeans like it's no big deal. "I heard about Charlie. Did mom and dad kill you?"

"Yeah, I'm dead. You're talking to my ghost."

"Ass," she mutters, dropping into the room and landing lightly on the carpet.

I sit on the edge of the bed while she hops up onto the built-in dresser under the window, leg swinging like she's 10 again.

It makes me nervous, the way she perches there, half in the window frame, half out, like one wrong shift will send her tumbling back into the yard.

I stood and moved towards the window, pretending to check the street outside, even though I wasn't really looking.

She didn't move, just kept swinging her legs, gaze somewhere far off. Thinking.

"I think mom saw us," I said, reaching for the blinds.

That got her attention. She hops down on her own and flops onto the bed, cross-legged and content.

I lower the blinds halfway and let the room dim. "How did you get here?" I ask again.

"May drove me."

I wrinkle my nose. "May Otico?"

"Yeah. She and Dylan are close now. I called him when I heard what happened. You know she and Willie are serious; he gave her a ring. He's acting like such a big shot." She paused. "I heard you broke Charlie's nose." She said, watching me at the corner of her eye. "Was it about Marie?"

I nod. "He was talking shit."

Rene's face shifts, her teasing gone in an instant. She looks down at her hands, then back up at me, her voice softer now.

"Thanks," she said. "For sticking up for her." She pauses again. "if you hadn't beat his ass, someone else would've."

I didn't answer. I just sat there, the weight of everything pressing down on my shoulders. I hesitate.

"I saw her… twice more." I say finally. "And the second time… it wasn't just seeing her. It was like I was her shadow. Or someone else's. I don't know how to explain it."

Rene blinks. "Wait, what?"

"I was looking out the car window on the way home, and there she was. Walking through the trees. I swear, Rene, it was her."

She sits up straighter. "You saw Marie? Like… really saw her?"

"I made Mom stop the car. I jumped out and ran down the embankment. I thought I could catch up to her."

Rene's eyes widen; her voice whispers.

"What did Mom do?"

"She was upset, but I was already gone. I called out to Marie. Twice. But she didn't answer."

Rene is silent for a long moment, then says, "Do you think it's real, or another dream / vision thing?"

Her question isn't one of judgment; it's honest, and it doesn't make me feel crazy. She leans forward, her elbows resting on her knees, eyes locked on mine with that familiar mix of curiosity and concern.

"It felt real. Until I realized she had disappeared again." I pause. "They're getting stronger, Rene. It wasn't like before," I say, my voice low. "Not a shadow. Not a flicker. I thought she was legit in the woods, just off the road. And in the dream…" I pause, watching her face shift from intrigue to something quieter, more careful. "I touched her. I felt her heartbeat under my thumb. And I said something… but it came out of someone else's mouth."

Rene sits back, her gaze dropping to the floor.

"Someone else's mouth?"

I nod.

"Not mine. Like I was inside someone else's head. Like I stepped into their body for a second and said something I didn't even know I needed to say. I know it was real, all of it."

She considers for a moment and nods, her brows drawn together, like she is trying to fit this new piece into a puzzle that has never made sense.

She doesn't speak for a moment, just stares at the worn edge of the rug like it might offer answers.

"So… what are you going to do?" she asks finally.

"I don't know," I said. "But it's real. I know it is. I think I need to figure out who he is. The guy I *saw* through? I think his name's Trey… or Traebhr. I've heard Marie say it before, but this time… it felt like it was mine. It has to mean something."

"Yours?"

"My name." I scoff at my own words. "it's crazy but I think…"

Rene nods. "Maybe you're connected."

We sit in silence, the kind that doesn't feel empty but full, like the air between us is holding its breath.

Then we heard footsteps in the hallway.

Rene's eyes dart to the door, and without a word, she slid off the bed and disappears beneath it.

"Don't tell on me," she whispers.

I nod and lay back, pulling the blanket up and letting my body go limp.

The door creaks open, and my mom peeks her head in.

"Logan," she breathes.

I open my eyes and stretch, feigning sleep.

"Hmm?"

"I called your father," she said. "He wants to talk to you after work. Until then, you're grounded to your room."

She steps inside, hands me a bag of frozen peas for my bruised hand, and lingers for a moment before closing the door behind her.

I wait until I hear her footsteps fade, then roll onto my stomach and lean over the edge of the bed.

"Ally, ally, in come free," I whisper.

Rene smiles and wriggles out, brushing dust from her shirt as she climbs back onto the bed.

I look at her. "I really freaked Mom out earlier. You think she thinks I'm crazy?"

Rene took a breath, then reached for my hand, her grip small but steady.

"I don't know," she says. "But it doesn't matter. I believe you. I know you're not crazy." She smiles, then glances around the room with mock appraisal.

"But if they do put you in a nuthouse, can I have your room?"

I raise an eyebrow.

"It's bigger than mine," she says, grinning. "And the view's better."

I laugh, the sound catching in my throat, and then stopped mid-chuckle, turning serious.

"Not a chance, brat."

The sound of her light and familiar laughter reminds me of something I hadn't heard in quite some time. Before Marie went missing.

Rene leans her head against my shoulder. The room is dim, the air thick with everything we haven't said, but it doesn't feel heavy anymore. It feels like something is shifting. Like the silence between us isn't just silence, it's agreement.

"I believe you," she says again, softer this time. "And if she's out there… we'll find her."

I nod, staring at the ceiling like it might crack open and show me the stars she was walking under.

"I think someone's helping me," I say. "Someone on her side. Trey? I spoke to her. And she heard me. I know it."

Rene didn't baulk. She just reached for my hand again, her grip firm.

"Then we start here," she says. "We figure out what's happening. We find the threads and we pull the shit outa them."

I look at her, and for the first time in weeks, I don't feel like I'm drowning.

Outside, the wind picks up, rattling the blinds.

Somewhere far away, Marie is walking toward war. And here, in a quiet, safe home in nowhere Pennsylvania, we are preparing to follow.

23

EPILOGUE

Logan

People think the world ends with earthquakes or fire or some cosmic event you can see coming from miles away.

But sometimes it ends with a knock on the door.

Funny, ain't it?

After everything I've seen, the visions, the dreams, the pieces of someone else's life bleeding into mine, you'd think I'd be ready for anything.

But I wasn't.

I used to believe that the world was safe, explainable if you just kept your head on straight, but the truth is that the world is so much bigger, and so much stranger than I had ever imagined.

I thought losing Marie was the worst thing that could happen.

I thought the visions were my breaking point.

Hell, I thought I was losing my mind.

But I wasn't losing anything; I was being found.

By him.

By people who've been watching me far longer than I realized.

If I'd known what waited on the other side of that knock, maybe I would've run sooner. But that's where this part of the story ends, with me standing in a doorway, staring into the eyes of a man who wasn't a detective, and realizing, too late, that the world I thought I knew was already gone.